As Shared by
Mark H. Newhouse
From the Journals of
Brodie S. Adkins

Illustrations by Dàn Traynor

An AimHi Press Production
Lady Lake, FL

Mark H. Newhouse

Published by AimHiPress
1042 Sayle Street
Lady Lake, FL 32162

www.aimhipress.com

Illustrations by Dan Traynor

Publishing Consultant and Editor:
Josh Newhouse

Welcome to Monstrovia

THANK YOU:

When you visit Monstrovia, you won't find many humans, so it is important I thank the humans who helped me with this nightmarish task. The seed of this series came from a play I wrote for my 6th grade class, so I thank those great kids from Central Islip, Long Island, New York, for their love and support.

I also thank my very human wife and family, as well as the members of my writing groups. Special thanks to my editor and guru, Josh Newhouse. Thanks goes to Erle Stanley Gardner and Raymond Burr, who gave me Perry Mason, my childhood role model, and Arthur Conan Doyle, whose Sherlock Holmes set the bar for all detectives. Monstrovia is a tribute to them. I hope they have a sense of humor.

Finally, thanks to my readers. Your support and reviews keep me inspired, even trapped in Monstrovia.

Happy Stories Always,
Mark

Mark H. Newhouse

CHAPTER 1

The jet is shaking like crazy. Terrifying bolts of lightning are shooting up all around and the thunder is deafening. I'm holding onto the armrests as the plane drops, leaving my stomach behind. We're diving straight to the ground.

Everything is happening really fast. So how can the guy next to me be snoring when we're going to crash?

"Mom! Why did you do this to me?" I wonder if she can hear me in China where she is selling those tiny rubber bands for kids' braces to dentists. Some summer vacation! I hope I make it to high school next year.

The plane is making clattering noises. Why haven't the air masks dropped?

I'm about to duck into crash position, tucking my head between my legs and kissing my butt good-bye when all the clattering and shaking suddenly stops. The wheels touch the ground with three surprisingly soft bumps.

I can't believe it. We've landed. I can't wait to get back on the ground. "We made it," I say to the guy next to me, but he's still sound asleep. I look around. Everyone else is sleeping too. They slept through the whole thing?

The pilot's voice announces, "Welcome to Key West, Florida. We hope you enjoyed your flight."

Is he serious? It had to be the worse flight ever!

The plane rolls toward the terminal. The seat belt light goes off, and I push past the passenger next to me who is still 'sawing wood'. I expect the aisle to be blocked, everyone pulling luggage out of the upper compartments and racing to the exit. Nobody is moving. *Am I the only one getting off? Maybe it's the wrong stop?* I peer at the sign on the terminal:

WELCOME TO KEY WEST, FLORIDA

Yup, this is it. So why do I feel like something's wrong?

"You! Human! Hurry!" The flight attendant, barely able to fit through the aisle—someone I haven't seen before—is eyeing me like I am an alien.

"Who me?"

He points at me and roars, "Yes, you! Now hurry! We haven't got all day!"

He looks furry-faced, like a giant bear so I don't dawdle. I thank him for the service he did not give me, and climb down the shaky stairs to the tarmac.

"Holy guacamole! It's hot enough to boil spaghetti out here!" My suitcase is the only one on the ground. "Where is everyone?"

I turn to the plane, but its' gone. I didn't hear it take off. I search the sky. No plane, no lightning…not one cloud. Is the sun frying my brain? Did the near-crash put me in shock?

It is too hot to stay here. Dragging my luggage toward the terminal, sweating like a pig, I hear footsteps racing behind me. Is someone coming to help me? I thought I was ready for anything, but not what I see barreling at me.

CHAPTER 2

"Welcome Master Brodie! Welcome to Monstrovia!"

I'm gawking at a guy who comes barely up to my belly button, has a stubby nose, greenish hair and furry caterpillar eyebrows over storm-cloud gray eyes. "I'll take that!" He is tugging my suitcase out of my hand!

I tug right back. "Let go! That's mine!"

This mini-dude is strong! He yanks the heavy suitcase from me as though I am not pulling on it at all. "Who are you? What do you want?"

"Relax. Relax."

But I'm not relaxed. I'm hoping he isn't some insane robber about to take off with my underwear.

He gives me a mouthful of crooked yellow teeth. "Yer uncle sent me. I be Silas Bumbernickle at yer service."

"Not my service! Where's my uncle?"

"Just follow me and ye'll be fine." He carries my suitcase in his gnarly hands like it's a feather.

I don't trust strangers, and he is as strange as anyone I've ever seen. *But he knows my name and says my uncle sent him.* "How did you recognize me?"

"Around 'ere you sticks out some." He lets out an evil-sounding laugh and veers like a rocket ship to the right.

"Isn't that the terminal back there," I ask, trying to keep up with 'speedy'.

Bumbernickle makes straight for a large red, white and blue object at the end of the terminal.

"Is that a UFO?"

"Ain't ya seen a <u>buoy</u> before?" Bumbernickle asks. He pronounces it, 'boy'.

"Boy?" *Where's his arms and legs?* "Boys have heads!" (Mom doesn't always think I do.)

"Not a 'boy', a 'buoy'…like what's in water. It is a famous landmark in yer world. You do know Key West is the Southern-most point of the United States. Or so most of ye' think."

"My world?"

"Oh never mind," he says, running at the buoy at break-neck speed.

"You're going to crash!"

Just as he is about to hit the wall, a door appears in the side of the 'buoy-thing' with a flashing, red, neon sign over it that says:

WELCOME TO MONSTROVIA
SPECIAL SECTOR!
KEEP OUT!
UNLESS YOU ARE SPECIAL!!!

"I'm not special! I'm not special!" I'm trying to pull back my suitcase before he sucks us into whatever this thing is, but I'm dragged toward that door like I'm a rag doll, flying behind this strange dude, without any chance of breaking free.

Did he say, Monstrovia?

CHAPTER 3

I grab the door handle and hang on. "I'm not going in there! Where's my uncle?"

"Ye'll be perfectly safe," He's yanking me through the door.

"I don't think so!" I keep trying to pull away, but before I know it, I am inside and the door slams. "I'm not 'special. I don't belong here!"

He's pulling me so fast I'm almost flying!

"We're nearly there," he shouts.

"Where?" I'm shook-up by the size of the inside of this thing. It is gargantuan! But that's not what's causing me to stare. He's dragging me past the strangest creatures I've ever seen. There are snake-headed bipeds racing around. They look like they're on roller skates! A trio of bearded gnomes in dark green vests give me a puzzled look, like I'm the 'weirdo'. A knight rides by on a unicorn! "Am I dreaming?" I ask my 'guide', as I'm almost crushed by a giant frog-thing hopping over us. Froggie sticks his tongue out at me and hops into the crowd.

This can't be for real? I'm in a different world. I don't see one other human being. "WHERE ARE WE?" I try to make myself heard over the racket.

"I told ye before, Monstrovia."

"I've never heard of it!"

"Shhh, Master Brodie." Bumbernickle pauses before two bear-like creatures wearing tan uniforms, with badges that announce they are Monstrovia Security.

"We don't need no more 'Humans,'" one growls, aiming a rifle with a pineapple shaped barrel at my face.

"'You're a human," Bumbernickle explains in a low voice.

"I know I am. This is ridiculous--"

"SILENCE!" The bear's breath is like a blast of garlic. "You're coming with us!" He grabs my arm. "WE DON'T LIKE YOU."

Not five minutes in this crazy place and I'm in trouble! So what else is new? Isn't that why I'm here? If I hadn't gotten in trouble with Principal Feeney maybe Mom would have taken me to China with her.

"We don't like humans," the huge guard says as he drags me away.

I don't like 'whatever' he is either.

CHAPTER 4

I'm being arrested by these 'goons' when Silas pipes up. "Gentlemen...."

They look around to see who he means. I do too.

Bumber...whatever, whispers, "Fellow Monstrovians, have ye never heard of Jasper Doofinch, Esquire?"

The guards glance at each other and then at me. "Sorry, Mr. Doofinch, sir, we didn't know it was you." It's like magic. They look terrified.

Now is not a good time to tell them I am not Mr. Doofinch, but his nephew. I guess my uncle must be super important if just the mention of his name sent these two hairy beasts into a 'tizzy'.

"Don't let it happen again," Bumbernickle says, and pulls me past the guards before they can recover.

I can't believe they didn't arrest me. I let out a big breath of relief. Who knows what kind of monsters are in jail in Monstrovia? I hope they don't come after me when they realize their mistake.

I am now in a cavern. The lights coming at me are the glowing eyes of more Monstrovians. They are all sorts, and everywhere, rushing at me like I'm in Times Square! I thought Uncle Jasper lived in Key West. This is definitely not it! This isn't anywhere in America I know about.

"Here be your 'chariot', Master Brodie."

I can hardly breathe as I stare at my... 'chariot'? It looks like a yellow mushroom on three large wheels. "Is this your car?"

He gives another maniacal laugh, tosses my suitcase into the mushroom, and throws me inside before I can make a run for it. "Strap yerself in, Master Brodie. Safety first. It's a jungle out there."

That mushroom takes off like a rocket, knocking me almost out the window. "Hey, slow down!" I strap myself in and hold on.

"No time. Like I says, it's a jungle out here!"

The roads are a jungle, a racetrack on ten levels crisscrossing the sky. The highways are alive with speeding vehicles, many resembling this maniac's 'mushroom', but others even stranger. A huge, metal elephant-shaped 'bus', roars by with five octopus-creatures hanging on to tall spikes on its top. "Get out of the way, slow-poke," the elephant shouts.

I turn away, afraid to look, as we zip around these 'vehicles' while they zip around us. I'm in a crazy video game, bouncing around, about to crash and burst into a million molecules at any instant…with no extra lives!

"We're 'ere," Bumbernickle blasts, minutes later. He slams on the brakes catapulting me nearly off the seat, even with the belts on. "Dis 'ere is de grand 'ome of Mr. Jasper Doofinch, Esquire!" He scurries to my door and pulls it open.

"Do I have to pay you for that ride?" I ask, trying to find my stomach.

"Glad you enjoyed it, but no need. Yer uncle is a respected man in dese parts. E's a ero!"

"'Ero? Do you mean 'hero'?"

He shakes his head so hard I think it is going to fall off. "Exactly, Master Brodie, E's a 'ero!"

Mom called Uncle Jasper a hero too, just before she left for China...right after she told me I was going to spend my summer with my Uncle Jasper in a suburb of Key West. Some suburb! Inside a buoy?

"Who?" I asked when she first hit me with this unwelcome news.

"Your uncle Jasper. I told you about him a thousand times."

"No, you didn't!"

"Of course, I did."

"No, you didn't." I knew almost nothing about this so-called uncle of mine. The truth is Mom never talked about her brother, except after some of our fights. Then she'd grumble, "Your Uncle Jasper is just like you. He loves to argue. Only he's successful at it!"

"Now out ye get, Master Brodie." the mad driver yanks me out of the mushroom. "Yer Uncle is a fine man. You'll soon get over his 'peculiarities'."

'Peculiarities'? How much more 'peculiar' can Mom's brother be than this character? "Sir, could you take me back to the airport? I'll pay you by mail when I get back to New York?" I must be desperate to ride in this maniac's 'car' again.

He lets out another maniacal laugh and guns his motor. "Good luck, boy!"

Doesn't anything move slowly around here? I'm alone in the middle of 'nowhere'. But 'nowhere' is Monstrovia. I don't know where it is, so how can I find my way back?

I hear a strange screeching noise and my eyes shoot up to the sky. Almost hidden by the sun, I spy a long black flying serpent. It's heading in my direction.

I have to get indoors, but I don't like the looks of the red brick building I've been dumped at by that maniac, Bumbernickle. It could be a prison, three stories tall, thick black bars on the windows, and a tall black fence with spear tips ringing the perimeter. The spiked tips of the fence remind me of the spears knights used to fight dragons. Dragons? I'm letting my imagination run wild, but no way do I want to find out what else might be lurking at night in Monstrovia.

The serpent is getting closer. I feel the wind stirred up by its huge black wings. I have no choice. I pull at the gate and it opens easily. Seeing more serpents, I drag my suitcase on a brick path toward a gargantuan pair of doors.

A plate on the wall by the doors catches my eye. It reads in large, black, letters:

J.D. Doofinch, Esq.
Defender of Monsters, Fictional Folk, Etc.

Below it, I see in much smaller print,
Monsterlish spoken here.

CHAPTER 5

"Monsterlish?"

I gaze at the puzzling sign when one of the doors swings open. Someone jumps out and I am eyeball to eyeball with a short, round-faced man in wire-framed circular eyeglasses. He is wearing a steel helmet with horns sticking out of its sides, and holding a sword bigger than he is, aimed at my nose. I don't move a muscle.

"Are you my nephew?" The man asks in a thunderous voice.

"You're Uncle Jasper?"

He shakes his head as if he's the one who is disgusted.

Seeing he isn't moving, I back my nose cautiously away from the sword tip. It looks really sharp. What have I gotten myself into? Correction: What has Mom gotten me into?

This character is studying me. Hasn't he ever seen a teen-ager before? He lowers the weapon, saying, "I must always be on guard." He gives me a 'squinchy' look. "You're skinny for a twelve year old."

"I'm not skinny! You're just…" I almost say, 'fat', but calling him 'fat' is a 'no-no' with a sword in his hand.

"Speak up, boy! I'm what?" He leans on the sword handle.

"You're a 'wide' man," I manage to say, not wanting him to throw me out with all those serpents flying around. "Your… er…grown-up size makes it look as if I'm skinny."

"No. Always tell the truth, boy! What you intended to say, but decided to not risk honesty, was that I am FAT. True? True? True?"

He is in my face, shouting at me, his eyeballs magnified by his eyeglasses. "I guess," I admit, cautious, because he still has the sword.

He has a big smirk on his face. "That's better. Honesty is the best medicine …or something like that." He glances up at the sky. "They get ravenous at night. You'd be barely a mouthful. We'd better go in."

I see something black flying along the horizon. "What are those," I ask, shivering as I see more flying snakes.

"You'll meet them later. Grab your bag, boy, I have work to do." Uncle Jasper is slapping along the brick walkway in floppy, blue slippers. He looks like a walrus. "Well are you coming or not?" Before I have a chance to answer, he charges inside.

Should I follow or run for it? The serpents are closer. I'd be hardly a mouthful. I see Uncle Jasper toss the helmet on a hat rack with a dozen other strange hats. I can't stop staring at him. Mom and that driver claimed Uncle Jasper is a hero. This gnome in grass-stained jeans, striped underwear showing above his baggy trousers, red, green, and yellow, plaid shirt, and bedroom slippers the size of elephant ears, looks more like a sloppy hero sandwich!

My smart phone! A way out!

Welcome to Monstrovia

The phone's face is blank. Absolutely perfect! Nothing works here. I can't even call my friends to help me escape.

"Are you coming or do you want to be snatched up?"

I drag my suitcase through the door, wondering what is waiting for me on the other side.

CHAPTER 6

Uncle Jasper leans the sword in a corner. Raising his eyeglasses to his forehead, he squints. "You have brown hair, like your mother, and you've got the famous Doofinch dimples." He smiles, showing off his dimples, and then just as quickly, frowns. "What am I to do with you? What was my sister thinking?" He lets out a deep sigh. "Well, I suppose I'd…we'd, better make the best of it."

I dodge Uncle Jasper's giant slippers. He could have been a kicker on the Jets. "Must get ready for work," he mumbles, and pulls open one of the doors that line the room.

The man is a tornado, grabbing a bright pink shirt, blue tie, red vest, and a pair of blue pants from a closet. "I was gardening. Do you garden? It's good for the soul and the brain. But now it's time to get to work. Leave your suitcase here. Go sit in my office. I'll be there in a dragon-swallow." He begins to dress behind the door.

How does he say so much in one breath? "Did you say 'dragon-swallow'?" I ask trying not to see his 'dressing jig'. He looks ridiculous! But he looked ridiculous in that helmet too. "You have dragons here?"

"Doesn't everyone?" He emerges from behind the closet, holding up his pants with one hand as he hops over to a red door marked in bold, black letters, "STAY OUT!"

I'm trying not to laugh.

"I've forgotten something," he says, and quickly grabs a pair of red suspenders from a hook. "Can't lose my pants, can I?"

I shrug. So uncool.

"What are you waiting on?" He bursts into laughter. "You have no idea where to go!" He shakes his head and his hair is flying again. "Take that yellow door, the one marked, "STAY OUT!". At the end of the hallway you'll find three more doors marked, "STAY OUT!" Enter the middle one and sit down. Be sure it's the middle one. And whatever you do, don't touch anything. Do you hear? DO NOT TOUCH ANYTHING! NOTHING! And stay out where it says, "STAY OUT", except of course when I tell you to go in."

What did he say? He is gone before I can ask even one of my many questions, like how am I supposed to sit down if I can't touch anything? How do I recognize which doors I can't go in or out, when they all say, STAY OUT!? Or what am I doing in Monstrovia, and how do I get home?

I shake my head, apparently 'inheriting' one of my uncle's rotten habits. After rethinking what I think he said, I pull open the yellow door warning in large black letters, to "STAY OUT!".

"What stinks?" My nose twitches. Monster B.O.? Nothing would surprise me. The door closes behind me. It is dark. I mean really dark. I can't see my hand! I can't see my sneakers!

But I do see something.

CHAPTER 7

Something is scurrying across the floor. Oh gosh! There's another!

I reach for the door knob. It is locked. That figures.

Something moves again. Did I go through the wrong door?

I hear the scurrying and see glowing, orange eyes. Rats?

Rats would be better than some Monstrovian monsters biting my ankles and toes while I wait for my uncle to rescue me. Like he will? The eyes are closer. I count thirteen. I can't stay here, but the door is still locked. I can't go back.

I feel my way in the dark, surprised to feel cold and 'rocky' walls. It feels like a cave? *Why is a cave in the middle of my uncle's house?*

"*Sniff. Sniff.*" Something is sniffing at my shoes. I wish I had my slingshot. Mom took it when I got in trouble with Principal Feeney again. "Rubber bands are okay for dental braces, but not for slingshots…not even for shooting spitballs," she said, and then gave a sigh that seemed to come all the way up from her toes. "Brodie, why can't you be good? Whoever heard of taking a slingshot to school? I don't know what I'm going to do with you this summer?"

I was looking forward to watching TV and sleeping late. It was going to be great…and then Mom dropped this bomb on me, and here I am, surrounded by all these glowing eyes.

"You're not scaring me!"

They seem to be everywhere, circling like wolves around prey. I have nothing with which to defend myself.

An idea hits me. "**CLAP! CLAP! CLAP!**"

The sound of my clapping stampedes the monsters and they race off in all directions and vanish. Did they go through the walls? Ghosts?

Spying a sliver of light coming from the end of the hallway, I head for what I hope is an exit. "Squish. Squish. Squish." It could be monster poop? I'm walking on monster poop!

"This place is weird," I exclaim.

"This place is weird…weird…weird…weird." It has a hollow sound, like an echo.

I love playing with echoes in tunnels, but I never heard of one in the middle of a house? "Hello?"

"Hello…hello…hello…hello."

"This place rots."

"You rot!" the echo barks back.

"Hey!" I don't think that's funny. I no longer hear the scratchy noises, or see the eyes, but I know they are near. Why does my uncle have a gargantuan cave inside his house?

I find the three doors my uncle described. Sure enough, they all have signs that warn in threatening black letters, "STAY OUT!". I'd love to take that great advice and head back to the airport, even if I have to hire that crazy cab driver, Bumperwinkle, or whatever his name is. I have no money, no phone…no hope.

My uncle told me to enter the middle door. I twist the knob. It opens a crack and I see inside. "This place gives me the creeps," escapes from my lips.

"You give us the creeps…creeps…creeps."

Something pushes me. The door slams. Goose bumps erupt on my body when it locks.

CHAPTER 8

Instantly I am hit by light. It went on by itself. I can't see after being in the dark cave. I hope some creature doesn't ambush me while I'm blind.

As my eyes adjust to the glaring light, I am amazed to see I am in a humongous room with a ceiling as high as my school gymnasium. The room is lit by a gargantuan lamp that looks like four dragon heads, hanging from a thick chain in the center of the ceiling. The dragon's eyes are shooting beams of light into the corners of the room.

"That's odd." Like what isn't? I've spotted a large doorway in a corner of the ceiling. Is that really a door?

Of course it's a door! Black lettering on the over-head door says, "STAY OUT!" Why is there a sign on the ceiling? Why is a door way up there? My eyes dart back to the dragon headed lamp. Is it possible? I'm not sticking around to find out.

But where can I go? The only 'normal' one I've met in Monstrovia is my uncle, oh yes, and that maniac driver, with his mushroom cab. They're not going to help me. I've got to wait for the right opportunity while I plan.

I decide to nose around the office. Something here might be helpful.

What a messy desk! There are papers everywhere. It looks normal, a big reddish wood desk. There's a dagger! It's just a letter opener.

The two red leather chairs in front of the desk look like my principal's chairs, only Mr. Feeney's legs are a lot shorter...I mean his chair legs, not his real legs. Anyway these chairs have seats as high as my chin and are made for big butts. I could use one to reach that door in the ceiling...

Behind the desk, there are black shelves running across the entire wall, reaching from floor to ceiling. How can my uncle reach the top? Maybe he stands on dragons? I laugh at the impossible picture of Uncle Jasper standing on a dragon, but one look at the ceiling makes me wonder again. Dragons need a lot of head room...

Maybe something on the shelves is cool? Nobody's around. What trouble can I get into just looking? My fingers itch to touch some of the weird items from the lower shelves...just curious, like any kid would be.

I am about to look at, okay, pick up, an ordinary bark-covered wood stick when my uncle's **booming** voice makes the walls shake, "I SAID, 'DON'T TOUCH ANYTHING! NOTHING!' DON'T YOU UNDERSTAND ENGLISH?"

I jump and land on a chair. How did he know? Does that sneak have cameras hidden in this office. Is he Mom's brother after all? She's sneaky too.

From my perch I search for any tiny hole that might hide a camera, but the only things on the walls are certificates and framed photographs. I'm stunned at what I see. "What the heck are all these ugly monsters doing with my Uncle?"

"I'm glad you asked that," my uncle says, bursting into the room. "I've helped every one of them!" He stands in front of the wall, his arms stretched wide, a big smirk on his face. "Without me, they would all be in 'grave' trouble!" He chuckles. "Grave...do you get it?" He fastens his necktie, a long snake-like creature embroidered down its front.

"Get what?" I have no idea what he is talking about.

"Grave...dead.,,trouble?" He chuckles again. "It's a joke!"

"Oh." *Rotten joke.* "Uncle, I don't understand all these... you know all these...these...."

"Fictional creatures." Uncle Jasper finishes.

"I was going to say 'ugly monsters'," I shoot at him, as I stare at a photo of a pimply gargoyle shaking my uncle's hand. Man, is he ugly! (The gargoyle, not my uncle... although Uncle Jasper isn't exactly what I would call 'gorgeous'.) Mom would have made that gargoyle cut his nails. They must be a foot long!

"Fictional creatures," Uncle Jasper corrects me. "They're my clients. That means customers. Actually, most are my friends. We don't have many humans here." He looks thoughtful and then smiles, deep dimples in his reddish cheeks showing as his voice rises, "Your uncle is the one and only Jasper Doofinch, famous defender of all fictional characters and mythical monsters in Monstrovia! Without me, many of these delightful citizens would be rotting in prison, exiled, or worse. I am their protector! I am DOOFINCH, THE DEFENDER!!!"

"You're kidding!" My mind returns to the elephant with all those octopus monsters hanging on for dear life, the two burly bear guards, and the other weird creatures I've already seen in my short time here. Are these the 'friends' he is talking about? This is too weird even for me. If this is what everyone is like, a voice howling inside my brain warns, I should have obeyed the signs posted all over this house and STAYED OUT!

CHAPTER 9

Sliding down from the giant chair, I walk to the wall to examine the photos of my uncle and his 'friends' more closely. There is a one-eyed cyclops, a three-headed serpent, even a witch in a black robe and tall, pointy, hat. "How do you know all these monsters?" They would have been great on one of those make-over shows. Wow! Great idea: Monstrovia Make-Overs!

Uncle Jasper smiles. "Do you know what a lawyer does?" He poses under a huge portrait of himself in a suit of armor, a helmet in one chubby hand, a large book in the other.

"You're a lawyer? Mom knows I hate lawyers. How could she do this to me?"

Uncle Jasper looks at me as if I am something he just walked in. "See here boy, I'll have you know lawyers are wonderful--"

"First, don't call me 'boy'! My name is Brodie Adkins. I'm named after my father, Brodie Adkins II. And two, there's no such thing as a 'wonderful' lawyer!" I shoot him one of my worst looks ever. I always knew Mom was sneaky, but sending me to stay with a lawyer! That's worse than sending me to Monstrovia!

Uncle Jasper adjusts his eyeglasses. "Brodie, eh? I have not had many dealings with human children before and your attitude--"

"Uncle Jasper, what am I going to do stuck here with you all summer? This wasn't my idea."

Uncle Jasper nods his head slowly with his eyes closed. He opens his eyes. "Good question. What can I do with a little boy?" He nods some more.

He's really getting on my nerves. "I'm not a little boy."

"Well, you are a teenager then, which is far worse. So I suppose you could do a little house work: cleaning closets, washing windows, filing files, shoveling dragon droppings--"

"DRAGON DROPPINGS? I'm a kid! There are laws about kids working! Big laws!"

He snorts, "I know the law! I'm a **lawyer**! Remember?"

"Do you mean LIAR?" It is like firing a mud ball at Principal Feeney's car. Direct hit! I can annoy any grown-up alive within ten minutes of meeting them. Mom says I have a real talent.

Uncle Jasper's thick, gray eyebrows pinch down over his large, round nose. "That's not funny, boy."

I am surprised how fast his face has gone kinda scary. His hair is standing up on top of his head like white flames. He looks like one of his monsters. Could staying in Monstrovia cause this kind of transformation? Can it happen to me if I stay? I have to get out of here, and fast!

"Lawyers are not liars." Uncle Jasper sounds as if he is choking back his anger.

"Right." Doesn't he know what lawyers did to me?

My uncle is twirling the end of his tie. "Brodie, I am going to explain this to you." He gives me a 'Mom look'. "When you get in trouble in school, and I have heard about your shenanigans from my dear sister, wouldn't you like someone to help you?"

"Mom told you about school?" So this really is a punishment. I can't think of a better one. Lock me away in a psycho world with a crazy uncle who is also a LAWYER!!!

"As I was saying." That stern look again. "When my clients are in trouble with the law they trust me to help them. I am very proud of what I do. They don't call me 'THE DEFENDER' for nothing."

Mom had called him a hero. Some hero!

Uncle Jasper sighs. "You don't believe me, do you?"

"If you say so."

"You're quite difficult," Uncle Jasper mutters.

"That's what they all say." How long will it be before I can frustrate him and he sends me back to New York? Not a bad plan.

There is a long silence. His eyes are measuring me…for a coffin. If a staring contest he wants, then that's what he'll get. I'm staring at him. He's staring at me.

Suddenly, he exclaims, "That's it! You'll soon see how I help others!" He bends down and I hear what sounds like a pig squealing in pain. "Skreeeeeeee!"

"What is that?" I yank my legs up under me on the chair in case some wild monster pig comes charging out from behind his desk.

"My desk alarm," he remarks, fishing something from a drawer. "This is for you." He reaches across the desk.

I'm suspicious. It could be a snake or anything evil. This guy hates me.

"Take it. It won't bite, although, you never know?"

I reach for a thin, leather case… cautiously.

"Open it. What are you waiting for?"

I unzip the case. "It's a feather. It's just a stupid, yellow, feather."

"No, boy, it's a treasure."

"It's a stupid feather."

"I'll have you know this 'feather' is the recording device I received when I graduated law school twenty years ago."

"It looks like a boring old feather to me." I tap the pointy end on the desk.

"Brodie, with this 'feather' you shall record my cases. You will be my historian, my key to immortality, my very own Doctor Watson."

"You're Wat…who?" I scratch the side of my nose with the feather. At least it has some use.

"You've never heard of Sherlock Holmes, a great detective, and his assistant, Dr. Watson? Marvelous mysteries!"

"No." I'd read Nancy Drew, The Hardy Boys, and Rockhound the Science Detective when I was a kid, but these days I'm more into video games and television than reading.

"What do they teach you in school these days? Sherlock Holmes was the greatest detective that ever lived, and Dr. Watson reported on all of their fantastic cases. You shall be my personal Dr. Watson!"

His wild eyes scare me. "You don't need me for that. You should buy a computerized recording device." I place the feather on his desk, eager to rid myself of it and him.

Uncle Jasper is waving his arms and full of smiles, ignoring me completely. "Yes, dear Brodie, you will record all my amazing cases! You shall soon see what a great man your uncle really is! The whole world will know of DOOFINCH THE DEFENDER!"

"But--" I begin to answer, then notice he looks like a racer waiting to take off, his eyes gleaming, and his teeth looking like those of a shark. Mom's warning comes back to me, "He loves arguing."

"Yes, nephew, you were about to say?"

He is itching for an argument alright. "Nothing." I'm not going to let this tricky relative I hardly know trick me into a fight... not until I'm sure I can't lose.

"Nothing?" He looks disappointed.

Gotcha uncle!

He's about to speak again when his door crashes against the wall. Something whooshes in and races for the only window. "I need help," the intruder says, peering through the blinds.

At the door busting open I jumped behind my uncle…to protect him of course. Now I am staring at this odd, 'whatever-it-is', in a gold raincoat and matching floppy hat, looking out the blinds. 'It' coughs. "Don't you ever dust? You've got 'dust bunnies' bigger than buffalo in here!"

Uncle Jasper smiles. "Brodie, get your feather. It's hero time."

CHAPTER 10

My eyes are on the creature glued to the window. I worry one of these monstrous inhabitants, even if a rather small one, is only a few yards away. Where is my uncle's sword when I need it?

At least Uncle Jasper didn't run like a scared rabbit when that door burst open.

"May I help you?" Uncle Jasper asks, seated in his chair, as if this weird stuff happens every day. It probably does.

May I help you? That's how you greet a monster? I try to see the thing's face, but it is hidden by the raincoat's collar and droopy hat.

Suddenly the hat is whipped-away.

Oh man! The 'terrifying monster' is just a girl with long, stringy, hair. She's dripping water all over the floor!

"I need a lawyer. My brother is in big trouble." She sees me and her eyes widen. "Are you a lawyer? How old are you?"

"Twe…How old are you?" I shoot back, thinking she is the first human—at least I think she is human-- I've seen in Monstrovia.

"Don't you know it's not polite to ask a 'lady' her age?" She shivers and water drips off her coat, like when a dog shakes after a bath.

"You're no lady. You're just a kid."

"Brodie," my uncle says, "A lawyer, and his 'assistant', never insult a client. Clients deserve our courtesy at all times."

Our visitor smiles. She won 'round one' and knows it.

"But she's not a lady."

"Brodie!"

As for the girl, she is strolling around like she owns the joint. She's still dripping water everywhere. She turns to my uncle. "You are Doofinch the Defender?"

I give my uncle a doubtful look. There must be another Doofinch the Defender! Another Doofinch?

Uncle Jasper glows, dimples showing like happy headlights. "How may I help you? Brodie, the feather…clockwise on…counter-clockwise off."

"I get it!" Who wants to do this all summer? Dr. Watson? Bleh! I wave the 'stupid' feather clockwise and am surprised by a slight vibration. The crazy thing might actually work? Now I'm going to be waving a spindly feather every time something happens around here? Talk about humiliating!

I attempt to hide the feather from the snob. I don't even know if she's a real human girl. Remember, we are in Monstrovia.

The girl twists her hat and more water hits the floor. Her voice trembles as she says, "My brother is wanted by the police."

"Why do they want him?" My uncle's desk drawer squeals again like a wounded pig as he pulls out a pen and thick pad of long, yellow, lined, paper.

"Beans," our visitor mutters, digging for something in her purse.

Welcome to Monstrovia

"Beans?" My uncle's eyebrows raise into question marks and his pen lifts off the pad. "My dear, did you say 'beans'?"

The girl wipes unruly strands of wet hair out of her eyes. "I meant to say... murder."

CHAPTER 11

Murder? Is she serious?

"Did you say, murder?" Uncle Jasper asks.

I hear sirens in the distance.

My uncle bounces to the window and peers through the blinds. He coughs loudly. "You're right, my dear, the dust bunnies are as big as buffalo in here." He gives me a disgusted look. "And the floor is wet too."

Why is he looking at me? I didn't do it. Does he think I'm his slave: shovel dragon droppings, clean dust buffalo off blinds, wash-up wet floors? Is this how I am going to spend my summer?

The girl rushes for the desk. "They're coming for me!"

What a drama queen!

She snatches a paper from her handbag and scribbles something. "Meet me here in an hour. You must." She hands my uncle the slip of paper.

"I didn't say I'd take your case." But he is scanning the note.

"You've got to help! I'm desperate!" She digs into her purse again and forces something into my hand. "The cops and banks have taken everything except this. We hid it. It's yours. Just help us? Please, help us?"

"Is this gold?" I ask, dazzled by the shimmering egg. "I don't have any change?"

"Change of an egg? That's crazy," she says and turns to my uncle. "One hour. You must be there!"

"But...but...but," Uncle Jasper stammers, as the soggy girl rushes out the door.

Uncle Jasper waddles to the window. "Gone," he mutters.

"What was that about?" I hand the egg to my uncle. "It can't be real gold?" Mom has lots of gold jewelry...all fake! This thing is amazing... if it is real?

"Interesting." Uncle Jasper examines the egg under his desk lamp. "Definitely interesting."

"But is it really gold?"

He walks to the wall and pulls away the large portrait of himself looking absolutely ridiculous in a suit of armor, revealing a slightly smaller painting of a dragon's head. "Brodie, can you keep a secret? You must never reveal this to anyone, not even if they threaten you with torture of the worst kind."

Reveal what? He looks silly wearing armor?

"Open sesame!" Uncle Jasper says loudly and gazes around, as if searching for spies. Instantly there is a roar, and the painted dragon's mouth opens wide.

"Holy crappoli!!!" This place is great for practicing jumping out of chairs. That roaring noise came from the dragon painting!

My uncle rolls up his shirt sleeve and shoves the egg, and his hand, wrist and arm, deep inside the gap between the dragon's razor-sharp teeth. He actually shoves his arm up to the elbow down the roaring monster's throat! You should have seen the size of those teeth! I wouldn't do that for a million dollars! I hardly breathe while his arm is in that dragon's mouth. One chomp and....

Mark H. Newhouse

Thankfully, a few seconds later, I see him pull his arm back. All the arm, wrist and fingers are still there. Maybe he is braver than he looks. As soon as Uncle Jasper retrieves his hand, the jaws slam shut and the dragon becomes a lifeless painting again.

"That will keep it safe." Uncle Jasper slides his portrait back over the dragon's head.

"I'll say." The vision of those ginormous dragon teeth around my uncle's arm is still in my brain.

"Don't you have a dragon vault at home," Uncle Jasper asks. "Everyone these days should have one. Even in this Special Sector crime has become a serious problem."

"No way would Mom allow something like that in our house." I'm thinking about dragon droppings and how Mom would react to that.

"Hmmm," he says, examining the paper with a magnifying glass.

"What did she write?" I ask it like 'normal', trying not to sound like I'm even a little curious.

This uncle I hardly know gives me an 'I know something you don't know' smile. I hate when grown-ups do that! But I refuse to beg for answers. I am sure that is just what my sneaky uncle wants. I'll bet he's thinking if he can get me interested in his dopey case, I might behave.

Uncle Jasper grabs his jacket and briefcase. "Gotta go."

He's leaving without me! I don't care. Well, maybe I do… only a sub-atomic little.

"Dr. Adkins, are you coming?" He is holding the door open. For me? "I told you, I do not waste time." He taps his foot impatiently. "Are you coming or not?"

"Do you know who she is?" I ask, rushing to join him before he changes his mind.

"Do you always ask so many questions?" He hands me the small rectangle of paper. "You be the detective. What do you make of it?"

As I guessed, she had scrawled an address on it. "No name." I look at the paper, still trying to hide my curiosity.

"Look on the other side. That's the important clue."

When I flip the paper over I am surprised to see it is a photograph. It is badly faded, but I can see what look like four scrawny legs on some kind of animal's body. I switch on my uncle's desk lamp and gasp. "It's a cow?"

"Brilliant detective work!"

I hate when adults are sarcastic. "It is a cow. Isn't it?"

"Read what it says below the photograph."

In very neat, hand-written, print under the photo, it says, "Elvira, we miss you."

"Holy cow," I exclaim, finding this really strange.

My uncle is tapping his elephant-sized shoe louder, clearly impatient. "Holy cow indeed! Now can you guess who our mysterious client is?"

"OUR client?"

"Yes, Dr. Adkins, my 'brilliant' assistant! I have a feeling this will be a very challenging case. I am going to need all the help I can get."

I figure he figures he's won me over, but I know 'sneaky' when I see it. At least he is taking me out of this insane office and letting me go with him. I am a little curious to see what this is all about, but as I speed after my uncle—everyone walks so fast around here- (I guess they don't want the monsters to get them?)-- I have a bad feeling I am going to need all the help I can get...and a truckload more. Now, I not only have to deal with monsters, and a weird uncle, but with a snobbish girl, who has a golden egg, and a faded photo of a cow, all in some secret place called, Monstrovia.

CHAPTER 12

We are outside the house rushing toward a large barn-like building at its side. I look up and spy what look like more of those serpents flying in the sky, but now they are illuminated by the moon, which makes them look like they have diamonds glowing in their skin. Their buzzing around makes me run faster.

My uncle stops at a humongous door, sharp metal spikes poking out of its dark wood surface. Of course, it has a large painted sign on it warning, "STAY OUT!".

Does Uncle Jasper have a crazed sign-painter client? I've never seen so many signs around a house before. Who are they, and these spikes, and spear-topped fences, designed to keep out?

"Wait here," Uncle Jasper orders.

He doesn't have to worry. I'm not going anywhere with these serpents flying around.

Uncle Jasper sucks in his breath and bellows, "Open Sesame" at the door.

"You think you're Aladdin?" I never read the story, but saw the Disney movie twenty times. (I'd kill for a genie of my own, but of course they're make-believe. Aren't they?)

"Don't you mean, Ali Baba? He lives in a palace not far from here. A bit stuck up for a newly rich young man."

"Right." I hear a scraping noise. The gargantuan doors are sliding sideways, revealing a huge, dark opening. "My garage," Uncle Jasper says.

"Where's your car?" I peek inside and pick up a strong odor, a bit like really stinky b.o..

"Patience is a virtue, nephew," Uncle Jasper replies, and waddles into the dark garage. He is gone a few seconds when I hear a low roar.

That could be a car motor?

The roar gets louder.

"You've got to be kidding!" I back away from the bizarro sight of my uncle seated behind handle-bars on the head of some gargantuan...dragon! The monster's large, v-shaped, head dips toward me with wide open mouth revealing two rows of scary, pointy, teeth.

"M...m...Meat-eater!"

"Don't remind him," Uncle Jasper hisses. "I've convinced him he's a vegetarian. It wasn't easy."

"I'm not convinced yet," I say, ducking away from the bobbing head.

"Nonsense. You'll be perfectly safe. You're in the sidecar." Uncle Jasper taps a white container at his side.

"I'm not going in that bathtub," I say, ducking again. "It looks like you put this whole crazy contraption together."

"I did! It's one-of-a-kind! You're wasting time! Hop up the tail. I'm a great driver!" He slaps his hand down and the horn on the handle makes a loud 'oogah' noise. "Where's your spirit of adventure? We must hasten to help our young damsel in distress!"

How could my mother leave me with this lunatic?

The meat-eater is still bobbing his head dangerously close, sniffing me with his flaring nostrils. Saliva is foaming on his lips. Vegetarian? I wonder.

"Stop playing with him. He won't bite you," Uncle Jasper says. "Now come on or wait out here until I return. I'll only be about…four hours!"

I glance at the sky and there are those swirling serpents. I recall my uncle's words, "You're hardly a mouthful". Dodging that head with its foaming mouth and mean-looking teeth, I reluctantly climb up over the tail, up into the sidecar. I don't like this dragon eyeing me like I'm a juicy human jelly donut.

"Don't forget your seat belt," Uncle Jasper helps me up. "Horace won't go anywhere unless you're wearing your safety belt and helmet."

"Who's Horace?" I strap on a helmet with a dozen pointy horns butting out from its bright yellow surface. *Yellow, the color of cowards. I hate wearing helmets on my bike and now I am wearing this horned yellow thing in public? No self-respecting dude would be seen in public wearing something like this!*

I am about to protest, but see Uncle Jasper is wearing a black leathery helmet with large red rubber balls glued to it, a real fashion statement. I can hardly keep from laughing. "I repeat, who is Horace?"

The dragon's head bobs toward me. Gulp… I think I know.

CHAPTER 13

The dragon's roar is deafening. Before I can get an answer, the 'dragon-vehicle' is jumping down the driveway, bumping noisily into the street. Within seconds we are no longer on our quiet road, but hurtling into that tangle of roads that is up, down and all around us.

"Not again!" I brace myself as the 'meat-eater' gallumps into traffic. My uncle's rude-sounding horn blasts, "Oogah! Oogah," as we charge in front of a speeding knight in armor, on what looks like a giant goat. The knight isn't very nice with his hand gesture's meaning being clear, even in armor.

Horns blare all around as we dart in and out of the strangest vehicles I've ever seen. There are more knights on unicorns and giant goats, carts pulled by huge pigs, speeding pumpkin-like-thingees, and more mushrooms, like Bumbernickle's, all traveling at incredible speeds. We weave in and out of these chains of odd-ball vehicles as if none of the others exist. "Oogah! Oogah!"

I hold onto the sidecar with white knuckles. "Slow down!" I scream.

"Yes. It is a nice town," Uncle Jasper replies, his scraggly hair peeking out of his helmet, as he uses the handlebars to steer the dragon in and out of the traffic.

No wonder he's a lawyer, I groan, hanging on, bounce after bounce, as he ignores every law I know about driving. Where are the Police when you need them? I'm rockin' and bumpin' all over the side-car.

Welcome to Monstrovia

Odd looking buildings are flying by so fast I can't tell if they are made of brick, stone or straw. Dust clogs my lungs and the noise of the dragon's massive feet is like the beat of a kettle drum. Aren't these people afraid of crashing? Oh, I forgot, they're not people.

Suddenly, the noise and congestion is gone. We are galloping on a beautiful one-level tree-lined road. There aren't any other crazy cars or contraptions. The road's surface is smooth, and the sky is blue and clear. I don't see even one of those horrible serpents. Are we back in Key West? Oh please?

"Whoa Horace!"

With a loud squeal, the dragon-bike, or whatever it is, comes to a sharp stop, throwing me and the sidecar forward.

When I straighten up, I see we are at a gate between two tall stone columns.

Uncle Jasper straightens his glasses and fishes out the photograph from his jacket pocket. He compares the card to a flat stone in one of the columns. "This is the address," he says, standing on his seat to peer over the spiked gate. He touches one of the spikes. "These would have made Vlad proud."

"Vlad?"

"Vlad...Dracula. You do know about him, don't you? Nice fellow really, once you get past his fangs. I'll introduce you. I defended him when accused of breaking into the blood bank. Unfortunately, he was caught 'red-handed'."

"Is that a joke?"

"Not at all. He served two lifetimes for that. We'll go there for dinner one night."

"No thank you." I'm still shaking from the worst ride of my life and he wants me to eat with Dracula! And what about this Horace? "Is 'IT' a real dragon," I ask, as Horace's head swings toward me again, mouth wide open, reeking of smoke. The smoke smells like Mom's cleaning junk, kinda thick and chokey.

"You can pet him," Uncle Jasper coaxes. "He doesn't bite. Lost his flying license, poor, old thing. One of these days I'll have to get it back for him. Age discrimination, you know. Go ahead, pet him."

"I'd rather not." I dodge the dragon's head as it dips toward the 'tub'. I wonder if he is going to tell me next that Dracula doesn't bite either. Nice fellow, huh? I imagine heads sitting on top of the spear-points on this tall fence. Will I be next? Not in this yellow helmet! I'd die of embarrassment...if I wasn't dead already from the vampire, dragons or serpents!

"Forgive him, Horace old boy, he's been reading too many fairy tales," my uncle says to the dragon, who lets out another puff of smoke.

"I do not read fairy tales! Those are for babies. Kids today don't bother with all those dumb make-believe stories."

Uncle Jasper looks shocked. "You don't like fairy tales? I used to love them as a child. I still do."

"That figures. Everyone knows all those stories are fake. No such creatures exist."

Welcome to Monstrovia

Then I remember where I am, and all I have already seen. A chill shoots through me.

Uncle Jasper leans down across Horace's neck, "My nephew has a lot to learn, Horace, old friend." He pushes a button on the right stone column.

I notice a faded square where a nameplate once was bolted to the column.

Uncle Jasper pushes the button again.

I hope nobody is home.

There is a loud buzzing noise and the gate creaks open. It reminds me of the gate at the cemetery. I wouldn't go in there, not even in daylight. I have a bad feeling about this.

333333333

CHAPTER 14

"Forward, Horace, my friend." My uncle gives me a smile. "Hold on. We're almost there, Kiddo."

I would yell at him for calling me that, but I have other things on my brain. I brace myself against the sidecar wall, expecting another 'rocket' ride, only to be surprised when we putt-putt down the long road with hardly a bump.

Horace's head barely avoids being struck by the branches reaching over the side of the road as if to grab us.

My uncle's eyes jump from one side of the narrow road to the other. "They have a lot of 'spaghetti'. That means lots of money, but it doesn't take Sherlock Holmes to observe something isn't right here." He looks at me. "Sherlock Holmes? Remember?"

"I know. The great detective." He is testing me! He actually wants to see if I paid attention when he talked about Sherlock Holmes earlier! What nerve!!!

"Very good. I knew you could do it, despite your dismal school record."

"Thank you." I clench my fists, refusing to get into an argument with him.

We pass several larger-than-life statues of a duck, pig, chicken, and of course, a cow. Some show cracks, all have green mold on their gray concrete surface.

"Yes, they had a lot of spaghetti," Uncle Jasper remarks again.

Welcome to Monstrovia

I understand he means rich, but why the potholes, the scraggly weeds, and wide cracks? Why do the statues have green gunk growing on them? Hey, why am I even slightly interested? I'm not. Well, maybe a little?

"There is something definitely wrong here," Uncle Jasper keeps mumbling.

There sure is, I think, glaring at my uncle, the lunatic lawyer.

The long road ends in a wide semi-circular driveway before a gargantuan three-story mansion. "This place is even larger than your house," I say, resentful Mom and I had to move into a small Brooklyn apartment after 'D' (Divorce) Day.

"Things will get better," Mom always said.

Right! I wonder how many of those teensy, rubber bands for braces Mom has to sell to Chinese dentists before I'll be able to live with her again. I just need to get away from my uncle's weird house and Monstrovia, which reminds me of something I had almost forgotten. "Uncle Jasper, what are those creatures in your hallway?" I remember the orange eyes and noises I heard when I was searching for his office door. "Are they rats? I hate rats."

"Oh them. They're just Scramblers," Uncle Jasper replies, as Horace moves slowly over the gravel driveway. "Every house has them. You know how when something is missing and you can't find it anywhere? The Scramblers snatch them. I can't tell you how many things I've lost because of those little rascals."

Really? Good excuse next time I can't find my homework. "So, they don't bite?" Not like the 'man-eater', Horace, who keeps looking at me like I'm hamburger.

"No, they don't bite. But you must put away your stuff carefully, or the little devils will grab it and trade it with each other."

Horace stops walking.

My eyes are traveling the width of an amazingly large house. It is twice as 'gargantuan' as my school!

"She can't possibly live here," I say, as the door opens and the girl herself, comes out and gawks at us. She is wearing a gold t-shirt over matching gold jeans, and you guessed it, gold sneakers. Spoiled brat, I'm thinking, struggling to escape the sidecar before she spots me. I don't want her seeing me in a bathtub for goodness sake!

Her hair, no longer soggy, is reddish, and tied in a pony tail. She looks different. With all the water off her face, she looks almost cute… until she opens her mouth.

CHAPTER 15

"Looks dangerous," Miss Smarty-pants sneers, poking her finger at the dragon, who shoots her a snort of purple and black smoke that smells like body odor.

"Danger is my middle name," my uncle crows, as he climbs down Horace's back. "May I tie him to a column on your porch? He won't pull it down."

"Jasper 'Danger' Doofinch? Some name for a lawyer!" I turn to the girl. "What's your name?" She has been studying me with her green cat eyes. I'm allergic to cats. I'm allergic to her too.

"I like your helmet," she purrs, then shakes her head, and laughs.

I forgot to take that yellow 'horror' off my head? How embarrassing! I pull it off and throw it up into the sidecar. I can't believe she saw me in it!

"Emily." She turns instantly toward the door.

"Emily what?" She is really rude! You don't turn away when someone is talking to you!

Uncle Jasper smiles. "Brodie, her name is Emily Beanstalk."

"Beanstalk? That's a dumb name." It just pops out of my mouth. Mom says that happens a lot to me. "Sometimes, Brodie, I think your brain is not connected to your mouth," I hear her say.

"Brodie!" My uncle looks shocked.

I've seen that look before, on Mom, my teachers, Mr. Feeney. I'm used to it.

"Well it is. Whoever heard of anyone being named after a bean stalk?"

My uncle looks annoyed. "Brodie, I'll have you know hers is one of the most rich and famous families in Monstrovia."

Emily frowns. "Everyone remembers the rich part, Mr. Doofinch, but we weren't always rich, and we're definitely not now. The bank took most of our stuff, but said we could keep this house. The cops took everything else as 'evidence'. We're really in a fix."

Right, I think, as I follow her into a tiled lobby with gold railings along twin staircases. *Not rich with a place this size? Who's she kidding?*

Emily leads us into a gargantuan room with floor to ceiling windows.

"You've got some palace. I bet your bathroom is larger than my whole apartment." Something's strange. I don't see any furniture.

"Brodie Adkins," Uncle Jasper hisses, looking like he's about to have a fit, "Will you please stop?"

Emily sighs. "Come with me. I want to show you something."

"Where to?" I'm imagining racing my roller blades down the long hall.

"You'll see," Emily says.

I hate when people say that.

As my uncle and I follow Emily, I see faded squares on the walls. Where are the pictures? Where is the furniture?

We walk through two tall glass doors and down four marble stairs, to a huge swimming pool, shaped like a star. It is empty, except for a coating of grunge.

"I guess you have lots of fancy pool parties?" What a show-off!

"Brodie!" Uncle Jasper snorts.

Emily points with a finger that looks like she bit the nail off...no polish. "Look back there."

"I don't see anything." I look harder and see a small building. It looks like a box. As we walk closer, I realize the 'box' is a shack. Its thatched roof is sagging over dark, planked walls.

"Is this your slaves' cabin?" I'm being sarcastic, but maybe they do have slaves in Monstrovia? Who knows what goes on here?

"Brodie!" Uncle Jasper groans.

Emily sighs. "You don't get it. This was our house."

"This was your house?" It looks like it was gutted by fire, walls black and brittle. If I spit on it, the whole mess will come tumbling down. I don't believe her for a second.

"Mom kept it here so we never forget how poor we were." She gives me a sad smile. "You don't believe me, do you?"

"Nobody is this poor."

My uncle says, "Oh, Brodie, you have a lot to learn."

How can he say that in front of Emily? I can almost see her keeping score: Two for Emily and a big, fat, ZERO for Brodie!

"Mr. Doofinch, do you have my photograph?" Emily holds out her hand. "It's very precious."

Precious? It's just a picture of a cow!

"That's Elvira." Emily takes the photo from my uncle, a tear dangling from her eye.

How can she cry over a cow, and a really skinny cow of all things? I can understand crying over a dog, a family cat, maybe even a dead fish, but a cow?

"Poor, poor Elvira," Emily moans, as she gazes at the cow.

"When do we get to the murder?" I want to get to the 'juicy' stuff already.

"Be patient, Brodie," Uncle Jasper scolds. "Patience is a virtue."

"Thank you, Mr. Doofinch," Emily says, smiling so sweetly at him I could strangle her.

"Thank you," I snipe at my uncle for helping her yet again.

"Patience is a quality you should learn, Brodie," my uncle drones on. "I was once young and impatient too, like you, dear nephew." He gives me a fake kind look that makes me even angrier. "Yes, it doesn't seem that long ago...."

Please, not another lecture? Emily is laughing in my face. I don't like her. I don't like my uncle. And I don't like Monstrovia. So how do I get out of here?

CHAPTER 16

Emily waits for my uncle's lecture to be finished before she speaks again. "My father, C.C. Bordenschlocker-- that was our real name until the 'beanstalk incident', when we changed our last name—Anyway C.C. ran off one night when Jack and I were little. We had to move from the big house back to this shack. We were poor. Heck, we were starving!"

"Bordenschlocker?" And I thought Beanstalk was a weird name? "What'd you do? Eat the cow?"

Emily Bordenschlocker, aka Beanstalk, looks shocked. "Of course not! We could never eat Elvira!"

"Brodie Adkins Junior!" My uncle sounds like he is barking at me.

"Eat Elvira? The very idea." Emily Bordenschlocker scowls at me. I scowl right back.

"No way could we eat Elvira." She gives me another shot with her eyes. "But Mom had to do something. So she told Jack to sell Elvira."

"Jack is your older brother," Uncle Jasper asks, giving me a warning look.

"Yes. He's fifteen."

So she's younger than fifteen...maybe thirteen?

"My brother met a salesman who wanted to trade for Elvira. Jack said no, but this peddler told him town is a long way off, and he might not find anyone who wants to buy such a sad-looking, sorry-smelling, (Elvira did have a serious odor problem), cow."

"So your brother traded your cow to the peddler," Uncle Jasper says.

"The sneaky peddler tricked Jack."

"I get it! Jack killed the peddler because he felt cheated. Case closed! Let's go home," I say, full of false hope.

"What? No! Jack didn't kill the peddler! He didn't kill anyone! Read this!" Emily shoves a newspaper clipping into my uncle's hand.

He reads the article silently and hands it to me. I never read the paper, but I'm curious, so I take it. The headline reads:

"Teen Thief Terminates Titan!"

"Sounds like a tongue-twister." I repeat the headline three times before my tongue gets all twisted up. "What's a titan?"

"A giant. Shhh! Just read it," Uncle Jasper scolds. "You give me a headache."

"Stop shushing me!" Like I said, I never read the paper and really didn't want to read it now, but Uncle Jasper is eyeing me. So is 'you-know-who'. "It says here, your brother is a thief and he killed a giant? Wait! You have giants here?" Why am I surprised? They've got dragons and bloodsuckers.

"Jack is not a thief. And he's not a murderer. He may be slightly d-u-m-b, but he's not a criminal." Emily frowns.

"Yeah right. Then why does it say Jack broke into the home of Mr. and Mrs. Eugene Bulk three times? Does that sound like a good kid to you?"

"He is a good kid. Jack said he was invited."

"Like dust buffalo are invited?" I slam her words back at her. One point for Brodie!

My Uncle shakes his head at me. "The paper says Jack killed Mr. Bulk, during the third burglary," he says, studying Emily's face.

"He didn't kill anyone, sir. It was an accident."

"Emily, I need to explain the law." He peers into her eyes. "When someone dies, even by accident, while a crime is committed, the perpetrator, the one who committed the crime, can be charged with murder."

I'm thinking Uncle Jasper looks like a sloppy St. Bernard as he gazes sadly into her eyes. "Do you understand?"

"I think so. But Jack swears it was an accident. I believe him."

Uncle Jasper sighs. "Emily, you don't get it. If Mr. Bulk died during a burglary, Jack will be charged with murder."

"I didn't know that," comes out of me.

"This is very serious. I should be talking to your mother. Where is she?"

Emily gazes down at her gold sneakers.

More bad news is coming.

CHAPTER 17

"Mom went looking for Jack," Emily says, still looking at her sneakers.

Uncle Jasper sighs. "Without your mother, I'm not sure how I can help."

Emily is trembling. Is she going to cry? I hate seeing anyone cry, especially a girl. Mom cried all the time before the divorce, and then after. I'd almost forgotten. I hated seeing her like that. Dad says it's wrong for boys to cry, and I don't think he's right, but I still hide when I cry. Emily, I can see she's fighting it, but her lip is giving her away. As much as I think Emily is a spoiled brat, I can't believe my uncle is saying he won't help her. What kind of 'hero' walks away from a crying girl? I should say something, but it's not my business. He's the lawyer.

Uncle Jasper pats down his hair. "I'm sure your Mother will return soon. Please, have her call me. I'd like to help." Uncle Jasper hands Emily an off-white handkerchief. "Let's go, Brodie. It's past your bedtime."

My bedtime? He said that In front of her?

"Can't we help her without her mother?" I have to get her attention off that last business about 'my bedtime'.

Emily blows her nose. "Mr. Doofinch, I can't wait for Mom. My brother is in real serious trouble. You have to understand that sneaky salesman tricked Jack. Do you know what my brother got for dear, sweet, Elvira?"

What could he get for a skinny, smelly cow?

"Beans...That slick, sly, sneaky, salesman gave Jack three gloppy baked 'farty' beans and convinced him he'd gotten a super deal!"

Some kids can be so dumb. I hate farty beans and wouldn't even trade my uncle for them. Well, maybe I would?

"What are farfy beans," Uncle Jasper asks.

I look at Emily and she looks at me, and we both burst out laughing. Is it possible someone does not know about the farty beans? "Not far-fy beans, but farteeeee beans. You know, 'Beans, beans good for the heart—'"

Emily chimes in, "The more you eat the more you--"

"Oh." Uncle Jasper interrupts quickly, looking embarrassed.

Emily and I shake our heads at the same time. (Now, that's scary!)

"So Jack came home with three...er...beans?"

Uncle Jasper just can't seem to say it. It's just a natural function. Some adults can't say 'burping' either.

Emily stops laughing. "Jack was holding up those gloppy fa-a-arty beans like he'd won the lottery. Mom was ready to kill him."

"I don't blame her," I say, "I'd kill him too. Who trades a cow, even a smelly one, for three crummy beans?"

"Shhh!" Uncle Jasper scowls at me. "Please continue, Emily?"

Emily nods. "That sly, slithering, snake of a salesman said the beans were magic."

"Magic farty beans? That's really funny!" I burst into laughter again. "Your brother must be real dumb."

"BRODIE!"

"The beans were magic," Emily says.

"I've never heard of magic beans," I reply. "Even non-farty beans."

"Emily," my Uncle says gently, "I've never heard of magic beans either... of any kind."

Emily nods. "That's why Mom screamed and shouted at Jack until our shabby shack shook. "How could you give away our sweet Elvira?" Okay, Elvira did have an odor problem, but she was a good cow, except she was too old to give milk, too weak to pull a plow, and she wobbled when she walked. Oh who am I kidding? The poor cow was a wreck! But to trade her for three beans? Mom lost it. Her hand smacked the beans sailing out the window." Emily's hand just misses me as she demonstrates.

"Hey," I shout, ducking the flying hand.

Emily ignores me as usual. "Mom sent Jack to bed without supper. What could we do now? My father, C.C., had vanished years ago without a trace, and Jack had now given away Elvira, our last hope."

"What happened next," my uncle asks, his eyes riveted on Emily.

She sniffles some more. "The next morning, I found a note from Mom saying Jack had run away and she was going to find him." Emily takes another trumpeting blast into the hankie.

"Your mother never came back," Uncle Jasper asks.

Emily shakes her head. "I was starving. I thought of Jack's gloppy beans and went out to find them, or some roots and bugs to eat. Instead I saw--"

"You eat bugs?" My stomach clenches violently. The beans were bad enough, but bugs?

"I was starving."

"I could never be that hungry."

"You really do have a lot to learn," Uncle Jasper hits me again.

Emily is on the rickety shack porch. She whips her hand through a web hanging across the doorway.

"She's going to eat that gross spider," I warn my uncle. I breathe a sigh of relief when she just passes below it.

My uncle tests the floorboards with his shoe. The rotted planks creak loudly. "Follow her," he says, stepping down from the rickety porch.

"Sure, give me the dirty work!" He should go on a diet, a big diet. Maybe then the porch won't creak.

A monstrous black hairy spider is in the upper corner of the doorway. It is opening and closing its mouth, staring down at me with its red eyes. It looks like it wants to get me before I get it. I can't move. It is like I am hypnotized.

"You're not afraid of a little spider are you?" Emily's Bordenschlocker eyes are looking right at me.

"Who me?" I glare at Emily, and then at the spider, then back at Emily. I'm not sure which one I hate more.

CHAPTER 18

Emily smiles sweetly. "Well, come on, Brodie, unless you're afraid?"

"I've never seen such a gargantuan spider," I stammer, eyeball-to-eyeball with its red eyes and dripping jaws. I hate Monstrovian spiders.

"Don't be afraid," Uncle Jasper, the brave hero, advises, safe on the ground, while I'm below 'bloodthirsty' here. This was the 'anti-Charlotte'! No way could I ever imagine a spider as a best friend after this ugly, hairy thing! E.B. White, you're a liar!

Emily laughs loudly. "Why that's just a little old wolf spider. If you think that's big...."

The song, "Who's afraid of the big, bad wolf?", instantly plays in my brain, as I stare at this monster hanging from a bug-filled web.

My uncle taps his foot and urges me on.

Emily's smirky grin is daring me.

"You'd better behave," I threaten the beast, ready to slug the bug if it moves just one hairy leg.

Am I really going to do this?

With both eyes locked on that eight-legged monster, I step toward the door.

I am almost there...almost...there.

"BOO!," Emily yells, bursting into rude laughter when I jump clear off the porch, almost knocking down my uncle.

Breathing hard, I glare at Emily, my heart pounding and my hands, now fists, shaking. Aren't girls supposed to be nice and gentle? Not Emily! She is such a 'stuck-up' brat!

My uncle is laughing. I'll fix him later. I stomp toward the door. "If you can do it, Miss Emily Brat-Bordenschlocker, so can I!"

Emily laughs again and disappears inside the shack.

I take a deep breath, duck under the spider with my hand above my head to protect my hair from sticky web goo. I almost wish I had that ugly, yellow, helmet. "I did it!" I am finally past the spider, glaring at Emily. "That was a nasty trick."

"I couldn't resist."

I can tell she's enjoying my humiliation.

"Let's finish this fast." I'm searching all around for more ugly beasts.

Emily nods. But of course she doesn't apologize. I'll get her back later. She doesn't know who she's messing with.

"This is the kitchen where Jack first showed us the beans," Emily says, as if she did nothing wrong. What a little angel!

I am so mad I can hardly concentrate. The place is a roach motel! I definitely don't want to touch the cruddy wood-planked tabletop in front of me, covered with dried leaves and other gunk.

Emily points to a rickety, worm-eaten window frame with crooked fingers of broken glass. "Mom slammed the beans through here when she got mad."

The floor sags. Spiders are everywhere and the webs stick to my hair and skin like stubborn, almost invisible, strings of already-been-chewed bubble gum!

Emily doesn't seem to mind anything. She scoops some decaying leaves out of the rusty basin with her bare hands. A fist-sized cockroach comes crawling up her arm. It is huge! I hope it bites her. I can't wait to hear her scream. But she cups it in her hand and puts it back under the leaves. I'm just glad she didn't eat it! How can she be so gentle with that ugly thing and so crummy to me?

I am itching like crazy, imagining thin spider legs crawling all over me. Scratch. Scratch! Scratch!

Emily keeps rattling on, "We lived here before my father struck it rich. He then built the mansion and changed our family name from Bordenschlocker to Beanstalk. He had always hated his first name so he called himself C.C. Beanstalk. Whenever anyone asked how he became rich, he told them he found the golden goose."

I am about to ask about this golden goose bologna when Emily, without warning, charges out of the shack.

I'm grateful to get out of there.

My uncle is bending down over something brown. Thank goodness his underpants aren't showing, for a change! It looks like a bug.

Emily picks up the 'bug' with two fingers and holds it up. "This bean's a dud," she says, handing it to my uncle. "But one of the beans was magic. It grew into a giant beanstalk. It grew and grew until it reached the sky."

"Giant beanstalk? She is kidding. Isn't she?"

"I wonder." Uncle Jasper's eyes are aimed at the sky. "Strange things happen in Monstrovia."

"Are the spiders poisonous?" I am reaching into the back of my shirt for a good scratch. I'm all itchy.

Emily looks serious. "Oh, Monstrovian spiders are very venomous. One bite and they turn you into a scratching post!" She bursts into laughter. She is really having fun at my expense.

I stop scratching. No way am I giving her the satisfaction! Not even if those itches kill me. (I will not scratch. I will not scratch.)

"Tell me about the beanstalk." Uncle Jasper is still staring up at the sky.

Sure, he cares more about a stupid plant than about his nephew being bitten to death by poisonous spiders! I have to scratch again, even if Emily sees me. I try so hard not to, but then... ooh, it feels so good. Scratch. Scratch. "Mmmm."

"That's what's left." Emily points to a stump a few feet high.

"It looks dead." I go to plop my butt on it.

Emily grabs my hand and slams it on top of the stump. "Does that feel dead to you? Does it?"

Why is she yelling at me? I am about to slug her when I feel something thumping under my palm. "Thumpa...thump...thumpa...thump..."

CHAPTER 19

I jerk my hand free. "It's a trick! Isn't it?" She played one on me before, so why not another?

"Thumpa…thumpa…thumpa…."

"That's her heartbeat." Emily lowers her hand gently. "It feels like jelly, doesn't it?"

I pull my penknife from my sock. Mom would have killed me if she knew I'd snuck it in my suitcase, but a pencil point is sharper.

"Who are you cutting with that toy?" Emily sniggers.

"I'm taking evidence, if you must know?"

"Oh no, you don't!" Emily blocks me.

"Oh yes, I do." Who died and left her boss of the world?

"Would you like me to cut a 'sample' off you?"

"That's silly!" I poke the tiniest slit into the bark.

"Did you hear that?" Emily grabs my hand.

"I didn't hear a thing." She's nuts. I pull free and cut a little deeper. "What's that?" I hear a low moan. The stump shivers.

"I'm sorry," Emily says to the stump and whirls on me. "Don't you know plants have feelings? All living things have feelings… except some **boys**!"

I am too busy trying to hold my penknife in the quivering stump to reply. And why would I even talk to someone nasty anyway?

Uncle Jasper bends towards me. He grunts and says, "Brodie, stop that, please?"

The stump lets out a long, ghost-like moan as I wiggle out my blade.

Emily tries to grab my hand again. "You hurt it! Say you're sorry!"

"I'm not apologizing to a dumb stump!

"An apology can't hurt you! Apologize!"

I hope she remembers that the next time she makes a nasty crack about me. "No! I am not apologizing to a stump!"

The shivering stalk moans louder. I'm getting nervous.

"APOLOGIZE NOW!" Emily looks like she is about to slug me.

I turn to Uncle Jasper for help. "It's just a dead tree."

"Apologize Brodie!," he orders.

"Are you serious?" I am tired of adding up Emily's 'points'.

He nods. "Apologize now, please."

"I don't believe this! I'M SORRY!"

"Again," Emily orders, her ear pressed against the bark.

"I'm sorry, sorry, sorry!" I look at my uncle. "Uncle Jasper, this is ridiculous!"

"Do as Emily says, Brodie. This confirms what I've long believed, plants have feelings. Now, apologize like you mean it Brodie. We have important work to do."

"I'm very, very, very sorry," I growl through gritted teeth, glaring at my traitor uncle. To my surprise, the shivering slows.

"Say it again!" Emily is really pushing her luck with me.

I feel totally stupid, but say it anyway. "I'm very sorry, oh beautiful stump."

The stump stops shaking. Just like that.

Emily listens a little longer. "Lucky for you, I think she's okay!"

Am I ever going to be 'okay' again? Not with all this craziness!

"Goodbye," Emily calls to the stump, as she drags me away, penknife still in hand. "Say goodbye, Brodie."

I refuse to say goodbye to a stump, but I keep looking back as we walk, which is why I trip and fall into a hole. In front of Emily!

CHAPTER 20

"Be careful! This is where that awful Mr. Bulk landed." Of course Emily warns me too late.

"I don't see anything!" I angrily pick myself up, with as much dignity as possible. First the yellow helmet, then apologizing to a tree stump, and now nose-diving into a hole. This is too embarrassing for words.

"You're standing in it," Emily says smugly.

My uncle looks down. "It has a human shape, Emily. Quite a large human...perhaps twenty feet tall? The giant?"

Emily nods. "Mr. Bulk, according to Jack, was a terrifying giant. The police say Jack killed him when he chopped down the beanstalk to make his getaway... while Mr. Bulk was on it."

I'm in a crater about knee-deep, shaped like a giant human being. "OMG!"

"Is that lawyer talk?" Emily offers her hand to help me out of the hole.

She's mocking me! I refuse her hand. "That's it! I've seen enough for one day!" Especially of Emily and my traitor of an uncle who I just met and wish I hadn't.

"I guess we have seen enough for now," Uncle Jasper says.

"Thank you for coming, Mr. Doofinch." Emily smiles at him. "I knew I could count on you to help us."

Mark H. Newhouse

Uncle Jasper smacks his forehead. "I almost forgot. I need to see your brother to help him turn himself in to the police."

Emily walks away.

"I need to talk to Jack." Uncle Jasper calls after her.

"I told you he ran away. I haven't seen him in days."

"But you must know where he is." Uncle Jasper is panting as he tries to keep up with her.

"I really don't know." Emily walks faster.

"Why didn't you tell me that before?" My Uncle's words pop through, between gasps for air.

"You didn't ask!" Emily is almost running.

My uncle's face looks red. "You knew I was coming here to help him! He has to turn himself in." He signals me. "Go after her, Brodie! Ask her where he is. He must give himself up before the Monstrovian cops catch him."

I catch up to Emily and grab her arm. "Where is Jack? Now! Spill it!"

"Let go!" Emily's eyes are blazing. "Let go now or you're fired!"

I release her gladly. Who needs her anyway?

My uncle is struggling up the steep hill. He can't hear me yet. "Go ahead! Fire us! Please fire us? This case is insane! Magic beans, giants falling from the sky, and skinny cows with odor problems! This whole case is bananas! Please fire us? I'm begging you!"

"Thank you, Brodie," my uncle says, giving me the evil eye. "I'll take over now." He is still panting.

"You don't have to." My eyes are shooting fire at Emily. "She fired us."

"Is this true?"

Emily sighs. "I can't fire you. I've tried everyone else."

"I see," Uncle Jasper says, looking sad.

"See, she doesn't want us. You were her last resort." I hope he takes the hint and we can drop this case and get to what is important: how I can escape and get back to my normal life.

Uncle Jasper stares at me and turns to Emily. "I've helped hundreds of Monstrovians. You came to me. I did not ask for this case. I am Jasper D. Doofinch, Defender of Mythical Monsters and Fictional Folk! I am a Monstrovian Knight! You can trust me."

Emily's eyes are tearing-up. "I wish Mom was here."

My uncle gives her a comforting smile. "Let us help you? They don't call me, Doofinch the Defender for nothing."

"Let's go." I'm pulling on his sleeve. "She doesn't want our help."

Uncle Jasper pries my fingers loose. "Please Emily, for Jack's sake, where is he? Let me help you?"

How can he beg her? I'm disgusted. Some hero! "Let's go? Let her figure it out for herself."

Emily kicks at the dirt. "He's in the one place nobody would ever look for him."

Uncle Jasper's voice is soft. "He'll never be safe. You can't hide from the police forever. Emily, dear, please tell me where he is?"

"Tell us already," I butt-in, unable to guess where he might be.

Emily lets out a deep sigh and points a shaky finger straight up. "He's up there."

Uncle Jasper looks up. "Up there?"

Emily nods. "He's back in the Bulk's castle. I tried to stop him. It's so dangerous, but he said no cops would go there. I hope he's alright. I couldn't stop him-"

"No wonder the cops can't find him. That is the last place I'd look for him." Uncle Jasper is still looking up.

"Maybe he's not so dumb after all," I mumble a bit too loudly, earning another dirty look from 'her brattiness'.

"I tried to get him to go to the police, but he's afraid. So am I. We don't know what to do."

Uncle Jasper puts his arm around Emily's shoulder. "You have been through a lot. I'm truly sorry. By now the police are searching for him. Jack was right, nobody would think he'd return to the Bulk's castle, but it's time for someone to get him."

Uncle Jasper and Emily both look in my direction.

"Please tell me he has a cell phone?" I don't like the way they are looking at me.

CHAPTER 21

"We have to go up and get Jack." Emily says, as if this is no big deal. She needs serious help!

"WE? UP THERE? HOW?" Now I am staring up at the sky too.

Emily wiggles her finger. "Follow me." She leads us all the way back to the rear of the ratty shack and those darn spiders.

"Here we are." Emily hunches down over the stump, her lips moving a mile a minute, as usual. "I didn't want to show you before…I wasn't sure I could trust you."

"What are you doing?"

"Shhh!"

"How many times do I have to tell you not to shush me?"

"Shush Brodie," my uncle echoes.

I am about to scream I've had enough, when I notice the top of the beanstalk is bubbling. It looks like the sap is boiling.

"One of you tell her a joke. I'm all joked-out." Emily looks up at us.

"You've been telling this plant jokes," Uncle Jasper asks.

"It's the secret. You mustn't tell." Emily addresses the stump, "Why did the cow cross the road?"

"Because stupid Jack traded it," I blab before I can stop myself.

"Brodie!" Uncle Jasper's bark is becoming familiar.

"That's not funny! My brother is not stupid! You should never call anyone stupid." Emily looks mad.

I think it was funny, but my uncle doesn't look too happy with me. I'm about to get another lecture, so I quickly ask, "Okay, why did the cow cross the road?"

"Because the chicken was 'eggs-hausted.'" Emily bursts into laughter. "Your turn."

"That's a terrible joke." I laugh anyway. I'm becoming as loco as Emily and everyone else here.

"Your turn," Emily repeats. "Tell it a joke?"

"Telling jokes to a plant? Not in this life!" I look at my uncle for support.

Uncle Jasper shrugs his shoulders. "Unfortunately, Emily, I don't know any jokes. There has not been much humor in my life, what with being one of the few non-fictional characters residing here."

"Say anything funny. I'm the only one who talks to her now that Jack's gone."

"Go ahead, nephew while I observe this fascinating phenomenon. I am a vegetation expert in this unique habitat, but I have never witnessed anything like this before. I'll pay very close attention."

"Sure you will!" I search my brain for a joke, but for a plant? As one cactus said to another, "That's a bit thorny." Sorry about that. "Okay, what time is it when a lawyer sits on a desk?"

"I don't know," Emily replies, looking puzzled.

"Is this a lawyer joke?" Uncle Jasper gives me a disapproving look.

"Do you want me to finish this joke or not?"

Uncle Jasper sighs. "Okay, what time is it when a lawyer sits on a desk?"

"Time to get a new desk!"

"Oy!" Emily groans, and then bursts into laughter. "That's terrible!"

"That's not funny," Uncle Jasper pouts. "If you're going to tell 'lawyer' jokes, I'll wait over there." He shuffles away. "I hate lawyer jokes."

The stump is quivering. *Is it possible? Is it laughing? It is definitely growing.*

Emily says, "Try another! I think she likes your awful jokes. I know I do."

"How do you get a lawyer into a car?" I give my uncle a snotty "I dare you to stop me" look.

"How do you get a lawyer into a car?" Emily asks.

"Very carefully," I say loud enough for him to hear, "or he'll sue you!"

"Your jokes are really bad," Emily says, laughing hard.

I think my jokes are awful too, but the plant is growing taller with each rotten riddle. I keep firing up those really dumb lawyer jokes, to get even with my uncle, until the beanstalk is way over my head. Twenty-five awful lawyer jokes later, my eyes search the sky for the top of the still growing plant.

"It's amazing!" Uncle Jasper shades his eyes with his hand. "It defies nature, growing without food, water or sunlight. It grows by itself. Amazing!"

"Not by itself." Emily's eyes remind me of the cow's eyes in the photograph. "The jokes make her feel 'loved'."

"This monster feels love? Give me a break!" I've heard everything now. Plants feeling love?

"Don't call her a 'monster'. She has feelings. All living creatures have feelings." Emily shoots me a mischievous look. "Except boys and especially, you--"

"Hey, you rotten, spoiled--"

"Brodie!" My uncle's voice sounds like thunder.

"You heard what she said!" He's taking her side again. I thought he's supposed to protect me? Isn't that why Mom sent me here for the summer?

Uncle Jasper is in my face, his face looking red with anger. "We don't fight with young ladies, and we definitely don't insult clients!"

Emily gives me a triumphant look.

"I give up!"

My uncle grabs my hand. He has a firm grip, a big surprise. "Stop wasting time. You have a large beanstalk to climb."

"ARE YOU KIDDING???"

CHAPTER 22

"Oh no! I'm not climbing this thing."

"Chicken?"

"I'm not a chicken." I spit it back at Emily. "Why doesn't he go up?"

Uncle Jasper pats his stomach. "Surely you don't expect me to climb at my age and...er... particular body configuration?"

He is definitely chubby and out of shape. I lean all the way back and still can't see the top of the beanstalk.

Emily laughs. "Okay, since you're afraid, I'll go by myself." She pulls herself up to the first leaf. "And boys are supposed to be brave?"

"Well?" Uncle Jasper nudges. "Well? You heard her. Go on then."

By now, she is over our heads. "Come down. You'll break your stupid neck!"

"It's easy. Just hold onto the stalk and climb up the leaves." She's waving at me. She's on that thing one-handed!

My uncle pushes me forward. "See Brodie, it's easy."

"Well, if it's so easy, why don't you do it, Sir Monstrovian Knight?"

My uncle shakes his head. "There are many forms of heroism. Someday you'll learn..."

I begin to climb. Anything is better than another one of his dumb lectures! Besides if that spoiled brat can do it so can I! I pull myself up to the first leaf slowly.

The leaf seems to be lifting me up so I can reach the next one. It is as if the beanstalk is helping me. Of course, that's impossible. Isn't it? "Thank you." I mumble, hoping Emily doesn't hear. I'd feel ridiculous if anyone heard me. Strange as it seems, the leaves seem to stretch even higher after that, lifting me from leaf to leaf until I am above the clouds.

"Don't look down, Brodie," my uncle warns from the safety of having both his large feet firmly on the ground.

So of course I look down. He looks like a miniature, bald, bowling pin from way up here.

"On second thought, Brodie come back," he shouts. "I was wrong to let you do this. It might not be safe. I'll find another way. Come down. Please?"

"Too late," I call down to him, determined not to let Emily think I'm chicken. Mom's going to kill him when I tell her about this. I can't wait.

The mansion looks like a tiny white box from up here. I wonder if the large, brown building near the river is my uncle's. It has a huge sign on the roof. I'll bet it says, "STAY OUT!"

I climb and climb until I reach the top of the plant. I made it. I look down through the cloud. I can see through it. How can it hold a giant's castle? It doesn't look like it can hold me. Arms wrapped tight around the stalk, I cautiously place one foot on the cloud. My shoe sinks in up to the top of my ankle. I'm going to fall through. "Emily? Emily?" Where is that brat?

"Jump down!" Emily is laughing, bounding toward me with super-high jumps. "This is fun!"

Is she nuts? I hold onto the stalk so tight it coughs.

"You're choking her! Jump off! If you kill her, we'll never get back." Emily shakes her head. "Trust me! Jump! JUMP!"

The plant's coughing is worse, but I'm not letting go. That's one long fall!

"LET GO NOW! JUMP! JUMP!"

Why do I listen? I close my eyes and jump.

I'm sure I'll fall through, but I don't! There is a hard surface under the foamy top layer. I take a few test steps, feeling the sucking hold of the cloud on my sneakers. It feels like walking on marshmallows.

Emily is running ahead. Nothing scares her. Maybe I'm jealous or maybe she's just crazy!

I trot after her, getting the hang of it, but still not trusting the cloud, or her.

Emily stops. What is she searching for?

My nose is twitching. "What's that smell?" The odor is familiar. "What's that awful smell? It smells like... farts!"

"Shhhh!"

I am about to rip into Miss Bordenschlocker for shushing me again, when I recognize the look of fear on her face. Uh oh!

CHAPTER 23

"Now what?" It's like we're standing downwind of an elephant!

Emily is sniffing at the air like some crazed bloodhound. "Do you feel that chill? It's the evil in this place."

"Ooh! I'm so cared! Really scared!" It is my turn to laugh. "I'm not falling for another trick".

"You'll see for yourself, wise guy!" She walks ahead cautiously. "Shhh. I think we're getting close. It's just like Jack described it."

"Stop shushing me! You don't hear me shushing you!"

"Shhh!" Emily peers ahead as she steps forward slowly, taking one step at a time.

I want to shut her up, but I can't speak because of the odor. It is syrupy and sweet, but powerful enough to knock your socks off. *Beans?* I inhale deeply.

"Shhh!" Emily points ahead. "Look!"

I am almost blinded by the sunlight bouncing off a tall fence with a towering building behind it. "Is that the Bulks' castle? It's magnificent!"

"Look closer," Emily whispers.

As we approach the castle, I understand. "I don't believe it! Who would build a castle from baked bean cans? It stinks!"

"Gross, huh?" Emily wriggles her nose. "Just like Jack said."

"I don't get it. Why would Jack come back three times if he wasn't a thief? This place is creepy and stinks like a garbage dump. I'd never come back."

"When you're desperate you do desperate things. You wouldn't know what that feels like--"

"Don't you lecture me! I've had enough lectures to last me a lifetime!"

"Yeah, me too."

Like 'Little Miss Know-It-All' ever gets in trouble? If only I'd behaved, I wouldn't be in this mess right now.

Emily studies the castle. "I guess we'll wait here. We don't want giants to eat us."

What did she say? Another one of her jokes? Is she trying to scare me again? The heavy bean odor is making me dizzy. "Is Jack really in there? I'd rather hide in a smelly boys locker room."

Emily laughs. "If you say so! I've never been in a boys locker room. I'm a girl, remember?"

It's funny how I almost forgot that.

"But you should smell Jack's room sometimes. He's a slob." She gives me a knowing look laughing. "He is my brother though."

Why are we waiting? I understand now why Jack is hiding here, but he's dumb to risk his life and sense of smell.

"We'll sit here." Emily is seated, cross-legged, on the cloud. She's quiet for a second and then, for no reason, asks, "Is Mr. Doofinch your father?"

"What? No! Of course not!" *How can she think that? He looks nothing like me.* "He's just my uncle."

"Oh?"

"I never met him before." I still wish I hadn't met him. I must be crazy, risking my life up here while my uncle, the 'hero sandwich', is safe below, probably stuffing his face.

"Where are your parents? Where are you from?" Emily asks. "I'm being nosy, huh?"

She is, but there is nothing else to do. "Mom is running around China somewhere selling those teeny-tiny rubber bands for kids' braces. That's why I'm stuck here. I never even heard of Monstrovia before."

"Oh. What about your Dad?"

I don't say much about Dad to anyone… usually. "My Dad is a soldier in the Middle East somewhere. He's been there a while."

"I'm sorry." Emily is looking at me with sad eyes this time.

She sounds like she means it.

I continue, "My parents got divorced 2 years ago. I don't see dad anymore."

Emily is silent for a while and then says, "My father left a long time ago. We never hear from him. I know how you feel."

"Thanks." I'm wondering why I told her. I don't even like her. There is no way she can know how I feel.

"We're a lot alike," Emily says.

How can she say such a dopey thing? I'm nothing like her! I wish the giant would leave so we can find Jack and get out of here.

"Yup, we have a lot in common," Emily continues. "We were both abandoned by our fathers."

I want to scream into her face that I wasn't 'abandoned', and I'm not a spoiled rich brat like she is, but what's the point? She'll never understand. Better to shut up and ignore her.

"I hope I never see C.C. again," Emily says so softly I hardly hear her. "I hate him."

Emily hates her father? That sounds so cold. She looks like she means it too. I don't know what to say. I would do anything to be with my Dad, even for a little while. He's a real hero, a captain in the army. And as for Mom? I don't want to think about how much I miss her, or how awful I've been to her. "You don't mean that," I am about to say, when I see Emily is staring wide-eyed at the castle. The huge door is opening.

CHAPTER 24

A black boot, the size of a cow, appears.

"Get down!" Emily orders, nearly pulling my arm out of its socket.

A giant shape is oozing through the door. Her head is the size of a small car. A wrecked car is prettier, much prettier! Her hair is green and standing up like snakes about to strike. Her face is round with gray cheeks that look like inflated balloons. Her teeth are pointy and stained with brown gunk. Beans? And her eyes are thin slits framed by greenish thick brows.

"Wow!"

"Shhh!"

I don't mind Emily shushing me for once. The giant is really gargantuan, and moving in our direction. Each footfall sends tremors through the clouds.

She stops walking suddenly.

"FEE FI FO FUM!" Her voice thunders across the mountains of cloud.

"What did she say?" I ask, fighting to keep my balance as the clouds shake.

"Shhhh."

This is not a time to argue. I stare at the fleshy arms and fatty fingers of the giant's hands. Her face lowers and I see her squinty red eyes searching.

"I smell the blood of an Englishman."

Her voice makes my heart pound. The clouds seem alive, churning violently, as the giant takes a large step, eyes peering down into the clouds like white marshmallow, nose sniffing furiously.

Welcome to Monstrovia

I think I've finally run into someone even my uncle would agree is a monster. What might this hulking creature do if she finds me? Are Emily's ridiculous warnings about cannibalism true? I can't stop staring at Mrs. Bulk's huge pointy teeth…

MEAT-EATER!

I'm not enough even for a snack.

The footsteps crash closer, louder. She is still sniffing and hunting the rolling, misty, surface of the clouds. Another step or two and she'll see us! What am I doing up here?

"Brodie, follow me." Emily is snaking through the clouds on her hands and knees.

"Are you nuts? She'll get us!" I make a grab for Emily's leg, but miss.

A boot crashes down.

"Emily? Emily?"

No answer.

"Emily?" I worm my way toward the giant.

A boot falls a few feet in front of me. I watch in paralyzed terror as it rises again. What is that sound?

Sniff. Sniff. Sniff.

CHAPTER 25

I hear the giant sniffing above, hunting for me.

Her boot drops like a rocket crashing. The ground shakes, bouncing me to my feet. Unable to think, I run harder than ever. I run, the marshmallow clouds sucking at my sneakers. I don't stop running until I am out of breath. I throw myself on the ground, panting, not believing what I saw.

When I look back, the giant is still there. I guess she has lousy eyesight or she would have caught me for sure. Pooped, but alive, I have escaped a gruesome giant, and have zero plans for ever facing that thing again! No kid should have to do things like this. And definitely not for a cowardly, lawyer uncle!

The giant scratches her butt and lumbers away, each step creating a new wave of aftershocks.

I wait to be certain she is gone. Then I call Emily's name again and again, scanning the clouds in the hope of spotting her. I want to scramble down that beanstalk and get out of here, but I can't do it... not without Emily. What's wrong with me? I don't even like her. I do admire her though, a little. I hate to admit it, but Emily showed a lot of courage, being first up here, and trying to help her brother. You gotta admire that kind of gutsiness.

I wait for her as long as I can. When she doesn't return, I walk all the way back, until I am facing that disgusting castle again. From a distance, the fence had looked like a wall of mirrors, but I can see it is actually thousands of can lids strung on razor-sharp wire.

Welcome to Monstrovia

I touch the ragged edge of a lid. It is sharp enough to tear through flesh and bone. I can't climb this. If Emily was here, she'd know what to do. Is she trapped inside these walls? Is she really that brave? Is she really that stupid?

I know the answer, and worse, I know what I am about to do. I know, as much as I don't want to, I have to get into that horrible castle. I have to find a way in there before Emily is chewed to bits by a two-story-tall, human-eating giant. Do I really believe in 'man-eating' giants?

In this crazy world of Monstrovia, I don't know what to believe.

The clouds are rocking again. "Emily, where are you?" I struggle to my feet.

If I can get the giant's attention, I might be able to lead her away from the castle until Emily escapes, and maybe I'll be able to beat the giant to the beanstalk and make my getaway, and then I'll chop that axe right into that beanstalk…

*And next, I'll be charged with **murder** too!* But there has to be a way to rescue them both.

Everything is churning wildly. It's like a tornado or a hurricane. I can't keep my footing. And the worst part: Beans! Beans! The smell is everywhere!

"What am I doing up here?" I scream, as I am knocked flat on my butt into the clouds again. There is nothing to hold onto so I am bounced up and down lying flat on my stomach. Footsteps! She is coming this way again! I can only pray she misses me as she lumbers by.

The earthquake finally stops. The giant is back in her castle. I am safe...or am I?

I can get away from here without any more trouble. I don't owe my uncle anything. I hardly know him. And as for Emily? She brought this on herself. *Why should I care what happens to her? I can escape. I'll just run down that beanstalk and get back to normal. That's the best possible plan.*

Of course, that's not what I do.

The air is heavy, as if a tombstone fell on my lungs. I search for anything I can possibly find to help me break into the castle, rescue Emily, and her brother. There is nothing I can use. Well, almost nothing. Emily's crazy stories about the giant's appetite makes me think there is one thing the monster might not be able to resist... ME!

CHAPTER 26

I gotta admit I'm terrified of meeting up with that giant, but I have to act now, or Emily and Jack will soon be... be what? Is Emily's fear a figment of her frenzied, teen-age brain? Mom says I have a 'runaway imagination'. Maybe Emily does too? Do I really believe giants gobble up humans, even in this crazy world?

Those pointy teeth might mean they are meat-eaters...like Horace. I wonder.

This is getting me nowhere fast. What would Emily do? Emily would do the bravest, stupidest, thing possible.

I get back on my feet, and like a fool, walk straight through the slowly closing gate, right into the front yard, as if I own the place. How much stupider can I be? I hate Emily! Why can't she be the one who's afraid? I always thought that girls aren't supposed to be brave. Maybe I do have a lot to learn.

The yard is cluttered with piles of empty bean cans, moldy debris, and decaying mounds of ripped up books and magazines. These giants need a dumpster.

I gag at the strong bean odor, but force myself to march right on up to the massive front door, telling myself I am just going to Principal Feeney's office again. I bang as hard as I can on the rough wood. Bang! Bang! Bang!

I bang again and again. My knuckles are raw from banging so hard. Bang! Bang! Bang! Bang! Bang!

"Who's making that racket?" A voice thunders, as the door flies open, crashing against the wall.

Falling to the ground, I find myself eyeball to ankle with Mrs. Eugene Bulk, in all her gruesome glory. What have I done? Emily, I'm going to get you for this...if we survive past today!

My eyes travel disbelievingly up from the creature's grime-coated fatty shins to the quadruple chins jiggling high above me. "I'm toast," I mutter, as the full impact of what I am facing hits me like a ton of beans, I mean, bricks. I hurry to my feet, my eyes reaching barely to her knees. "Excuse me," I shout as loudly as I can, "EXCUSE ME?"

Perhaps Emily's bravery is rubbing off on me? I sure hope not! Emily is crazy, and now I am doing something completely crazy too.

"Who are you?" The creature bellows, a glob of brown spit landing on my head. "What do you want here? We don't have no kids come up here!" She looks past me, her mouth dripping foam, and her voice lowers real scary-like. "Are you alone?"

That makes me really nervous. I reach up and barely able to control my hand from shaking, I hand her my uncle's business card. I notice brown stains on her fingers, forearms and skirt as she fumbles to hold the flimsy card with those huge fingers.

"What's it say? I can't read no midget writing!" Her eyes are all squinty as she struggles with the tiny print.

"It says I'm a lawyer!" I shout through cupped hands. "LAWYER!"

"You're a lawyer? A shrimp like you?" She gnashes her teeth. "We don't like lawyers up here."

"Who does?" I joke, having trouble keeping my knees from banging together. "I'm here on your case." I deliberately don't reveal I'm on Jack's side. Who knows what she'll do if she finds out?

She grunts and picks something out of her nose. "Oh rats! I guess you better come in then."

It takes all my courage to follow her through the door, knowing I may never come out. "What a lovely home you have." I jump out of the way of a flying giant, brown, booger.

The inside of the castle is made up of bean cans too. There isn't a flat wall surface anywhere. "Interesting wall covering… all bean can labels. Very nice." Am I kidding? It's gross!

"My husband loved baked beans. It was one of his favorite foods." She looks at me and lets her tongue run across her lip again.

I try not to think of what his other favorite foods might have been.

Mrs. Bulk scoops up a pile of books from the floor. The place is cluttered with them. How bad can she be if she is a book lover?

CHAPTER 27

The 'book-lover' tosses the books into the fireplace where flames leap up to consume the pages.

Even I, hardly a reader, think what a sad waste of books! I'm horrified as the fire flares dangerously close. I can't miss seeing a huge cooking pot dangling over the flames. It is big enough for an elephant, maybe even two!

"Sit there!" She points her finger at a gigantic chair with a yellow plastic cushion, and badly rusted chrome legs.

I jump to obey. Unfortunately the chair legs are covered with greasy, brown, bean juice. I keep sliding off as I try to climb up the legs.

"Midgets!" The giant curses, seizing me and tossing me onto the yellow chair. "You're not even a mouthful!"

Holy crappoli! That's exactly what Uncle Jasper said. I hope she keeps that in mind if she gets hungry.

I am sitting by the grungiest, greasiest, grossest, table I've ever seen. I can barely see over the stacks of bean cans and trash in tall, tippy, piles. The smell is overpowering. I have to rescue Emily and Jack and get out of here fast. But how?

"Mrs. Bulk," I shout. "I need to know how old you are."

"It ain't polite to ask a lady her age," she roars, giving me an angry scowl.

Where did I hear that before? "Okay. I understand Jack Beanstalk stole some valuables from your castle?"

She grimaces, which adds to her 'beauty'. "That little rat stole our golden harp, our goose that lays golden eggs, a bag of our hard-earned gold…"

"Is that all?"

Mrs. Bulk's massive fist slams on the table. The table jumps off the floor and the garbage threatens to tumble down and drown me. That's when I catch a glimpse of Emily, peering at me from behind the door of the next room.

"Is that all?" Mrs. Bulk's eyes grow furious and she screams in a shrill voice, "That boy is a rotten thief, and he murdered my dear Eugene! They should let me take care of that Jack pipsqueak and his miserable mother myself!" She lets out a loud, croaking, laugh and crushes her fist on the table again. "I'd fix that rotten murderer and his whole family!"

Emily springs from her hiding place swinging her fists. Is she crazy? A skinny hand shoots out and pulls her back. It must belong to Jack. At least she found him. He must be crazy to come back to this place…or so guilty, he does not want to get caught by the police even if it means risking his life. Why else would he come back here? And three times before?

The giant follows my eyes. I turn back quickly. "I see," I shout as loud as I can. "Mrs. Bulk, you do know murder is an extremely serious charge? Are you sure it wasn't an accident?"

"ACCIDENT?" She slams her fist on the table again. "What kind of a lawyer are you? It was MURDER! MURDER! MURDER!" The table jumps three times and so do I.

"I see, I see, I see," I say, terrified, her huge face just inches away. I smell beans on her breath. "Would you mind telling me exactly what happened?"

"I told the Giant cops everything already." She is pulling the lid off a large bean can with her bare hands! She digs two sausage-sized fingers into the can and pulls out one bean. She holds the syrupy, gloppy, brown bean up and takes a long look at it. She then rolls it between her fingers very gently.

"Shucks," she mutters, shakes her head, and surprisingly gently, places the bean in her mouth. She chews very, very, slowly, with her mouth wide open. Yuck! It is like watching a garbage truck swallowing dirty diapers. Why doesn't she down the whole can, I wonder, as she repeats the painstaking process with three more beans. It is like she is testing each bean before she chomps it to smithereens.

"Mind if I try one?" I run for a bean that has fallen out of the can.

"No! They're mine! They're all mine!" She grabs the bean and pops it into her mouth before I can reach it. She tongues it slowly before she eventually bites down.

I've never seen anyone chew so carefully.

"I only want to taste one," I say, reaching for another bean.

"I said no, and I mean NO!" She holds her huge fist over my head. "Do you get me kid?"

"Okay! Okay! Sorry about that. I'm just hungry." I stare up at the huge fist, expecting it to crash down on my skull at any second.

"I'm hungry too," she replies, that tongue rolling around her mouth as she pins me down with squinty eyes. "You can eat after you leave, little lawyer...and that better be soon. It's close to my supper time!"

I have a pretty good idea of what she might be thinking about having for supper, and it isn't just beans.

CHAPTER 28

I'm sweating rivers. I still haven't figured out a way to distract Mrs. Bulk and get Emily and her brother out of here. Mrs. Bulk is eyeing me like I'm candy.

It's Jack's own fault if I leave him here to rot. Who would ever come to this place to escape cops? Jail would be better. Well, I think so... but maybe not being imprisoned with the horrifying creatures of Monstrovia.

"You know," the giant coos sweetly, "You could stay for dinner? Wouldn't that be delicious?" Her eyes narrow and her voice drops. "Have you told anyone where you are?"

"Yes, of course! My boss, the police, my mother, my father, my Uncle Jasper, my Aunt Lizzie..." I didn't know I could say so many words in one breath. "Horace the dragon, the President, the marines..."

"Okay! I get it already!" She eyes me with one eye closed, like a starving hawk. "Maybe another time." She picks up her knife and fork.

I feel a chill race through my body. It is time to get out of here. But how can I get Emily and Jack out? If only I was bigger than Mrs. Bulk. But how can a kid, a human one at that, fight someone so big?

Suddenly I remember how much trouble Mrs. Bulk had reading the small print on my uncle's business card. My mind begins to work...*small things give gargantuan giants gigantic trouble. If I can't beat her because she is so powerful and large....*

Welcome to Monstrovia

Don't ask me where it came from, but I have the tiny seed of an idea. It is very, very, risky, but I have to try something, anything, and fast. "Mrs. Bulk, can I trouble you for a drink of water," I ask politely.

"Ain't you leaving?" She twirls the knife point on the surface of the table.

I do not like that one bit. "I have a few questions left, but my throat is really dry." I force myself to let out a fake cough. "You've got dust bunnies as big as dragons out there." I cough again. "Water." I gasp. "Water."

"I ain't going all the way to the well for water for you! You don't need no water." Her eyes are menacing and the knifepoint is drilling into the tabletop.

I fake a serious fit of coughing. "Cough, cough, cough, cough!"

She jumps from her chair. "GERMS! I don't need your disease germs! I'll get your water, or I'll never get you out of here. Lawyers! Bleh!" She picks up a bucket big enough for an elephant's drink, and then looks angrily at me and mutters, "This won't work. Where can I get a glass small enough for such a pipsqueak?" She trudges into the kitchen.

I hear her grumbling on and on, as she rummages in her filthy kitchen for a container small enough for my drink. "I got nothin' for this midget!"

My plan is working. "Emily! Emily! Get out now!"

Emily runs out of her hiding place in the next room. Jack is already scrambling to the door. He is very thin. He looks like a weasel.

"She's coming back! Duck!" They run back behind the door.

"Is this small enough for you?" The Giant stomps in with a spoon the size of a kitchen sink.

"That's a swimming pool! Don't you have anything smaller?"

"Smaller?" A dirty look and she stomps back to the kitchen, grumbling, "What a pain men are, even when they're puny pipsqueaks."

"Wait behind the door! She'll open it to get water from the well." I hope I'm right.

"How's this, you germ spreader?" She's back, with a white bottle top the size of a manhole cover. It looks like it is from a pill bottle. I get another crazy idea. "Wow! That's a bathtub!" Like she would know what a bathtub is.

"Listen! I'm done slaving for anyone now that Eugene is gone! I hated waiting on that dummy! All them rotten beans? Bleh!"

She looks mad. This is getting very, very dangerous.

CHAPTER 29

I don't know how much longer I can push her before this giant loses her cool. I take a fast glance at the huge cauldron in the fireplace. I have to think fast. Small things give big trouble to big giants! Can I push her just one more time? I cough again really hard.

Mrs. Bulk backs away from me, venom in her eyes. "I don't want your germs. Why don't you just go?"

"I've an idea. Do you have any pills?" I know this is a long shot, my last chance.

"You want my medicine now too?" She is beet red.

"Of course not. But you could pull a pill capsule apart and use half to get me a little water? That would work great."

"Waste my good diet capsules on you?" she bellows, the knife point digging into the table. "No."

Diet capsules? Well, they're not working anyway. I force another loud string of loud coughs. "Sorry. Sorry. It's worse when I'm upset. Cough…cough…cough…."

She swats at my germs like they are squadrons of attacking flies. "All right! All right!" She storms back to the kitchen. "Fi! Fi! Fo! Fum," she rumbles. I can't hear the rest.

I spy Emily and Jack crouching behind the door, waiting for my signal. I peer into the kitchen. The clumsy giant is having a terrible time trying to break open a fragile medicine capsule without demolishing it.

It is funny seeing her struggling to pry the thin capsule apart with those giant fingers. She can't even hold it. If she grips too hard, it will shatter. She turns the capsule this way and that, sweat beading on her face. Sure enough, the capsule explodes in her fingers, spilling medicine all over the floor.

She curses at the flimsy remnants of the capsule still in her hands and throws it on the floor. Another capsule falls out of the bottle into her palm, and she tries to pry it open with her huge, clumsy fingers.

I'm amazed as capsule after capsule explodes into useless fragments, spilling contents all over her 'nice clean' floor. (I can be sarcastic too.) Those capsules are probably the smallest things in her entire castle, but are giving her the biggest challenge. Her fingers are too large to get a good grip on them. "This is impossible," she screams, shaking the walls, as she tussles with all her brute strength against her miniscule, fragile, foe.

"Very interesting," as Uncle Jasper would say. Here, I have been so frightened of this gargantuan monster, and a tiny object, a fragile medicine capsule, is giving her the battle of her life and the 'underdog' is winning. There are broken capsules and bits of medicine all over, making the floor slippery. The noise is deafening as she bangs into cabinets and walls trying to chase the runaway pill capsules on all fours.

I don't want to laugh, but I now realize that small as we are, Uncle Jasper and I can 'topple the titan', 'crush the colossus', and 'bash the behemoth'!

Welcome to Monstrovia

All we have to do is use our intelligence against hers, and despite her overwhelming size and strength, we will win! And then, just as I am feeling confident, I see half of a capsule shell fall to the floor in one piece, and hear a thunderous, "Ugh, I did it!" Maybe I shouldn't feel quite so confident?

The giant lumbers back, a sloppy, triumphant grin on her face. "How's this, you puny pest?" Stinky sweat is dripping off her bare arms. "It was tough, but I win. I always win," she shouts.

I am afraid she is going to smash that capsule right into my face. "Perfect!" I quickly say. "Thank you! Cough! Cough! Water! Water!"

"Germs! Germs!" She backs away, screaming at me. "YOU STAY!" She flings open the door and at long last, runs out. The door crashes against the outside wall and unfortunately, begins to swing shut.

"Oh no! It's closing! Get out now! Hurry!"

"What about you?," Emily calls. That weasel, Jack, is too busy running to care about anybody else.

I want to escape. There isn't time for me to get off this chair and get to the door before Mrs. Bulk comes roaring back. "If I'm not out in ten minutes, call the police! Call the army! Call the marines!" Then say your prayers."

"There are no phones up here," Emily replies, hesitating at the door.

"Get going! She likes me! She's getting me water!"

Emily doesn't answer. She's gone.

The door is nearly shut. I'd never have made it. I'd never be able to outrun Mrs. Bulk to the beanstalk anyway. It is more important that Emily and Jack get away.

"Am I nuts?"

The shaking of the floor and walls are scary clues the giant is almost back. She isn't very dainty.

CHAPTER 30

"Here's your blasted water!" She throws open the door and it smashes against the wall again. She glares down at me as she holds the capsule full of water between two filthy fingers. "Drink slowly. I wouldn't want you to **CHOKE** on it!"

"Thank you." I reach for the large capsule, and deliberately let it slip out of my hands. "Oh gosh, I'm sorry! I'm soaking wet!" I let out a burst of sneezing. "Kachoo! Kachoo! Kachoo! Kachoooooeeeeee!"

"Keep those germs away from me!"

I sneeze some more, for good measure. "Ka...ka...choo! Kachoo! Ka...choo! Kachoooeeeee!"

"You are the germiest, clumsiest, thing ever," she growls, jumping out of the chair. "I've never seen such a pain! You're worse than Eugene! I'm glad you ain't his size!"

"I'm so sorry. I'd better go home and change my clothes before I catch pneumonia. We can finish the questions when you come down for the trial." I get up before she can protest. "Could you open the door for me please? I don't want to drip water all over your nice clean floor."

She looks surprised, undecided and hungry.

I hold my breath. One swipe of her hand and I am dinner, or at least an appetizer. "Thank you so much again. I enjoyed meeting you."

Her face turns hard as granite. "Are you sure you can't stay for supper?" She blocks the doorway with her body.

I let out another volley of hacking coughs and sneezes. "Oh, no thank you. That is kind of you, but I have a lot of people waiting for me. I really have to go. I wouldn't want you to catch my GERMS! Toodleoo, goodbye, au revoir, ciao, shalom, adios, see ya."

I am finally out the door, walking backwards, eyes constantly on her face, making my way to where I hope the beanstalk will still be. I pray Jack hasn't chopped it down again or I might be stranded up here forever, or as long as forever lasts when you're trapped with a hungry giant. "Thank you again." I call back. "Let's do lunch one day?" I wave. "Maybe we can go shopping? You have wonderful taste!"

She does not wave back. Mrs. Bulk fills the doorway of the bean can castle, following my every move with the eyes of a cobra just before it strikes.

I'm trying not to run, to not make her suspicious of how badly I want to get away. I never plan to set foot in this nightmarish castle ever again! Not for all the beans and golden eggs in the Universe! Not for Emily! And definitely not for my coward of an uncle! What was my mother thinking sending me to stay with him? Wait until I tell her he sent me on a wild giant chase up a beanstalk! Wait until I tell her about all the crazy things I've already experienced in Monstrovia! Ooh, she's going to kill him! I can't wait! But first I have to get out of here.

Thinking I am a safe distance away, I run as fast as I can on those churning clouds toward the beanstalk, praying I don't hear Mrs. Bulk's thundering boots behind me.

CHAPTER 31

I have had my fill of this cloud-world of smelly castles and ravenous giants. I want to wash that revolting bean smell off my aching body. "Beans! Blecch!"

My hands and sneakers are flying down that beanstalk as I imagine that hideous giant crushing the clouds, trying to chase me down.

I keep looking up, praying I won't get a view of Mrs. Bulk's underpants as she clambers down after me. When I finally reach the ground, I am tempted to chop down the beanstalk, but recall the life force in that plant, and can't do it. Besides Emily will kill me if I hurt her precious 'friend'.. Emily? What a pain! But I hope she is alright. She really was brave, risking herself, for that no-good brother.

"You certainly took your time," I hear my uncle's voice, as I jump off the twisty stem.

I feel like strangling him, but my fingers would never go around his thick neck. "So sorry I made you wait, sir, but I was a little 'busy' with a ravenous giant, running on clouds, almost barfing on baked farty bean stench--" I'm really ready to let him have it!

"No. You don't understand. I'm sorry I let you do that." Uncle Jasper looks flustered. "Brodie, I was very worried…very worried. I'm not used to children. I forgot how young you are. I'm truly sorry."

He's apologizing? I don't know what to say. I'm not used to anyone apologizing to me. "Where's Emily? Did she and her brother make it down okay?"

"Thanks to you, she and Jack are safe. She said they'll meet us back at the mansion." He looks like he wants to put his arm around me, but I back away. I'm not ready for that. I'm still angry, and I don't trust him.

Uncle Jasper drops his arms and begins to waddle up the hill. He is walking slowly, breathing hard. I can see he looks exhausted. I am too.

I reach the house a few steps ahead of my uncle and find the rear doors are locked. I bang on one of the doors. "There's nobody here!"

My uncle mops his forehead with a handkerchief. "I'm sure they're inside." He tries to pull the doors open. "They're definitely locked," he mutters, a worried expression on his face. "We'll try the front. Emily said they needed to wash up."

The front door is locked too. Nobody answers our frantic knocking. My uncle peers into the dusty windows and sighs. "They'll be back. We just need to wait." He sits on the porch and undoes his neck tie.

I tap my toes and stare down at him, thinking angrily how he just let them go.

"Brodie, don't say anything! Understand?"

What can I say? I'm disgusted. I risked my life for nothing. I am surprised, flabbergasted, disgusted that Uncle Jasper, DOOFINCH, THE DEFENDER, famed lawyer for monstrous mythical monsters, fictional folk, etc. was so easily fooled by a mostly ordinary little girl. It is funny, but not really. A terrible thought occurs to me. Is Jack guilty? Did Emily know all along? Is that why they aren't here?

"Brodie, we're in serious trouble," Uncle Jasper mutters after several minutes, getting up and walking toward Horace. "We should have contacted the police as soon as we learned Jack's location."

"WE?" Why is it always "we" when he gets us in trouble? I feel like screaming that I risked my life, climbing a dangerous beanstalk, facing a terrifying giant, and an even scarier bean stench, while he, my great 'hero' of an uncle, sat on his butt, safe and sound, and LET THEM ESCAPE! I keep quiet. He looks miserable without me jumping on him too.

Uncle Jasper lets out a deep sigh. "It's my fault. I let them get away." He slowly climbs onto the bike seat atop Horace. "I'll take the blame when I speak to the authorities."

I climb up into the sidecar, put on that stupid yellow helmet, and brace myself for what I know is going to be a bone-rattling ride. I'll never complain about the school bus again.

"I can't believe she fooled me. Let's go, Horace, old friend, but take it slow. I'm feeling a bit under-the-weather."

To my relief, Horace does not leap away like a bucking bronco, but trudges slowly and almost smoothly through the quiet, wealthy neighborhood. 'Lots of spaghetti' here, as Uncle Jasper would say. Why am I quoting him?

Even when we reach the city, and weird-looking vehicles with weirder-looking drivers start honking to get Horace to speed up, my uncle keeps him at a decent speed.

I keep expecting Uncle Jasper to kick the dragon in gear and bounce me out of the bathtub-shaped sidecar, but he seems in no rush to get back. He still has that awful sad look on his face that makes me feel kind of sorry for him. He looks like I look after my softball team gets whipped bad in a game, or after Principal Feeney gets finished with me after I pull one of my stunts. "Maybe she left a message," I say hopefully, as he steers Horace into the driveway.

My uncle sighs. "Horace and I are getting old. He forgets where he's going, poor thing. That's why he lost his flying permit." Uncle Jasper pats the dragon's face affectionately. "Poor old dragon."

Poor dragon? Poor us! Emily used us! She tricked us! She bamboozled the great Jasper Doofinch! Where is she and that thief of a brother?

Uncle Jasper pulls open his office door, picks up a padded envelope from the floor, and slumps down in his chair. "Why did I trust her? Why? Why?"

He really sounds beaten. I've never seen him like this and don't know what to say. Why should I say anything? I still don't like him.

Uncle Jasper pulls a bunch of papers out of the envelope. "It's the case files the District Attorney sent." He shakes his head. "Brodie, never trust anyone. Emily must have had this whole thing planned right from the beginning."

I never trust anyone anyway, but I really was beginning to think Emily was different. I'm still not convinced about my uncle, but maybe he is growing on me a little too.

Uncle Jasper is spreading the papers on his desk and shaking his head. "This is really bad. I can see why they might not want to get caught. There's a lot of evidence here against Jack."

"Can I see?" I expect him to say no.

"You're my assistant." My uncle slides several papers toward me. "But you mustn't tell anyone anything you read, or what a client tells you. Lawyers must never reveal a client's secrets. That's part of our job. Anything they say is completely safe with us. We need to keep everything top secret."

"Like a spy?"

"I never thought about it that way, but I suppose. We must keep their secrets so our clients trust us."

"Like Emily trusts you?"

My uncle gives me a funny look. "You really can be rather difficult."

I nod, happy he realizes that. It will make it easier for me to leave.

CHAPTER 32

Uncle Jasper looks at me, shakes his head, and dives back into reading the evidence against Jack. Suddenly he pushes back his chair. "Wow! The D.A. has a good case against Jack! Maybe Jack is smart to run away? Maybe this is one case I should pass up?" He puts down his pen and leans back. "Brodie, I have the D.A.'s list of witnesses. It looks bad, very bad."

"What is the D.A.?" I stifle a yawn.

"I'm sorry. I assumed you knew. D.A. is short for District Attorney. He, or she, is the government's lawyer. In this case, the D.A. is trying to prove Jack is guilty of murder. And he's doing a darn good job too."

"So the D.A. is your enemy," I say, wondering if I am still his enemy too. I have only been with my uncle for a few days, and I still think of him as a pudgy gnome. He looks nothing like a great hero should look like. I can't wait to leave Monstrovia, even though I am a little curious how this crazy case is going to end.

"Is the D.A. my enemy? Well, yes and no. The D.A. wants to put Jack in jail, to punish him, but it's just his job. Do you understand? It's not like we hate each other. Although sometimes it seems we do."

"I hate all lawyers." I shoot at him on purpose.

"You said that. Maybe you'll change your mind someday, when you see the good things we do."

"Right. Like that will ever happen."

He shakes his head. "Let's get back to the witnesses. You already know Mrs. Eugene Bulk of course?"

"Too well." Fear races through my body just at the name.

He scratches his head with the pen top. "This is some crazy list: a singing harp, a peddler, and an Annabelle Goose? I'll have to see all of them before the trial to know what they are going to say in court."

"Oh goody."

He ignores me. "We need witnesses for our side, but without Jack, we have no case."

"So why are you doing all this work?" Why would anyone do work if they don't have to? Not doing my assignments was one more reason I got in trouble and ended up here **in this insane Special Sector**. If I only could do it over again I'd never have thrown those mudballs at Principal Feeney's car either.

Uncle Jasper frowns. "Jack and Emily should never have run away. The police will catch them. They always do. Then they'll need us to be ready to help."

"You're still going to help them?" I couldn't believe it! This man was no hero! He was a door mat!

"That is what lawyers do. We help people in trouble."

"Even if they use you? Even if they lie to you? Even if they step all over you?"

He nodded his head. "Even if you think they are guilty you have promised to help them. That is the lawyer's oath. Do you understand?" He was studying me with his eyes again.

"I don't know. The only lawyers I know made my parents get divorced. Who'd that help, huh?"

He looks down at his hands. "Brodie, you need to understand, lawyers do not make couples get divorced." He sees my angry face and says, "We'll discuss that later. For now, I made a list of the evidence. Tell me if you notice anything, anything at all." He points to each item on the list with his pen as he reads the list aloud. Item 1: Jack's fingerprints-- found all over the Bulk's castle.

"Stop! How could they find anything in that dump?" I can still see the dirt and grime of the Bulk's disgusting castle and am amazed anyone could find any clues in that mess.

"Good question." My uncle makes a note on his yellow pad. He looks at me as he is thinking aloud. "Fingerprints are okay since Jack admitted being there."

"He admitted that?" Case lost. Even I know never to admit anything.

Uncle Jasper is still writing. "Being in the castle doesn't mean he committed a crime. Brodie, you were there too, but that doesn't mean you robbed them."

"I see what you mean. That makes sense."

He smiles and moves his pen to Item 2: Stolen property found in Beanstalk mansion.

"That's bad isn't it?" I wonder how he can wiggle his way out of this one. I am beginning to see lawyers are pretty smart at getting out of almost anything. I could have used a good lawyer like my uncle with Mom and Mr. Feeney.

Uncle Jasper scratches his brow with the pen. "This one could be very bad…hmmm? But anyone could have left that stuff there."

"Like who?"

"I don't know. Anyone…even…even… Emily. Hmmm? Emily?" He starts writing again.

"Emily? You don't really believe that she was the burglar?"

Uncle Jasper has the strangest smile on his face.

I don't like it one bit.

CHAPTER 33

"I asked you, do you really believe that Emily could be the burglar?" I don't believe that for one second. She is a real pain, but not a burglar, definitely not a killer.

Uncle Jasper aims his eyes at me. "No. Of course not."

I breathe a sign of relief. "I know Emily didn't do it."

"I agree. But it's a possible defense. You have to understand, as a defense lawyer, all I have to do is create a 'reasonable doubt' that Jack didn't do it. One way to do that is to show somebody else could have—"

"So you blame it on Emily? What a sneaky lawyer trick."

"I don't really want to cast blame on her, but if even one juror of the twelve in a murder case doubts that Jack did it, he'll be set free."

I find myself drawn into thinking about this case against my will. It is like being sucked into helping someone solve a challenging jigsaw puzzle, but lives are at stake here. "So if you can make even one person on the jury think there's even a tiny chance Emily did it...."

"Jack goes free." My uncle smiles.

I think he looks like a chubby-cheeked devil. "But you know she didn't do it. So isn't that lying?"

He shakes his head hard. "The point is Emily **could** have done it."

"But you and I both know she didn't."

"Brodie, we 'think' she didn't. The truth is we never know for sure. Our job is to work for Jack. We are his lawyers, not Emily's."

"But couldn't Emily end up in prison for something she didn't do?"

"That would take another trial, and they would have to find a whole lot of evidence to prove Emily did it. I'd help her if it came to that."

"Blaming Emily doesn't seem right. It's like Dad said, 'Lawyers are liars.'"

Uncle Jasper looks like I stabbed him. "Brodie Adkins, your father was angry about the divorce, just like you are. I think it is time you understand that lawyers are not liars--"

"But you're going to lie and say Emily did it!" I have him this time! I have him good.

"No, I'm not!" Uncle Jasper's eyes are fireballs. "I must do everything I can to help Jack. Everything! That is my job! That is the promise I made to become a lawyer!"

"Even lie?" I am enjoying using his own words, twisting the knife into him. "A lie is a lie." I am confident he can't win this argument. I have him beat at last.

He doesn't answer. He sits back, closes his eyes and a few seconds later opens them again. "Brodie, will you admit it isn't a lie if you can't possibly 'know' the truth?"

"Huh? What are you talking about?"

"Be honest. Do we know for sure who stole all those things out of the Bulk's castle? DO WE REALLY KNOW FOR SURE, BEYOND ANY POSSIBLE DOUBT?"

His eyes are blazing and he is in my face firing one word at a time at me.

I try to 'weasel' out of it, but there is only one possible answer. "No," I say weakly.

"Aha!" he shouts. "NO! Is that correct? Is that your final answer?"

"No…I mean, yes…I mean….yes, it is impossible to know for sure."

"So Brodie, if we don't know for sure who took those things out of the castle, it isn't a lie if there is a chance, even a teensy-weensy chance that Jack didn't do it? Is that correct?" He is pushing his nose right up to mine. "Is that correct?"

I feel like he is backing me into a corner. I hate losing. "Yes," I mutter, disgusted I didn't see this coming.

"IS THAT CORRECT?"

I can see how someone he is questioning could feel over-powered. He is like a bomb about to go off if I don't give the right answer. Suddenly, my little, pudgy uncle is a pretty scary dude. "Yes… You're right." I try backing away, but my chair is up against the wall.

He grins broadly and seems to be able to turn off the pressure like he's switching off a light bulb.

"That is correct, nephew. And therefore it is not a lie if I do my job to protect my client and try to show jurors someone else, even your sweet, little, Emily, had the motive, opportunity and ability, to commit this crime. I owe it to Jack to do whatever I can to help him. Do you understand now?"

"I…I understand." I feel like I've been shrunk to about half my normal size.I still believe lawyers are liars, and my Uncle Jasper is the worst of the species. Like Mom said, he loves arguing and is good at it.

"Now let's get on with this," he says, an annoying victorious grin on his face. He moves his pen to Item number 3: One (1) wood-handled axe, the murder weapon.

"We could tell them it's a hatchet. Maybe you can convince them that Indians killed Mr. Bulk. Hey, I can play this lawyer game too." I am not ready to give up needling him yet.

Uncle Jasper frowns. "That's not slightly funny. I've helped many Native Americans. They are among the nicest people I've ever met."

"It was a joke. Can't you take a joke?"

"Not funny," he repeats, and continues with his examination of a photograph of the axe. "The police claim Jack deliberately used this axe to chop down the beanstalk, causing Mr. Bulk's fall and death. The police found the axe a few feet away from the body of Eugene Bulk. Its blade was coated with beanstalk matter and Jack's fingerprints were on the wooden handle, proof that Jack used the axe to chop down the beanstalk to kill Mr. Bulk."

I shake my head, peering down at the axe. "I guess that proves Jack is guilty. Go directly to Jail."

Uncle Jasper is still staring hard at the photo of the axe. "There isn't much point in fighting the fact that Jack used this axe to chop down the beanstalk…"

"So he's guilty." Not even my uncle can weasel out of this one.

"You give up too easy." He gives me a 'here comes the lecture look', but instead continues thinking aloud about the axe. "Let's suppose we admit Jack chopped down the beanstalk with that axe… we could still argue he wasn't trying to kill the giant…"

"I don't get it? Jack used the axe on the stalk but not to kill the giant? Murder by mistake?"

"Exactly. Thank you, Brodie. It was an accident, just as Jack told his sister."

"An accident?" I shake my head just like Uncle Jasper usually does. "So Jack accidentally picked up an axe, and accidentally swung it, and accidentally chopped down the beanstalk, and accidentally killed the giant? Sounds like an accident to me. Very convincing. Not! I think the jury would buy the Indians better than this crazy story."

My uncle shoots me an annoyed look. "We can argue Jack didn't know the giant was following him down the beanstalk. What do you think?"

I am about to ask how anyone could not know a giant was following them down a beanstalk, with all the noise and vibration a giant would make, when I see my uncle's eyes dart toward his front door, the only entrance without "STAY OUT!" printed on it.

Someone is twisting the doorknob very slowly.

"I have lots of enemies," my uncle hisses, reaching for something inside his desk.

I almost burst out laughing. He is pointing that bark covered twig at the door. What does he think it is? A magic wand?

CHAPTER 34

The door opens slowly. There isn't even one tiny squeal. Someone does not want to be heard coming into my uncle's office.

"Thank goodness!" my uncle gushes, replacing the ordinary looking twig into the back of his desk drawer. "Where have you been? We've been waiting for you forever!"

Emily is anxiously peering around the door. "Are the cops here? Did you tell them?"

"How could you do that to me? I trusted you," I shout at her. Then I see Jack. He looks like a nervous weasel, peeking at us from the hallway, almost hidden by his sister. He smells awful!

Emily rushes for the blinds and separates them enough to see the street below. "I had no choice."

"Looking for dust buffalo again?" I ask angrily.

Emily throws me a dirty look.

"That I presume is Jack," my uncle says with surprising calm. "Jack, come in. It's safe."

Jack still has that frightened weasel look as he inches past the door, his eyes searching the office. Does he think we have giant Monstrovian cops hidden under my uncle's desk, waiting to ambush him?

"Did you call the police," Emily repeats.

"They've been looking for him for days. He was right. Nobody in their right mind would think he'd go back to that horrible giant's castle. It worked."

"It may have, but I should have called them after what you did!" Uncle Jasper says. "But I still had faith in you. You let me down."

"I needed time to talk to Jack alone." Emily looks like she knows she did the wrong thing.

"Be honest. The truth is you still didn't trust me," My uncle says, shaking his head. "Always tell the truth, Brodie."

I am glaring at Emily, still furious, even if my uncle, the doormat, is playing nice with her. Lawyers will do anything for money, my father said. Is my uncle like that too?

"He's my brother," Emily says softly.

She isn't apologizing. It is as if she thinks everyone should understand what she did was right, just because she's Jack's sister. Even though I'm still mad, I kind of envy Jack. I'd like a sister to protect me too. As long as it isn't EMILY! I have never met a girl who annoys me so much. She drives me crazy. One minute I admire her, and the next I hate her.

"I guess I can understand your desire to help your brother, but don't ever do that again," my uncle says. "I'll do everything I can for you, but no more messing around. Nothing! Do you understand? Complete honesty. Everything you say here is our secret. You must trust me if you want my…our help."

"Okay." Emily gives her brother a glance. "Just please help us?"

I am still boiling, but my curiosity is getting the better of me. "And by the way, how did you get into that disgusting castle? The door was massive. No way, not even you, could climb that fence." I shiver at the memory of those razor sharp tin can lids, bristling from the fence posts.

"Don't ask," Emily mutters.

"There you go again! My uncle said 'honesty'. Complete honesty! If you can't trust me…"

"Okay! Okay! Just no lectures! If you really must know, I climbed through a pipe on the back side of the castle."

"What pipe? There was a pipe? Why didn't you go out the same way instead of making me risk my life to rescue you from that horrible Mrs. Bulk? Do you have any idea what I've been through for you? Do you?"

Emily looks flustered, unusual for her. "IT WAS THE TOILET PIPE! Okay? Do you really expect me to go back out through the toilet?"

"Oh."

"Brodie, you have a lot to learn. A lawyer never asks a question unless he already knows the answer," Uncle Jasper says, shaking his head as always.

Not sure what to say to Emily, I turn to Jack. I get my very first good view of this 'wanted' killer. He looks dirty, black grime embedded around his neck, wrists and fingernails. One whiff confirms that he stinks of beans. "So this is the mighty giant killer?"

"I didn't do it! I didn't kill nobody! It was an accident." He is talking so fast he sounds like a machine gun firing words instead of bullets.

"You see, Brodie, I said it was an accident." My uncle is all smiles. He likes being right. We have that in common.

Welcome to Monstrovia

I can't find much I like about Jack, narrow eyes, sharp pointy nose, and the craters of one hundred pimples on his face. Are he and Emily really related? His weasel looks alone could convict him. And that voice! Scratchy, screechy, and annoying! How is my uncle ever going to prove this kid isn't a murderer?

Emily is staring hard at Jack. I can tell she's afraid. She cares. If my uncle does not win this case, Emily will have to face losing her brother. She will hurt like I did when my parents got divorced...when Dad left for the war...when Mom left for China. I don't want any kid to feel the way I've been feeling. I don't want Emily to lose her brother, even if that means I have to stay and help her.

CHAPTER 35

"Brodie, are you okay?"

"Yes, Uncle Jasper, I was just thinking."

My uncle gives me a curious look, like he doesn't believe I can think, and then turns his attention to Jack. "Jack, sit here. I need to go over some questions with you." He points to a leather chair in front of his desk. "This is my nephew, Brodie. He's my assistant. Don't mind him recording you." He nods at me.

Not again! I dig out the feather. "It's a recorder," I explain to Emily, embarrassed at whirling the feather over my head to start the darn thing.

Emily shakes her head. "And you think Monstrovians are crazy?"

Jack's lips curl into a sneer. "You're just a kid."

I'm about to answer him, but to my surprise my uncle jumps in, "But I'm your lawyer and the cops will be here any minute. You're in giant trouble, son, so let's get started."

"Listen to him, Jackie," Emily coaxes from her post by the window.

Jack plops onto the chair, his gangly legs hanging over the armrest.

Uncle Jasper is fast. "Sit properly, feet on the floor, the way you will in court."

Jack bolts upright and places his feet flat.

"That's better. The police could be here any second so I'm going to jump into the 'toughies' right away." He looks at me. "Brodie, take over by the window."

I move past Jack's dirt-encrusted sneakers like I'm moving past a coiled rattle snake.

"Thank you, Brodie," Emily whispers, as she moves to the second chair.

Is she being nice to me? That's a change, I think, peering through the blinds, but listening to what is happening.

"Okay Jack. Let's get started." Uncle Jasper levels his eyes on the 'weasel' face. "Jack, did you plan to kill Mr. Bulk?"

"No! I didn't plan to kill nobody!"

"Good answer. Jack, did you plan to steal from the Bulks?" Uncle Jasper gives Emily a quick smile.

"I didn't plan to steal nothing. It just happened. I dunno."

I almost fall over. His answer sounded incredibly d-u-m-b! My uncle looks surprised too.

"I guess..." Jack adds after a long silence.

My uncle is waiting for more...waiting...waiting. He has a long wait.

Jack is fidgeting. Suddenly he speaks again, "When the giant started saying that crazy rhyme...."

"Rhyme? What on Earth are you talking about?" Uncle Jasper interrupts. "Concentrate! Focus on the question. Keep to the subject."

"I dunno." Jack scrunches up his face, "Something like Fee fi...fee fee or something or other. I dunno. My head hurts."

"Come on, Jack." Emily leans forward. "Try hard!" She turns to my uncle and whispers, "I think he hit his head."

"Stop playing with your fingers!" My uncle barks, "You're even making me nervous." He loosens his shirt collar. "Let's get back to the subject. What happened in the Bulks' castle?"

"I dunno. I can't remember. I dunno." He points to his head and his eyes swim up toward the ceiling.

What is wrong with this kid? I'll never forget one instant of my visit with that gross, gruesome, giant. It was a nightmare! No kid should have to go through something like that.

My uncle leans closer. "Jack, speak clearly. It's not "I dunno". It's "I don't know". And don't say, "I don't know" because the jury will think you're hiding things."

I can tell the great lawyer is simmering, like a volcano about to erupt, but holding it in. Dumb Jack has succeeded when all my efforts to upset my uncle have failed. Maybe he can give me lessons so I can get out of here.

"He's trying his best, Mr. Doofinch," Emily says.

My uncle removes his glasses, not a good sign. "Okay. Okay. What happened next?"

"I think I felt like I was in danger." Jack looks at Emily.

"You think you felt?" Uncle Jasper sighs, clenching his fist. "You **think** you felt you were in danger? What kind of danger do you think you felt you were in?" My uncle looks at me with desperation in his eyes. "I think I feel I'm going to kill myself," he mumbles.

Emily jumps in again, her voice very gentle. "Jackie, what did you think Mr. Bulk was going to do to you? I know your head hurts but please think. It's important."

"I think I felt he was going to eat me for dinner." Jack says, picking at a scab on his nose.

"Keep your hands in your lap!" My uncle hisses. "You don't expect a jury to believe that, do you?" He throws up his hands. "This is awful! This is a disaster!"

Jack jumps out of his seat. "It's the truth! I'm telling you the truth! That monster, I think he was going to eat me! He was going to grind me up and make bread with my bones!" Suddenly he looks confused again, dazed. "I can't remember everything! I just dunno...I DON'T KNOW!" He looks to Emily for help.

Uncle Jasper has his hands in his head...I mean, head in his hands. Is he going to cry?

I know how he feels. After Jack's performance, I wonder if I've misjudged Mrs. Bulk? Maybe she isn't a monster? Maybe I have just been prejudiced against her? It is Emily's fault. She told me they were cannibals, but maybe that was part of her sneaky way of getting us to help her? Anyway, if I don't believe Jack, and Uncle Jasper, his lawyer, doesn't believe him either, how can we expect a jury to believe such a crazy story? Jack really is a terrible witness.

Emily places her hand on his dirty palm. "Go ahead, Jack, finish the story."

Even though Jack is older, I can see Emily is absolutely in charge. Why am I not surprised?

Jack gives her an anxious look. "Em, I ran away…to escape… before I was supper. That's all I remember. I think I banged my head when I was hiding." He points to the top of his head again. "It hurts."

I close my eyes. The other lawyers will tear him apart. A baby could tear his story to shreds. He is uncertain of everything. How on earth are we ever going to win this insane case?

CHAPTER 36

My uncle looks like he is ready to tear his hair out, what little he has left. He is pacing the floor, glaring at Jack. "When did you steal the gold coins," he finally asks.

"The giant fell asleep," Jack replies.

Emily groans.

My uncle grits his teeth. "Jack, you just admitted 'stealing' the gold coins."

Jack looks at Emily. "Did I?"

She nods her head. "You need to listen to the questions very, very, carefully."

My uncle sighs and shrugs his shoulders. "Let's try again. When did you steal the harp?"

"I dunno. The harp asked me to take him. He said the giant had cold hands…"

"Cold hands?"

I bet Uncle Jasper wishes his hands were around Jack's throat!

Jack whines, "It's the truth. The harp said the giant had cold hands…so did the goose."

My uncle looks at Emily with desperation in his eyes. "This is hopeless."

"Please keep trying. He's innocent," Emily begs.

My uncle shakes his head. "What about the goose? That was the last thing you stole?"

"Yes."

"NO!" Uncle Jasper screams, throwing papers in the air.

"Don't admit you STOLE anything! You! You..."
He is so fuming mad he can't even think of something
awful to call Jack.

Jack shifts from foot to foot like he has to go to
the bathroom. "That goose was the noisiest thing,
clucking everywhere..."

"Clucking?" I interrupt, trying to help. "Geese
do not cluck, Jack. They honk."

"That goose clucked. She clucked all the time,"
Jack replies.

I look him squarely in the eye. "Jack, listen very
carefully. Geese do not cluck. Got it? Geese honk.
Honk!" I imitate the honking of a goose. "Honk. Honk."

"What do you call it when someone says,
"Cluck, Cluck?"" Jack asks, looking confused.

"Stop it!" My uncle stamps his foot. "I don't
want to hear anything about clucking geese ever
again! Nothing! Understand? Just tell me what else
you remember. What a case!"

Jack shrugs his bony shoulders. "Anyway,
whether she honked, clucked or farted..."

Jack continues on his stumbling way. "I
couldn't take her. She was much too fat for me. I'm
not exactly Superman, you know?"

That much is true. His arms look like spaghetti.

"So what did happen," Uncle Jasper asks,
holding a hand against his throbbing head.

"When I stole the goo--"

Uncle Jasper shoots him a deadly look.

"Sorry," Jack mumbles. "When I didn't steal the
goo--"

"NO! NO! NO!" My uncle bellows, throwing his pad across the room. "Don't even say the word 'steal'! Do you understand? No 'S' word!"

He looks pleadingly at Emily. "He's hopeless! We'll never win if he takes the stand."

Emily looks stunned. She is speechless, rare for her.

Jack is still rattling on. "That goose was just clucking its fool head off. I said shut up, but cluck, cluck, cluck all the time! Cluck, cluck, cluck!"

"Geese don't cluck!" I try one last time, trying not to lose my cool. "GEESE HONK! " I grab a breath to calm down before I wring his neck myself. "Jack, are you sure it wasn't a chicken? Chickens cluck."

"Is he sure of anything?" My uncle asks.

Emily comes out of her trance. "Jackie, you know geese do not cluck. You know that. Now please, please, focus. It's very important you get this right."

Jack looks hard at his sister. "Em, I didn't think geese clucked either, but this one does. She does it all the time."

"Wow," I shout. "A goose that clucks?" I felt like I was in a fist fight and being clobbered. Yes, I had gotten into a few fights in school too, which is another reason why I am stuck here in insane Monstrovia, on this cracked case.

"I don't believe this." Uncle Jasper moans. "Let's move on. A goose that clucks? What next?" He shakes his head again. "Jack, please, what else do you remember?"

Jack's eyes are squinched shut and his face is crinkled. He looks like he is thinking. It looks like it hurts. "Well, I fell down from the beanstalk. I think that's when I hit my head?"

He must have hit it really hard.

"When I woke up I saw Mr. Bulk's body and I saw the goose. She was running all around in a panic and clucking away. I had such a headache from all that clucking…"

"Back up a minute!" My uncle looks hopeful. "This is really important. Think carefully before you answer. You sound like you were surprised to see the goose. Did you steal the goose?"

"Yeah. I mean, no. I took the gold and I took the harp, but I didn't steal that goose. Nope, I definitely did not steal the goose."

"How can you be so sure? You're not sure of anything else."

"I wouldn't take that noisy thing. It never stops making noise! Don't you listen to me?"

My uncle is writing furiously on his pad.

I don't understand why this is important. Jack admitted to almost everything under the sun, but not taking the goose. Why is he refusing to admit he stole the goose? Could he be smart enough to know he is safe from a murder verdict as long as he doesn't admit to stealing the goose? Holy chickens! I am starting to think like my uncle! Worse yet, I am getting really hooked on this case! I don't believe it! I am acting like a lawyer! No!!!

CHAPTER 37

I've been 'bitten' by the 'mystery bug'. I really want to know how this case will end. Was that my uncle's sneaky plan from the beginning? I am hooked like a fish and can't break free until this mystery is solved. Or is it I can't break free until we have helped Emily?

"Jack," my uncle says after thinking a while, "I understand why you went to the giants the first time, but why did you go back?"

Good question. I'd never go back. I still smell the rotten beans every time I think of that awful place.

"I dunno," Jack whines.

"Was it the gold?" Uncle Jasper is circling Jack. "Tell the truth. Was it all that gold?"

Gold? I remembered the gold egg. If that was real, it was worth a lot of 'spaghetti'. Could that be why Jack risked everything to visit the giants?

"Was it the gold, Jack? You couldn't resist it. Could you?" Uncle sounds like a spider luring a fly, his voice soft and syrupy.

"Gold is pretty. I like the way it shines."

"It was because you planned to steal the gold?"

"No! Not really....I stole...."

"The 's' word," Uncle Jasper warns.

Jack shifts in his seat. "Mrs. Bulk was nice at first. Real nice."

Uncle Jasper stops circling. "Did you say nice?"

"'She was lonely' she said. 'I made her laugh', she said."

"Then what made you steal from her? The District Attorney is going to push you until you tell the truth." Uncle Jasper eyes Emily. "You understand?"

"I told you I didn't go there to steal--"

Uncle Jasper startles me by shouting at him, "What made you go back? What made you risk your life like that? The gold! Right? It was all that gold!" He is shouting in Jack's face. "You wanted the gold!" He pushes harder. "Tell me the truth! Tell me the truth before we go to trial and the whole world finds out what a murderous little lying thief you are! It was the gold! The gold! THE GOLD!!!" He is screaming at Jack, inches from his face, forcing Jack back into his seat, a terrified look on his weasel face.

"STOP IT! STOP IT!" Emily pushes toward my uncle.

My uncle whirls on her. "He's got to tell the truth! The D.A. will force it out of him!" He turns back to Jack while restraining Emily. "Why did you go back? Why? It was the gold! Just tell the truth! Just say you were after the gold! Just tell the truth! Say it! You wanted the gold!!!"

"Tell him Jack! Tell him the truth!" Emily urges, my uncle still holding her back.

I want to stop my uncle, but understand he has to test Jack's story before the D.A. does a lot worse. I try not to look at Emily who is reaching for her brother.

Jack's eyes look wild, pinned to the back of the chair by my uncle who is almost in Jack's lap and still shouting. "Your greed got the best of you! You had to have the gold, even if it meant killing the giants!"

Uncle Jasper's eyes are blazing and his whole body is quaking. Jack looks frightened, panicky. He is being pressed relentlessly, with Emily unable to help. Suddenly he stammers, "Fa...father...my father...."

"What? What did you say?" My uncle screams at him even louder. "Don't lie to me! Tell the truth!"

Jack's hands are gripping the armrests as if he is in the electric chair. Emily is reaching for his hand.

My uncle throws her hand back. "Leave him alone! You can't do that in court!" He turns his eyes full blast on Jack. "What did you say, you little liar? FATHER? DID YOU SAY FATHER?"

Jack jumps up and the chair is hurled to the ground. "Damn you! Damn you! I went back...I had a hunch..." Jack's face looks demonic in the orange office light. "That giant knew something...something about what happened to my father! He did, Em! He did!" Jack's body is shaking, tears streaming down his face. "Emily, I really thought he knew what happened to our father!"

I fall back in my chair, a balloon with all the air let out. If Jack is finally telling the truth, he didn't go to the Bulks to steal their gold at all. He returned to that horrendous place to learn about his missing father. I stare at this sniveling, pathetic, filthy kid, and feel sorry for him for the first time since we met. He risked everything for the one thing that might have made me risk another visit to that bean can castle, a chance, even a slight chance, to be with my father. Was I wrong about him all along? What other secrets is he keeping from us? What does Emily know?

CHAPTER 38

Emily looks like she was struck by lightning, staring at her brother and trembling. I wish I could say something to her, but she speaks before I can think of anything. She sounds bitter. "You know he abandoned us. Jack, he left us. He just left us. Get over it. I did."

"I didn't want to believe that, Em. That's why I went back."

"I...I...I had no idea," Uncle Jasper says, letting Emily loose.

Emily hugs her brother. "Haven't you done enough," Emily rasps at Uncle Jasper, her face stone cold.

"The District Attorney would have found out. I was trying to help--"

"Let's go, Jack. It's enough." Emily aims furious eyes at my uncle.

He doesn't speak. My uncle, speechless?

Emily pushes Jack toward the door. "Keep the egg. We're done here."

"You can't go." Uncle Jasper wakes up.

"Who's going to stop us?"

"Jack, you've got to turn yourself in to the police."

"No way! Are you crazy, after what you just heard? They'll lock him away and throw away the key! He's a terrible witness!"

Uncle Jasper aims his eyes at Jack. "Jack, if you didn't do anything wrong, you'll be okay. I'll help you."

"No," Emily snarls. "He'll never stand a chance."

"If he runs away, Emily, they'll catch him and nothing will help! They'll convict him of murder!" Uncle Jasper says, signaling me to station myself against the door.

Emily sneers. "Are you going to try and stop me Brodie?" Her hand reaches for the knob.

"He's got to turn himself in," Uncle Jasper repeats, approaching the door. "Trust me, it's the only way."

"No. You're just a mean, old, lawyer! You don't care! It's just money for you."

I could tell that hurts my uncle. I'm surprised it bothers me too. "He cares. Trust him." Trust him? Am I really telling her to trust my uncle? A lawyer?

Emily doesn't take a second to fire back at me, "You're his stooge. You do whatever he tells you. Trust him? I don't even trust you."

My uncle sighs. "Brodie, let her go. If she wants to run for the rest of her life...just let her go."

Emily and I are glaring angrily at each other. "You heard him! Move!" Emily grabs at my arm.

"Emily, Uncle Jasper won't let anything happen to Jack," I say, refusing to let go of the knob.

"Let them go if they don't want our help," Uncle Jasper repeats. "Brodie, we tried."

I dropped my hand from the knob. "Don't do this, Emily. My uncle wants to help your brother. He's your only chance. He's the best lawyer there is."

Uncle Jasper looks startled.

Nobody could be more surprised than me. I don't know exactly when things changed, and I might never ever say it again, but at this moment, I really believe Uncle Jasper is the only person on earth who can save Jack. "Emily, don't make the biggest mistake of your life."

My uncle smiles at me. "Emily, you are free to leave if you don't trust us, but please think before you sacrifice your brother's life and your own. You'll be on the run for the rest of your lives. Please, Emily?"

Emily's hand is still on the door knob. "Jack, this is your life."

"Em, what should I do?"

"I don't know. I really don't." Emily looks at my uncle. "Do you promise you'll take care of him? Promise?"

"I won't let anyone hurt him. Not anyone."

"Jack isn't a murderer," Emily says, her eyes still defiant, but her voice softer, full of doubt.

"I won't stop fighting for him until he is safe," Uncle Jasper says.

For the first time since meeting him, I don't see his bald head or his short, fat, clumsy body, not even his red suspenders. I see a man who sincerely wants to help people, a man who has the determination and skill to stand up against evil, even Monstrovian giants. I have to admit, it is a shock. "I believe my uncle completely. I trust him. I really trust him." Just the look on my uncle's face makes me feel I am right.

Emily takes her brother's hand. "I want to do what's best for you, Jack. I wish Mom was here."

She burns her eyes into me. "He could get far away. He'd be safe…"

She is begging me to let her go. I feel sorry for her.

"He might be safe for a little while, but for how long?" Uncle Jasper gently removes her fingers from the doorknob. "Where would he spend his life? In hiding? Back in the Bulks' castle? Is that the life you want for your brother or for you?"

"What if you lose?" Emily finally asks the question that is on all our minds.

"He won't lose," I say. "He is Doofinch the Defender. He won't lose."

"Jack, what do you want to do?" Emily still looks ready to run.

She really loves him. Even with a weasel face.

"Jack, will running away prove your innocence? We will win," Uncle Jasper says, smiling at Jack.

Jack lets out a sad smile. "Okay. Okay, Em?"

"Okay, Jackie." Emily wipes away a tear.

Jack seems to have a dignity I didn't see in him before. "I didn't do nothin' wrong. I didn't kill no one. I'm really scared, Em, but I don't want people to think I'm no murderer for the rest of my life. No more running away. I want to fight. We will win."

Uncle Jasper nods. "I have to be honest with you, Jack. They have a lot of evidence against you. I'm not going to lie to you. Think what could happen," my uncle says calmly, almost unraveling all he had accomplished. "You must be sure. I need you to be sure."

Jack bites his lip. "I did some dumb things in my life but I never killed no one. I'm sure. I swear it."

"Are you sure Jack?" Emily sounds like she isn't certain.

"I didn't do nothing," Jack says.

"Say you're innocent," my uncle corrects, sounding gentle for a change.

"I'm innocent!" Jack repeats loudly.

"Well, let's get back to work." Uncle Jasper picks up his pad.

Suddenly there is a loud bang on the door. "Open up! It's the police!

"You promised to protect him." Emily wraps her arms around Jack.

"I never break a promise," he replies, letting the officers in.

"Is you Jasper Doofinch," the hugest police man I ever saw asks, as he stoops down to get through the door. "You is the guy what gets everybody out of jail. Isn't you?"

"I am Jasper Doofinch, famous defender of mythical monsters and fictional folk," Uncle Jasper says, beaming at Emily.

"I told you it was that rat," the other policeman, another huge giant says, as he lumbers into the office, knocking his backside against my chair.

"Excuse me," Uncle Jasper exclaims, "I am not a rat, sir. I am a lawyer!"

"Same thing," the first giant says, glaring at my uncle with the look you give a pile of poop you just stepped in. "You is the guy what gets bad guys out of punishments, aintcha? So you is a rat in my book."

"And this time, Mr. Ratfinch," the other says, "We got so much stuff on your killer here you ain't got no chance of winning."

I grab Emily's hand, as the gigantic officer, two times my height, places handcuffs on Jack's wrists. "You're going to Giant Court for what you did." He pushes Jack out the door. "And no little midget human lawyer is going to save your skin."

"Now come on youse," the other giant roars. "Your runaway days is over." He eyes Uncle Jasper, "You is lucky I ain't no meat-eater no more. I can't wait to see you get beaten bad in Giant Court." He heaves a laugh that makes the pictures on the wall rattle. "You is gonna lose so bad."

Jack looks terrified. I am just glad these two uniformed creatures are leaving. They scare the beans out of me. *Beans?*

"Yeowtch!!!" I feel Emily's fingernails break skin on my arm as she says, "We are going to win. Aren't we? Well, aren't we?"

I gaze at my uncle, who looks red with anger, and pray. I still don't like him that much, but I do not want him to lose this case. Emily is a pain-in-the-butt, and Jack looks like a weasel, but nobody threatens my family like that and gets away with it. Not if I can help it. Look out Giant Court, Brodie Adkins is coming your way, and it isn't going to be pretty!

CHAPTER 39

I never realized how much work a lawyer has to do. Every day the office gets more deliveries of folders and books. I've never seen anyone work so hard or so many hours. When Uncle Jasper isn't visiting Jack in jail, (I'm not allowed), he is hunched over his desk, working on his homework, much more 'homework' than I ever got at school. But strangely, he enjoys it. "It's like a big puzzle, Brodie," he explains. "Once you start it, you can't stop until you figure the whole thing out."

Even while I am trying to get to sleep in my small room on the third floor, I can hear Uncle Jasper ranting and raving about this frustrating case, as he works downstairs. I find myself staring at the gargantuan posters of Perry Mason, a lawyer from an old television series, my uncle has hanging on all the walls, wishing the famous lawyer would materialize and help my insane uncle solve this even more insane case. (By the way, Perry Mason never lost a case, but he sure can cause nightmares when his penetrating gaze hits you from every wall in your bedroom. I'm going to ask my uncle if he can buy a few posters of my favorite girl singers or something. This Mason guy's eyes can give you the 'heebie-jeebies'.)

Uncle Jasper is packing his beat-up leather brief case when I join him. He gives me a weak smile. "You know Brodie, I usually feel confident before a trial, but this time, I'm not sure. Just don't tell anyone. Okay?"

"Okay. But I know you'll win." I have to say that even if I have my doubts.

"If only we could find Emily's mother and the goose? Nobody is able to locate them. I hope they haven't left Monstrovia."

We walk to the garage. "Can I open it," I ask. "Open Sesame," I shout, but nothing happens. "Open sesame," I repeat louder. "Why isn't it working?"

"The troll only recognizes my voice. "Open sesame?" The heavy doors rise, as if by magic.

"Why does the troll work only for you," I ask, wondering if Horace could ever help me get out of here. Not if the garage doors only open for my uncle.

"He owes me for a case he had against three silly billy goats who were trespassing on his bridge," Uncle Jasper explains, climbing onto Horace, who snorts greenish smoke and bobs his head dangerously close to me. "Old Horace is a bit under the weather today. Don't worry Horace, old boy, we'll get your flying license back after this crazy case is over."

I lift my body into the sidecar and brace myself. And yes, I strap on my helmet with the silly horns and bright yellow paint. The way I bounced in this contraption the last time, I have no choice, even if it musses up my hair and looks ridiculous.

"Don't worry," Uncle Jasper says, "I'll take it easy. I don't want to get arrested for speeding on today of all days." He strokes Horace's neck. "Take it slow, Horace. I'll make it up to you. I promise."

Horace lets out a puff of smoke.

To my grateful surprise, we move smoothly on the crowded roadways until we arrive at the largest building I have ever seen.

It is white with three large gold domes on its roof. There are statues all along the exterior of various gigantic figures. Horace rears on his hind legs and spits a flicker of flame at the base of one of the statues. "Hey, what's going on?"

"That's the Dragonslayer," Uncle Jasper says, holding Horace's reins tighter. "He positively hates that statue. He's been after me to sue for equal rights for dragons. He wants the statue of a dragon placed here too." Uncle Jasper places a finger against his lips. "Not much hope. We'll talk about that later. Horace is sensitive about this issue."

The dragon gives a snort and a puff of smoke rushes from his nostrils.

"Horace, you leave that knight alone," Uncle Jasper says gently.

"Does he really understand you?" I ask in a low voice so Horace doesn't hear.

"You'd be surprised what our animal friends understand."

Nothing surprises me anymore.

"We're here," Uncle Jasper announces, as he pulls his dragon-bike into an underground parking lot. "Whatever you do, stick close to me. And don't touch anything. And Horace, my dear fellow, you stay here too. I don't want to hear about you knocking over that statue again."

My uncle jumps off the dragon and pushes me ahead of him onto a moving walkway.

"Hold on," he warns, as a sudden draft lifts us off the walkway and plunks us down several floors above. "We're in court room G14," Uncle Jasper says. We move on another walkway to the largest doorway I've ever seen. "Don't be afraid. This is Giant Court."

"Giant Court?" Why am I shivering?

"Giant Court was established to handle cases between giants, and for giants against other fictional characters, humans, etc. It keeps things fairly peaceful. That is the purpose of laws you know. Without law and lawyers the world would be chaos."

"Thank you for the infomercial." I cut him off.

He shrugs. "I'll just say then, that since Mr. Bulk was a giant, the trial must take place in Giant Court. That's obvious, isn't it?"

I am hardly paying attention. We're in the courtroom and I get why it's called Giant Court. The doors are at least twenty five feet tall and most of the chairs on one side of the court, and many on the other, were obviously made for gargantuan backsides. Everything is gargantuan, except for one small section.

"That is the human and smaller citizens section," Uncle Jasper explains, making his way toward the smaller of two tables at the front of the massive court room. "You will note the very tiniest of chairs are for the mini-folk of Monstrovia. We're very respectful here of individual differences, unlike in some areas of the rest of the country."

We sit down in two hard wood chairs behind the front table in the human section. Uncle Jasper, sitting up completely straight, begins to inhale and exhale deeply, with his eyes closed, and his palms flat on the table.

"What are you doing?" I think he has gone completely nuts.

"I'm doing relaxation exercises. Breathing deeply relaxes me before a trial."

"You look like a balloon blowing up."

"What's he doing?," I hear a familiar voice ask.

I turn and see Emily staring at my uncle who really does look like a round balloon inflating with air. I hadn't seen her in a week and was almost looking forward to seeing her again. I don't know why. "He's doing his exercises," I explain, still wishing he would stop.

My uncle pauses, and stares at Emily. "You're wearing gold?"

Apparently everyone else has noticed too. Pixie Photographers are flying in from the gallery, flashing pictures of Emily all dressed in a gold suit with a diamond tiara. Their wings are buzzing around me like flies as they snap photos that will be used by newspapers and television across Monstrovia.

"What are these things?" I'm tempted to swat them away.

Uncle Jasper barks, "Sit down now, young lady!"

Emily jumps into the chair next to me.

"What are you thinking, dressing like that?" Uncle Jasper hisses at her, his face red and his eyes bulging. "Do you want jurors to hate you?"

Emily gives him a sly look and hisses right back, "Maybe that is exactly what I want."

Uncle Jasper looks sharply at me. "Did you tell her?"

"Tell her what?" And then I realize what he means and reply, "I'd never do that." Of course I'd never tell her my uncle had thought of setting her up as a possible suspect to save her brother. How could he even think I would rat on him? Lawyers are like spies; we never give away our secrets. That's what he taught me.

Uncle Jasper scowls at Emily. "I told you to dress 'simply', and you dress like this?"

"I'm not dumb," Emily whispers. "I know you need to shift the blame." She waves to a particularly obnoxious pixie reporter who is flapping her wings much too close to us. "Jack is my brother, and I'll do whatever it takes to save him, even if it means making them think I did it."

How did she figure this out? I never said a word. Emily must be pretty smart. I am about to tell her that, but she has the most stubborn face.

Uncle Jasper wags his finger at her. "Miss Beanstalk, the next time you come up with a bone-head idea, check with me first. Do you understand?"

"I thought..." Emily begins.

"The problem is, young lady, you didn't think! Your actions reflect on your brother too. If they hate you because you're rich and flashy, they'll hate him as well." He shakes his head. "I told you to wear a tan suit, and no jewelry, nothing fancy-schmancy, for a reason. Next time, obey me!" He turns away from her, but I see he is still fuming.

"You enjoyed that, didn't you?" Emily's eyes are hot flames as she glares at me.

"Why are you picking on me? This is your fault! You're stubborn, spoiled and you're...you're...I don't even know what you are!" I am furious she can lash out at me after all I have done for her...after I was beginning to like her...sort of. Oh, I don't know.

"Don't talk to me," she hisses.

Fictional folk! Special Sector or not, they are enough to drive me crazy. I wish she'd sit someplace else. Maybe in Siberia...or Saturn. I'm plotting how to ship her to Alaska in a box when I hear a lot of noise in the rear of the courtroom.

"Here he comes," my uncle hisses. "Now, Brodie, you're in for a show."

"Oh my goodness!" Emily gasps, looking as if she's about to faint.

CHAPTER 40

"What's wrong with you?" I ask Emily, seeing she is flushed and leaning on the table.

"L…L…Look." She points a shaky finger to the back of the courtroom.

The pixie photographers instantly all beeline it to the back of the massive chamber, their tiny wings fluttering like crazy.

I am craning my neck to see what the commotion is all about.

"That's the District Attorney, Mr. Hugh B. Goode. He's one tough lawyer. He has a perfect record," my uncle whispers, looking nervous.

I turn again to the rear of the courtroom, expecting to see an elderly, round-bodied gentleman like my uncle. My mouth drops open as I take in the sight of a man about fourteen feet tall, who looks like a handsome movie star. Holy Crappoli! He looks like Perry Mason! He is stunningly dressed in a dark blue suit, with a red, white and blue American Flag design knit on his tie. He is surrounded by a whole group of reporters and pixie photographers. He has slick, jet black hair, combed back, and a thin black moustache on his tanned face. I can't find one zit, pimple or acne spot. All the women are staring at him and drooling.

Uncle Jasper whispers again, "He wants to be Governor of Monstrovia. And I suspect, maybe President of the United States. Winning this case will be a big step toward his ambitions."

"Have you ever wanted to do more than just be a lawyer," I ask, still not believing how everyone has flocked around the 'movie star'.

"Yes. When I was your age I wanted to be a brave knight and rescue fair damsels from distress, and--"

I can't help it. I burst out laughing.

Uncle Jasper sighs. "You still can't see me as a hero? I suppose Hugh B. Goode over there is more your picture of what a hero should look like?" He shakes his head. "My dear boy, someday you will learn to look past appearances and see what lies beneath. Remember, you can't judge a book by its cover."

"Sorry, Uncle Jasper," I say, thinking how many times I've heard that before, and wondering why my uncle doesn't see Goode's resemblance to Perry Mason, his television idol.

My uncle looks surprised.

I realize I have never apologized to him before for anything. It wasn't as hard as I thought it would be.

District Attorney Hugh B. Goode does look like a hero though. He is tall, slim, (for a giant that is), and dressed in a very sharp suit. As he walks toward the front of the courtroom, he smiles brilliantly at the spectators, definitely like a movie star, and makes humorous comments to the reporters which I can't hear. I do hear the reporters laugh. I have an awful feeling they are laughing at my uncle. It makes me feel ashamed that I laughed at him too.

He is right. I have judged him by his cover. Could I have been wrong? Is there a hero under that unlikely body?

Emily is wide-eyed as the D.A. approaches. "Who is that hot guy," she asks.

"He's the District Attorney," Uncle Jasper whispers.

"Who?" Emily looks like she is in love.

"He's the guy who wants to hang your brother," I hiss at her.

Emily's face turns pale and I regret what I said.

"Brodie Adkins!" Uncle Jasper waggles his finger at me. "What did I tell you?"

D.A. Goode saunters over to our table and extends his hand to my uncle. He has a huge black ring on his finger, a white skull and crossbones on its surface. He is also wearing a large wristwatch that almost blinds me with its flashing jewels. "How are you, Jasper," he says in a rich baritone voice. "And who might this lovely young lady be?" He is looking at Emily, all dolled up in gold.

What a show-off! I hate him at first sight.

Emily blushes as he takes her hand.

I feel my fists tightening. She makes me so mad!

Goode's teeth are bared, blinding and dazzling, like a shark. "Don't tell me this is Miss Beanstalk? Oh, you are charming. I love your gold outfit. I hope you will enjoy my performance today." He frowns. "I really do wish we had met under happier circumstances. I never lose a case."

Holy Perry Mason! I'm getting sick.

The smarmy D.A. turns to Uncle Jasper. "What a charming young lady. I hate to see her suffer so. If her brother is anything like her, I will feel most regretful locking him in prison for the rest of his life. Perhaps, Jasper, we might make a deal and avoid the pain of a trial…which of course you will lose."

I am simmering like a teapot about to boil over, but suddenly very afraid we might actually lose to this smarmy character.

CHAPTER 41

I am bristling with anger. Goode reminds me of a snake, all slick and slimy when he smiles.

Emily looks terrified at his threatening words.

"No deal," my uncle says firmly. "Thank you for the kind offer, but my client is innocent and nothing else will do."

"Good for you, Uncle," I exclaim.

Uncle Jasper quickly gives me a silencing look.

It is too late. The D.A. is staring at me with ice-cold penetrating eyes. I try not to flinch under his gaze. If he wants a staring contest, I'll give him one.

After a good hard look at me, Goode whispers something to his female assistant. She whispers back and they both laugh. "Who are you little boy?" Goode asks, as if he's talking to a kindergartner.

"I'm Brodie Adkins," I announce a little too loudly, "I'm his--"

"Assistant!" My uncle comes to the rescue. "My brilliant nephew is going to become a fine lawyer someday. First class!"

What did he say? Me, a lawyer? I'd never thought about that before.

"I have decided to employ him this summer as my assistant."

"Here little boy," Goode says, slime dripping from his lips, handing me an 8x10 signed glossy photograph of himself surrounded by trophies and certificates. "This should give you something to inspire you in your future endeavor. I am proud to serve as a role model for so many precious children."

I'm bristling with even more anger. Man, is he smarmy!

My uncle gives me a warning look again and says, "Thank you Hugh. That is very considerate of you."

"My pleasure, Doofinch." Goode turns his attention back to Emily. "This ordeal shouldn't take long, my dear." He pokes my uncle in the ribs. "You should have taken my deal, Jasper. This case is a loser! Trust me."

I can't wait until my uncle gives him a good solid thrashing. Instead Uncle Jasper nods his head and says softly, "We'll see, Mr. District Attorney, we'll see."

That's it? That's your best reply to this smarmy character? 'DOORMAT!' I am fuming, but Uncle Jasper is holding me back with his hand on my wrist.

The D.A. smiles again, teeth like a dragon... *MEAT-EATER!* "Child, your uncle is a fine lawyer. It's a shame you'll be seeing him take a whipping."

Who you calling, 'child'? I'm fuming. "We're going to win," I hiss, handing the photo to Emily.

The D.A. sighs dramatically. "I so admire loyalty, my dear boy, but you should always be loyal only to winners." He winks at his female assistant who winks back, and then he slithers to his table, placing his shiny suitcase down, and waving grandly to his many supporters in the gallery.

I am going to be sick. Please don't let Mr. Smarm beat my uncle, I pray.

"Are you okay, Brodie," Uncle Jasper asks.

"I'm fine. Let's beat this guy bad!"

My uncle frowns. "It's not about beating him. It's about helping Jack."

"Aren't they the same thing?"

Uncle Jasper leans closer. "Goode wants us to get angry. Angry people make mistakes. Don't let him get to you. Control your emotions. Think."

I now understand why Uncle Jasper hasn't reacted. He isn't weak or afraid, but is not letting that show-off trick him into making a mistake. "I get it," I say, smiling at Uncle Jasper. "I'm going to try hard."

"I know you are." He opens his bag and pulls out a fresh yellow pad and a silver pen.

I should have asked him if I can have a pad too since recorders aren't allowed in court. It doesn't really matter since Uncle Jasper is the lawyer, and even though he told everyone I was his assistant, I know better. I am just his nephew, a twelve year old boy, a problem to my mother, sent for the summer, the 'feather holder', the history recorder, and nothing more. I prepare to sit and watch, another spectator.

Uncle Jasper slides the pen and pad toward me. "This is for you, my loyal assistant."

"This is for me?"

Uncle Jasper smiles. "Brodie, I'm counting on you to pay close attention and make notes of anything you think will help us, no matter how silly or small a detail. You are my brilliant assistant. I need you. Remember, one tiny, over-looked, detail can solve a case. So write down everything you can. You never know what will solve a mystery."

"Thank you, Uncle Jasper." I know it is just a pen and a pad, but I feel a little choked up. "I'll do my best."

My uncle smiles, but suddenly his smile vanishes. He is staring at the front of the courtroom where a large door is opening.

CHAPTER 42

The court is silent, as a massive giant police officer booms, "ALL RISE! His honor, Judge I.M. Fair is entering the courtroom!"

He is one of them! He is a GIANT!

In his long black robe, Judge Ignatz Miguel Fair appears, a dark mountain of a man, almost as tall as Mrs. Bulk, but not as fat. His heavy jowls and thick, gray eyebrows add to his stern appearance. He is two stories tall of unsmiling stone-faced judge. I wouldn't want to be a criminal facing him. I don't want to be me facing him. "Is that the judge," I stammer, thinking everyone in Giant Court looks like Perry Mason, except my uncle.

"Are YOU defending this case?" Judge Fair's voice is deep, booming, and scary.

"Jasper Doofinch defending Jackson Beanstalk, born Jackson Bordenschlocker," Uncle Jasper announces, trying to close the middle button on his blue jacket, but of course it doesn't reach. I'm grateful his underwear isn't showing over his trousers for a change.

The judge grunts. "Doofinch, you know children aren't allowed in my courtroom!"

Who is he calling a child, I think, but no way am I going to say anything to this mountainous guy! Mountains can be volcanoes...

"This is my nephew, Brodie Adkins. He is assisting me on this case--"

"Is 'he' a trained legal assistant? If not, 'he' can sit with the other spectators. Shoo little boy!"

I hate when I'm called 'child' or 'little', but remember my uncle telling me not to show any anger.

"Your Honor," Uncle Jasper says calmly, "The defendant in this case is a youngster, and Brodie has proven invaluable in helping me provide Mr. Beanstalk the best defense he is entitled to. If you take away my assistant, I will have grounds to appeal any verdict reached in this trial."

"Grrrr," the judge snarls, clearly not pleased. "What do you say about this, Mr. Goode? Do you have any problem with a 'juvenile' assistant?"

The D.A. stands and smiles for the gallery. "If Mr. Doofinch can't afford a better assistant, I have no problem whatsoever with his using his nephew." He lets out a muted guffaw and an amused glance at the audience.

The Judge nods. "Thank you Mr. Goode. It is good to see you again."

"Good to see you too, Your Honor," Goode replies.

"Bring in the defendant," Judge Fair orders a giant police officer.

"Bring in the defendant," the officer shouts.

A door in the front of the room opens and two giant guards standing on either side of Jack usher him into the courtroom. He looks tiny and pitiful as he shuffles toward our table flanked by the two huge guards. He is dressed in a pink polka-dot prison suit, (yuck!), and has thick iron shackles on his wrists and ankles. The chains and shackles are very noisy as he moves closer.

The judge shakes his head and I hear him say, "tsk tsk".

"Good morning, Jack," Uncle Jasper says.

I give him a quick nod, but don't like the look of the shackles.

Jack doesn't wave back. He looks terrified. I don't blame him. I'm not even on trial and I'm terrified.

"My mom?" Jack asks in a low voice.

"I was hoping she'd be here," Uncle Jasper says.

Jack doesn't react. He looks like we've lost already.

I whisper to my uncle, "Do you want me to wait outside in case his mother shows?"

"No. Stay here. Keep Jack calm. He looks like he's falling to pieces." He turns to Emily. "I need you and Brodie to keep your brother calm. And tomorrow, you will wear something tan or gray."

"I really thought I was helping."

"Don't help and don't think. That's my job now. Just follow my instructions and we'll get Jack out of this mess."

"Hrumph," Judge Fair rumbles. "Are you quite ready, Mr. Doofinch? If you like we can send for tea and cookies, perhaps order breakfast, while you continue your nice little chat?"

Uncle Jasper looks startled. "What?"

The judge shouts, "CAN WE START NOW?"

I nearly jump out of my chair. Jack looks like he's ready to collapse. This judge is one scary dude.

"Sorry, Your Honor," Uncle Jasper says. "The defense is ready."

Judge Fair bellows, "I'll be the judge of that!" He aims his dark eyes at Jack. "And you! Are you satisfied with this lawyer?"

"I am satisfied, Your Honor," Emily whispers.

Jack repeats it. "I am satisfied, Your…Honor."

"Thank you for your confidence," Uncle Jasper whispers to Emily.

"I hope I know what I'm doing," Emily mumbles, puncturing his balloon. The Judge sighs.

"Mr. Goode, you are ready as always?"

D.A. Hugh B. Goode stands up in one smooth motion, casting a disdainful look in our direction. He speaks with a slight Southern drawl. It makes you feel like you are sitting in his house having a friendly chat before the fireplace. He really is very good. He begins by going through each piece of the story as if only a moron could doubt Jack's guilt.

"Don't we have to fight?" Jack whispers to Uncle Jasper as we wait to see what evidence the D.A. is about to present.

"I explained this to you," Uncle Jasper replies. "This is a pre-trial hearing. If they can't offer enough proof against you, we don't have to do anything. Without evidence, they have to set you free."

"Why can't I tell my side of the story?"

"It's simple," Uncle Jasper replies. "In our system of law, you're innocent until proven guilty. You don't have to do a thing unless they have enough evidence against you."

Jack whined, "But that isn't fair. I want a chance to tell my side of the story."

Uncle Jasper has amazing patience, but it is wearing thin. His lips are tight as he whispers, "Jack, the whole idea is to make sure every person, no matter how rich or poor, no matter their religion or race, giant or pixie, is considered innocent until there is no doubt of their guilt. That is a very good thing."

"So I don't have to prove I didn't do nothin' unless someone else proves I did do somethin'," Jack asks.

"He's got it," I say to Emily, wondering how anyone can be this dumb.

"But that means I can't say anything until everyone thinks I'm guilty already. That's not fair. I should go first," Jack says in his whiney, scratchy, irritating voice.

He doesn't get it at all! Maybe I can help. My uncle looks like he's eaten a hot pepper and is barely keeping himself from exploding. "Jack, you can say anything you want, but you don't have to if you don't need to...to prove you didn't do it." I look at Jack to see if I made a dent. I'm not sure a sledge hammer could penetrate his brain.

Luckily for all of us, Goode begins to speak. He is holding the axe, explaining how Jack's fingerprints on the handle prove beyond any doubt he murdered the poor, unfortunate, kindly, Mr. Bulk. "It is the axe that hammers the coffin, Your Honor. It proves Jack murdered Mr. Bulk."

Goode thanks the Judge for listening and strides confidently back to his seat. The giants filling the gallery behind him are applauding wildly.

"You cut that out," Judge Fair roars. "I'll have no noise in my courtroom!"

I'm surprised. That was very fair of Judge Fair. I am beginning to have a little more hope we have misjudged the judge. Uncle Jasper warned me this giant judge hates criminals and defense attorneys, especially human ones. He has a reputation for being hard on kids who commit crimes.

Judge Fair glares at Jack. "These are very serious charges, young man."

I have a very bad feeling. Emily must have too. I feel her nails suddenly dig into my arm. "Hey, cut it out," I rasp, pulling her nails out of my flesh. She has claws like a cat.

"Brodie, I don't like this," Uncle Jasper whispers to me.

The trial has barely even started and I am already scared to death.

CHAPTER 43

Judge Fair reads the charges aloud. "These are very serious crimes, Mr. Doofinch. Very serious."

"Jack is innocent, Your Honor. He should be set free immediately. There really isn't any evidence. He is innocent."

"That's what they all say," Judge Fair replies, his penetrating eyes aiming at my Uncle's hopeful face. "I believe there is sufficient evidence to warrant a jury trial. In addition, the police inform me that Jack ran and hid from them. They also tell me they can't locate his mother? Is that true?"

"Your Honor, that has nothing to do with Jack." My uncle looks anxiously at Emily.

"I disagree," Judge Fair replies. "This is a very rich family, rich enough to make it possible for the defendant to escape to some far-off land where we can never catch him."

"Your Honor, this is a first offense. Jack has never--"

"My mind is made up. The defendant will remain in jail until the trial is over."

"It's because your Mother isn't here," Uncle Jasper hisses to Emily. "How can she miss her own son's murder trial? Where is she?"

Emily pinches my arm hard.

"Stop pinching me. You're like a cat." I rub my arm.

"Your Honor," Uncle Jasper sputters, "Jack is just a frightened little boy who should not be in jail at all. I will guarantee his appearance in court."

Judge Fair interrupts my Uncle's protest. "No bail. That's final. And one more thing: I am ordering Jack to stand trial as an adult."

Uncle Jasper's hair goes wild. "But Your Honor, you know that could be life in prison, or even death! He's just a child!"

Emily digs into my arm. "My brother could die? Is that what he said?"

I am too shocked to say anything. I don't understand.

"Your Honor," Uncle Jasper is now shouting, "My client is a child! This is a first offense! The D.A. hasn't proven Jack PLANNED to commit murder! It was an accident at most!"

The Judge frowns, standing over his desk. "I must send a message that crime will be punished. Being young is no excuse! Court adjourned until one week from today." He slams his gavel and starts to leave.

My uncle isn't stopping. "Judge Fair, please? Surely, you don't believe a child should be given the same punishment as a grown up?"

The judge sneers at him. "I do. Absolutely! Don't you?"

Emily's nails are drilling for oil on my arm. "What is going on? What's happening to my brother?"

"Stop pinching me!" *Is my uncle screwing up?*

"If he's old enough to kill someone, he's old enough to be punished. Court adjourned!" Judge Fair roars, "Now let me leave or I'll have you thrown in jail too!"

Uncle Jasper is standing in front of the Judge's high desk with his mouth wide open and his hair standing on end.

Two guards lock the shackles back on Jack's wrists and ankles.

"What is going on," Jack asks, panic in his face.

"You is going back to jail," one giant guard smirks as he pulls Jack by the chain to the door that leads to the cells.

Emily is out of her seat. "How could you let this happen?"

"It's not as bad as you think," Uncle Jasper says. "Shhh."

"What's worse than life in jail or..." Emily can't bring herself to say the word, "execution"?

Uncle Jasper reaches for her hand, but she pulls it away. "You promised you'd protect him! You promised."

My Uncle whispers, "Don't show any sign of weakness." He indicates the gallery behind us and the pixie photographers flying all around, flashes popping everywhere. Boy, are they annoying!

"I don't care about them. I care about my brother. He could die because of you!"

"Emily!" My uncle's voice is sharp. "Be quiet, young lady, and listen! Judge Fair may have done us a favor!"

"A favor? Are you nuts? What kind of favor?" Emily's face is furious.

How can Uncle Jasper possibly think the judge did us a favor? "Keep your voice down, Emily." I smile at the reporters and the pesky pixies. "I trust my uncle."

Emily glares at me. "You have no choice. He's your uncle!"

Uncle Jasper hisses louder. "Emily, calm down. I know it looks bad, but this could actually help us. Show you have confidence. Smile at them. Do it now."

Emily smiles for the cameras, but is tapping her foot, never a good sign.

Uncle Jasper leans closer, still smiling for the pixies. "A lot of people, even giants, don't like the idea of sentencing a child to death. All we need is one juror who can't stand to see a kid get a grown-up punishment..."

I understand. "So even if a juror thinks Jack did kill the giant, they won't vote guilty..."

"Yes. Because they don't want a kid to get this kind of horrible punishment," Uncle Jasper says. "How many people want to see a child executed?"

Emily's foot-tapping stops. "That's very risky," she whispers, faking a smile at another photographer.

"It's not the way I want it, but it may work in our favor. The Judge's unfair decisions could give us a shot at an appeal too if we lose...which we won't," Uncle Jasper adds quickly.

"Well, I'm just mad!" Emily rasps through her fake smile. "I just hope you're right!" She walks at a fast clip to the rear of the court where reporters jump all over her like a swarm of bees.

"I have every confidence in my lawyer," I hear her say to the gaggle of reporters.

I lean toward my uncle. "Do you really believe what you told her, or are you lying again?"

Uncle Jasper falls back into the chair. "The United States Bill of Rights condemns cruel and unusual punishment. Well, I can't imagine anything worse than being a child with the horror of having an execution hanging over him or her. Sometimes prisoners wait years on death row. What a nightmare! Brodie, all we need is for one juror to feel that way… one caring juror."

"Uncle Jasper," I keep my voice low. "But some people feel harsh punishments, especially the death sentence, are the only way we can stop crime."

Uncle Jasper nods. "Nephew, I think such punishments are mostly meant to get revenge. To be honest, I never thought Jack would be facing this kind of unfair and cruel punishment."

"So you are worried? You lied to Emily?"

"I fibbed. I didn't want to frighten the poor girl any more than she is. It really could work the way I said. All it takes is one caring juror…one person who is against this kind of cruelty."

"I hope we have one," I say, wondering how fair a trial in Giant Court will be. "It is apparent that the giants hate us, so will Jack get a fair trial?"

Uncle Jasper packs his papers into his leather case. It looks beat up, pretty much the way I feel. "Let's go," he says softly, "Tomorrow is another day."

As we walk out, I hear a television reporter say, "You've just heard Judge Fair lace into defense lawyer Jasper Doofinch. Mr. Doofinch, often called, Doofinch the Defender, is up against famed District Attorney, Hugh B. Goode, often likened to the great Perry Mason. Neither has ever lost a case. After today's performance, one has to wonder if Mr. Doofinch has lost his magic touch? Ouch!"

I wonder too. I wish there was something I could do. I keep praying that I can perform a miracle and somehow help my uncle win this case. Once he wins, I can leave. I can't do that now, not when he seems so beaten by that bully Goode.

"You have been a big help to me, Brodie," Uncle Jasper says as we head for the front steps of the court house where a few reporters are still waiting for him. Most appear to have left once Goode departed.

"Thanks." Every time, I think of leaving, he says something that changes my mind...at least for a little while.

CHAPTER 44

The phone squawks shortly after we return to the office. "Is your Uncle available?" Emily asks.

She doesn't even say hi or anything. "Sure, I'll get him."

My uncle listens for several minutes. "Is that what you want?" He shakes his head. "Do you have any idea where your mother is? Emily? Emily? Miss Beanstalk?" He looks puzzled. "She hung up."

"What did the pest want?" I wish he had a speakerphone instead of this old-fashioned phone. Monstrovia is a hundred years behind the rest of the country on a lot of things. Annoying.

My uncle closes his folder. "She wanted to know if it was too late for a deal."

"What kind of deal."

"Let's talk about it later." Uncle Jasper pushes his chair backwards.

There is one thing still bothering me, something I've been afraid to ask. "Uncle Jasper, I hope you don't think this is a stupid question. Do you think Jack is innocent?" Why should we be doing all this work if Jack is guilty?

"That's a good question. Truthfully, I wish I knew."

"You don't know either? I thought I was the only one who's not sure."

"I'm almost certain Jack didn't plan to kill the giant. He doesn't seem like a murderer. But I suspect he went back to that castle deliberately to steal the goose."

He shrugs his shoulders. "If that's true, and Mr. Bulk died during that burglary, Jack is guilty of murder." He shakes his head. "I wish I knew what is in his head, but do we ever really know what is in anybody's head, dear Brodie?"

I wonder what he means by that look he's aiming at me. "But why doesn't Jack admit he stole the goose? He admits all the other burglaries. Why not that?"

He makes an arch with his fingers. "There are two possibilities. First, maybe he really didn't want to steal the goose, or second, maybe he's smarter than we think. We can never know for sure, so we must do our best for our clients, even if we think they are guilty."

"So you'd help him even if you know he's guilty?"

"You know, Brodie, you've hit on something interesting. Jack admits the first two thefts, but not the third. That could be a good sign since it is the third crime, the stealing of the golden goose that resulted in the death of Mr. Bulk. He also refuses the District Attorney's deals. That may be another good sign."

"You mean if he was guilty, he would have taken the deal offered by Goode for a lighter punishment?"

My uncle nods. "You're a smart boy, Brodie. Not taking a deal, helps make me believe Jack isn't guilty. The problem is I don't know if I can prove him innocent of that goose burglary. That's the tough one."

"You'll do it."

"I've just got to find his mother and that goose." He frowns. "You know, I've had a horrible thought for several days. Maybe the mother doesn't want to be found."

"Why? What mother wouldn't want to help her son in a situation like this? Mom would be there for me, even if she had to come home from China."

"Yes... China," Uncle Jasper says and sighs. "I agree, but maybe Jack's mother doesn't want to testify?"

"Why not? She'd want to help her son." I think of Mom and all the times she'd gone to school to help me. Even sending me here was a way to help me I realize, even if I don't like it.

Uncle Jasper looks worried. "Brodie, you mustn't say this to anybody, not even Emily."

Like I'm going to tell Emily anything? "I won't. scout's honor." I'm not a scout, but I really want him to feel he can trust me...at least until I leave.

He leans closer. "Have you ever wondered if his own mother thinks he went back to kill the giant on purpose?"

"Oh, wow! Then she'd want to hide. I never thought of that."

"That's my job. I think you're beginning to understand what a lawyer does."

I won't admit that my opinion of lawyers is changing, but I can see it's not easy. "So do you think we should try for a deal? If we still don't know that he's not guilty, wouldn't a deal be a good...deal?"

"I'm afraid we had our chance. Goode's confident. He won't make a deal when he thinks he's going to win. With the mother and the goose missing, he has a good chance."

"He walks around like he's won already," I say, remembering how smarmy the D.A. looked.

"You know, his being too confident is actually good for us. Remember the tortoise and the hare? I guess I'm the tortoise," Uncle Jasper says with a wistful smile.

"You're not the hare," I joke.

"Definitely not the hare." He laughs and looks like he is about to place his arm around me, but drops it down instead. He asks me to phone Emily back.

I don't want to, but he did ask. "Hi, my uncle wants to talk to you." I hand the phone over. "She said, "About what?" Man, she sounds cold."

My uncle nods and I hear he's being very polite, as always. "Good day, Emily. I think it's prudent to go over what you are going to say as a witness. We always want to make sure witnesses don't say the wrong things because they're nervous or caught by surprise." He lets out a little laugh.

I haven't ever seen anyone try so hard to protect someone. That does take a hero, doesn't it?

My uncle is squeezing the phone. "Emily, it is not cheating. I need to prepare you for the tough questions I predict the D.A. will ask." I can see from his face Emily is giving him a hard time. "No. I repeat: it is not cheating! It helps make sure you and I don't get surprised."

His face is turning redder and puffier. "Now you listen young lady, of course I want you to tell the truth, but I've already had enough surprises on this caseto last me a lifetime! So when are you coming so we can rehearse this--"

I hear the phone on the other end slam from all the way across the room.

Uncle Jasper looks stunned. "She hung up on me again. That's the second time--"

"I told you she's a stubborn, pain-in-the--"

"Brodie Adkins Junior!"

"Sorry Uncle Jasper." *Did I really say that? So easily?*

He shakes his head and bites his lip. "She said, "Don't worry about me, I know what you want me to say." He looks as if he is in pain. "What I want her to say? Does she think I want her to lie?"

"Has she heard from her Mom?" I ask, deliberately changing the subject.

"No." He pushes himself out of the chair. "This case is driving me nuts." He walks out the door without another word.

Emily Beanstalk strikes again. The poor little rich girl is driving him crazy too! One minute she is sweet and gentle, almost likeable, but then.... POW!

My uncle's papers are all over. I sit in his chair, and begin to read. Most of it is boring, but I know even my wise uncle may have missed something. I remember him repeating, "A case may be won on one tiny detail, which one eye sees, when the other does not." Wouldn't it be great if I found that detail?

173

My uncle finds me, my head on his desk. He gently shakes me awake. "I'm sorry Brodie. I need the files."

"Did you sleep?" I yawn, achy from having my head on the hard surface.

"No," Uncle Jasper replies, working to un-crumple the papers I've been sleeping on. "I still can't decide how to prove Jack's innocence." He gives me a tender look. "I've outlined a few possibilities, but they're all risky…very, very risky."

"Do you want to try them out on me?" I let out a yawn, as I pull out my feather recorder.

Uncle Jasper smiles. "Shut off the feather, dear nephew. What we say here is 'Top Secret', strictly between a lawyer and his trusted assistant."

I feel surprisingly proud when he says that, but also afraid of what his Top Secret strategy might be.

CHAPTER 45

The first day of the trial the butterflies in my belly are the size of horses, and they are galloping. We still haven't found Jack's mother or that goose.

Monstrovians of all kinds have already filled up one side of the courtroom. There are only a few human-like spectators on our side. Reporters are clogging the entrance, and pixie photographers are fluttering near the back doors, annoying everyone with their flashing cameras. Of course I don't see one reporter with a feather recorder. That is, unfortunately, my unique device. I keep it in my backpack since we aren't allowed to record in the courtroom.

The District Attorney arrives with Pixie cameras recording every move. Again, he is dressed perfectly, in a dark blue suit and an American Flag tie. He is showing-off a huge smile with a fortune in gold capped teeth. My uncle's checkerboard jacket and blue pants look shabby in comparison. "This is a good day," Goode says, twirling his moustache. "We should be able to finish in record time. I have a dinner party and match. Monstrovian tennis champion, you know."

I turn away from Goode's 'circus' when two gargantuan guards enter with Jack in handcuffs and ankle shackles. They seat him between my uncle and me.

Jack is wearing a white shirt, no tie or jacket. Uncle Jasper explained to Emily that juries like neat, clean defendants, but in this case, a suit would make Jack look like an adult, when we want to show he is still a child, and should not be punished as an adult.

"It's judging a book by its cover," I remark.

"You are a smart boy," Uncle Jasper says. "That is why today you are wearing a button shirt too. You look very nice."

I look dorky, but if it helps Jack, no problem. "Thanks for letting me wear my sneakers," I say, still annoyed about having to wear the fancy shirt, but he is studying his notes. He never stops working.

As I look Jack over, I wonder for the thousandth time if he really is innocent. You really can't judge a book by its cover or you could tell just by his weasel looks that he did it. It doesn't really matter if he did or didn't. In Uncle Jasper's words, "If you love the law you must believe that everyone deserves a fair trial. That is the lawyer's oath. To be a lawyer, you must believe this above all else."

"But what if you really knew Jack was guilty? Would you help him then?" I was sure not even my uncle would help a man he knew without a doubt was guilty. He couldn't be that bad as to help a person he knows committed a crime.

"Brodie, my dear nephew, have you ever been accused of doing something you didn't do?"

"Many times," I said, guessing he knew about my troubles from Mom.

"Uh huh. So you see, Brodie, that is why I have to do everything possible to help Jack, even though I may still have my doubts about his innocence. In the United States, you are innocent until proven guilty! Period!"

"I understand now," I said, but still wondered if I could defend someone that I knew was guilty of a terrible crime. I think it's wrong. I turn to Jack who is rubbing a red mark on his wrist from the handcuffs. I notice beads of sweat on his face. He looks as scared as I am. "Remember, Jack, you're innocent unless they prove you are guilty, and they won't be able to do that." I say it as if I am certain. "Just remember that and you'll be fine."

Jack gives me a weak smile.

Emily is seated next to Jack, in a gray pant suit. There is nothing flashy about her today. She obeyed for a change. "Good morning," I say, trying to sound cheerful. "You look okay." I don't want to say she looks 'nice', but she does. Something inside me is changing about her too. That bothers me since I don't understand girls at all.

"So many giants!" Emily sounds worried, but smiles at Jack. "We're going to win! Right bro?"

The room becomes silent. Eyes are aimed to the rear of the paneled chamber. I turn and almost flee from the room.

Trying to shove through the huge door is Mrs. Bulk, but her body, larger than even most of the earth-bound giants in the room, is wedged-in tight. "Holy Winnie-the-Pooh! She's stuck!" I can hardly keep from laughing.

"Brodie, be kind," Uncle Jasper says. "Even giants deserve our respect."

Be kind to that? "She's not even one of your clients!"

"Shhh."

What's the use?

Mrs. Bulk is wriggling from side to side, with everyone staring. With one mighty shove, she finally pushes her way in.

A shiver races through me at the sight of the gruesome giant in bright red lipstick and wearing streaks of thick green eyeliner around her beady eyes. The best makeover on T.V. wouldn't help her.

One of Goode's assistants hurries toward Mrs. Bulk, who Goode explained was not in court previously because she was in "mourning for her dear, departed husband".

"This way, Mrs. Bulk," the assistant says, as chairs bounce off her huge body. Even the giants seated next to the aisle are backing up, afraid of being crushed.

"Here's your place." Goode's assistant indicates a chair constructed of thick steel girders, at the end of the District Attorney's table. There is a great sigh of relief from the audience when she finally lands her caboose on the cushion.

Mrs. Bulk is panting when unfortunately she spies me. "What are you doing with them," she mouths menacingly, her teeth like a row of crooked razor blades coated with brown stain.

I try to smile friendly-like, but her eyes look like flame-throwers.

The clerk announces, "All hear. Monstrovian Court, Giant Division, is in session. All rise for the honorable, Judge I.M. Fair."

The Judge scowls at the crowded room, and says, "You may be seated."

The clerk reads aloud the list of crimes allegedly committed by Jack. The most important charge is "murder committed during the theft of one Annabelle Goose, aka The Golden Goose".

"Not guilty," Uncle Jasper responds loudly into the microphone on our table.

"Oh yes, you are!" Mrs. Bulk screeches, rising from her seat, which is stuck to her bottom.

Goode and his three assistants are bounced out of their seats. Spectators jump away from the roaring figure. Her arms are a furious windmill as she screams like an enraged hurricane at me, "I see you, Mr. Smarty-Pants! You tricked me! I won't forget! I won't--"

"SILENCE!" the Judge shouts. "Mrs. Bulk, contain yourself until it is your turn."

"That monster killed my--"

"BE QUIET, I SAID!" The Judge aims rock-hard eyes at Mrs. Bulk. "Even if you are a Cloud Giant you must obey the rules of this court! IS THAT CLEAR?"

She aims her fist at me, but it is her eyes that make me shiver with their murderous fury.

"I SAID SIT DOWN NOW!" The Judge towers over us like an angry demon.

Mrs. Bulk finally drops to her seat. But her eyes never leave me.

Judge Fair addresses the court. "I expect EVERYONE to behave in my courtroom. I'll clear the court if there is any further outburst." He skewers them all with his dark intense eyes. "Now let's get on with this. Are you ready for the defense?"

Uncle Jasper whispers to me, "How can I be? I can't find Jack's mother or the goose." He stands up, looking confident, but I know the truth. "Ready," he replies half-heartedly into the microphone.

The Judge turns toward the District Attorney. "Mr. Goode, you may begin."

The District Attorney rises, clears his throat, smiles for the press and giants, and approaches the jury as if he is an actor on stage.

I get a look at the jury, the men and women who will decide Jack's future: two male and five female giants; one human type who looks scrunched-in among the others; and two I-don't-know-what creatures, with scales and horns, who just look scary.

"This isn't fair," I whisper to my uncle. "Look at all the giants on the jury."

My uncle replies, "Good observation. There are very few humans in Monstrovia so the jury must reflect that."

I realize my uncle is like a little fly against these monstrous giants, and Mrs. Bulk is aiming her deadly swatter eyes right at me.

CHAPTER 46

"A court trial is like two gladiators fighting it out with words and ideas in an arena," Uncle Jasper whispers. "Watch your opponent and learn how he fights, and you can win. Take notes of anything you think will be important, even the unimportant, and you may have that one clue that can save your client. Remember one eye may see what the other eye misses."

I pick up my pen, ready to take notes, as the battle for Jack Beanstalk's life is about to begin.

District Attorney Hugh B. Goode bows his head to the jury, smiles warmly, as if he knows each one personally. He begins his opening statement. "Your Honor and honored members of the Giant jury. It is a tragedy for the family, friends, and society when a youngster goes wrong. Nobody likes punishing a child, certainly, not me."

The jury members were nodding in agreement. Uncle Jasper was right most people do not feel comfortable punishing a child with the death penalty.

Goode continues. "Unfortunately, trying to be kind to these violent young criminals, we forget the victims, their families, friends, and the terrible effects of crime on the nation we love." Goode stuck out his chest so his American flag tie was more visible. "A criminal allowed to get away with murder, even a young criminal, is a green light for others to commit horrible crimes. Nobody is safe! Nobody! Not me, not you, not your family."

I am impressed and scared. Goode speaks clearly and makes his points easy to understand. My uncle is doodling on his pad. I thought I was the only one who does that when in trouble.

Goode is smiling at the female giant jurors. "Mr. Beanstalk admits he visited the Bulk family of his own free will, not once, not twice, but three times. Three times! Does that sound like he believed the Bulks were dangerous and evil?"

Goode allows the jury time to fill in the obvious answer and continues, "Why would Mr. Beanstalk return three times if the Bulks were so horrible? That makes no sense! Every witness will prove that Hortensia Bulk and her dear, murdered husband, Eugene, offered Mr. Beanstalk every kindness, even feeding him!" Goode smiles at the jurors as if each is his special dinner guest. "And how did Mr. Beanstealer...I mean Beanstalk...repay this kindness? He stole Mr. Bulk's few personal treasures, and kept coming back for more and more and more!"

How can my clumsy-looking uncle beat someone smooth like this guy? He is everything heroic my uncle isn't. This is going to be a massacre.

"We all know children can be ungrateful. They're children." He lets out a kind smile at Jack that hides razor blade teeth. "But Mr. Beanstealer...I mean Beanstalk...wasn't just ungrateful, he was poisoned by greed, poisoned by the selfishness of his mother. Why, she isn't even here in court for her 'wonderful', 'innocent', son. How can this be? What kind of mother--"

"Objection!" My uncle shouts.

"Objection sustained," Judge Fair says. "Mr. Goode, please do not mention the missing mother again, even though I cannot possibly understand how anyone who calls themselves a parent could miss the murder trial of their own child."

Emily jumps out of her seat. "She'd be here if she could!"

I reached for her, but it was too late.

The Judge shouts at Uncle Jasper, "Restrain her or I'll hold you responsible."

"Emily," I hiss. "Sit down. You're not helping!"

She scowls at me, but sits.

"You can't say anything," I write on my pad for her.

She looks away.

She's so difficult. Why does that sound familiar? I realize that's what a lot of people think of me.

Goode sighs dramatically. "Mr. Beanstalk deliberately plotted to steal from the Bulks, who believed with all their heart, he was their friend. They trusted him. They showed him love…yes, my friends, love! Perhaps the first true love he had ever known. Why else would Mr. Bulk reveal his most beloved treasure, the goose that lays golden eggs? They loved and trusted Jack like their own child; the child they could never have. This is why he came back. Stealing everything from these kind and trusting folk, was his disgusting plan all along." He shakes his finger at Jack. "I feel sorry for you."

"Objection!" My uncle is on his feet again.

"Sustained."

Goode is holding the entire courtroom in a trance. He is a hypnotist. "It was while he was stealing this incredible golden goose that Mr. Beanstealer... I mean Beanstalk, murdered innocent, defenseless, sweet, Eugene Bulk, leaving his wife a poor, helpless widow alone...without hope." He dabs at his face with a handkerchief and tears appear in his eyes.

I bet there's onion juice on his handkerchief. I've tried that trick on Mom.

"Mr. Beanstealer...I keep saying that...I'm so upset...Mr. Beanstalk, murdered the kind and gentle Eugene Bulk, leaving his widow alone and defenseless." Goode places an arm on Mrs. Bulk's shoulder and is searching each juror's face for sympathy. "Imagine if this was your husband or wife brutally murdered? How would you feel? HOW WOULD YOU FEEL?" He surveys each juror with his penetrating eyes.

"Of course Mr. Beanstalk says it was an accident. An accident? But he plotted to burglarize the kindly Bulks! There can be no accidents when someone **plans** a crime! The law correctly states that if a victim dies while a crime is being committed, the person who commits that crime is guilty of MURDER!" Goode hammers his fist into his palm. "I hate this part of my job. Punishing anyone is painful, but a child?" He dabs at his tearing eyes again. "What is it we say when we spank our children? This hurts me more than it hurts you?"

I never believed that one, but several jurors nod their heads. I feel like spanking Jack myself. Goode is really good.

"Well, Jack, you greedy, little man, this does hurt me more than apparently it hurts you!" He is eyeing Jack with pity. "You don't seem to feel anything for what you have done, not one sign that you are sorry? Not even a teensy, weensy, apology? Sad, very sad. But justice must be done! A brutal murderer cannot hide from his punishment by claiming he is a child." His voice rises. "You gave up the right to be a child when YOU swung that axe with the intent to kill Mr. Bulk! You gave up the right to be a child when you committed an adult crime! You gave up the right to be a child when you MURDERED! MURDERED! MURDERED!"

Goode makes it easy for the jury to see his lips quiver and his tears fall from his downcast eyes. What a great actor! I feel like applauding. How can my uncle match this performance?

Goode waits to be sure everyone has been affected by his speech and continues, "We will prove beyond any doubt that this greedy man is guilty of a terrible murder. All we ask is that you search your soul to bring a fair ending to this tragic story of a widow losing her beloved husband to the twin devils of envy and murderous greed."

Goode passes his eyes across each juror's face one last time. He humbly accepts the praise of his female assistant as she hands him a 'well-earned' glass of water and a handkerchief to wipe his brow.

This is going to be a tough act to follow.

My uncle closes his jacket button and straightens his tie. He pats down his wildly wandering hair and shuffles toward the jury. After the poise and physical perfection of Hugh B. Goode, my uncle is going to have to work hard to win the jury over. I don't think he can do it. I don't think Perry Mason could!

"Good morning Your Honor and distinguished members of the jury. Thank you for giving your time for justice." Uncle Jasper stops to pull up his pants.

A few jurors smile. The judge is silent. I am embarrassed, afraid to hear what he's going to say.

"My client is a boy who was in the wrong place with the wrong people. What happened to him would have happened to anyone here in the same situation. All the lawyer speeches and fancy arguments won't change the truth that Jack is a child. Jack is just a poor unfortunate child. Calling him an adult is a lawyer's trick…and we all know about those, don't we? Mr. Beanstealer indeed? This poor child's name is Jack Beanstalk."

There are a few giggles, but mostly silence and stone faces. Goode doesn't look amused. Neither does Judge Fair. In fact, they both look bored.

Uncle Jasper hikes up his pants. "Jack is just a very unlucky young boy. The Bulks deliberately fooled him, pretending to be his friends. That's why he went back. There's nothing evil or sneaky about wanting to visit friends. He trusted them, just like any child would. Jack never planned to murder anyone. That's just ridiculous!"

He walks over to Jack and smiles. "Mr. Bulk's death was a terrible accident. No plan. No intent. No murder. Just a trusting boy, tricked by two evil creatures he thought were his friends. Jack is innocent. I know you will see the truth and send this poor boy home to his family where he belongs. Thank you."

Uncle Jasper looks shaky as he sits down. The chair makes a loud belching noise.

"That's it?" Emily whispers. "A bit short, huh?"

My uncle shoots her a look and hisses, "Write your comments. No facial expressions."

Emily glares at me.

I hope the jury doesn't notice. Why is she taking it out on me?

The Judge speaks. "Prosecutor, open your case."

Goode stands up and opens his briefcase. "It's open, your honor."

The Judge sighs, "Not your briefcase! I mean, call your first witness."

"Oh," Goode says, his face flushed. "I will only need a few witnesses. I call Mrs. Hortensia Bulk."

My stomach tightens. Can butterflies in the stomach become dinosaurs? The real battle is about to begin. I try to picture my Uncle Jasper in that suit of armor he wore in his portrait, about to slay the evil Mrs. Bulk and the slimy District Attorney, but it doesn't work. All I see is a poorly dressed gnome in red suspenders, striped underwear showing, about to be crushed by a throng of meat-eating giants.

CHAPTER 47

Mrs. Bulk wraps a white shawl over her shoulders. She looks like a frail, old lady, as she stoops over and shuffles toward the witness chair. When she passes Jack, she hisses, "I hate you. I hate you. You killed my sweet hubby-wubby!"

The guards nudge her forward. It is like nudging a truck, but the giant finally moves on. At the witness chair, leaning on a cane, she grimaces as if in pain. What an actress!

"Are you all right?" the Judge asks.

The giant lets out big, noisy, sobs, "Woe is me! Woe is me!" She is about to sit, but the Judge shouts, "WAIT! WAIT!"

The giant freezes, her huge backside half-launched toward the chair.

"Get this lady a…a …more roomy chair," Judge Fair orders in the nick of time.

Two giants carry a chair of steel girders to the front of the courtroom. Mrs. Bulk grunts and lowers her bottom onto the cushions. The girders sag, but thankfully they hold.

Goode hands Mrs. Bulk a giant tissue and she makes a big show of wiping her eyes. "Thank you, kind sir. Unfortunately I must depend on the kindness of strangers now that dear, sweet, Eugene was murdered."

"We all know what a terrible experience you've been through," Goode declares. "Are you well enough to answer a few questions, my dear?"

I am going to barf.

Mrs. Bulk makes a questioning gesture with her arms. "You'll have to speak up. I'm going deaf because of all I've been through."

Oh brother! I wish my uncle would do something about this.

"You're very brave!" Goode shouts into the microphone.

"You've got to be kidding," escapes from my lips.

My uncle gives me one of his famous 'don't' looks. "Listen and learn," he says.

Goode begins. "You're the widow of the late Mr. Eugene Bulk?"

"Yes. He's gone now. Thanks to that rotten killer over there!"

"I object," Uncle Jasper calls out.

The judge glares at him. "Jurors, I forgot to explain something important to you. When a lawyer feels an opposing lawyer has said something unfair or unimportant, he may object. I'm sure you've seen this on television shows. If I feel he is right, I say, "Objection sustained." If I judge he is wrong, I say, "Objection overruled." He looks at the jury and continues. "It's like baseball. Overruled means the lawyer objecting has a strike against him, while sustained means he has a hit." Fair straightens up. "In this instance, I feel Mr. Doofinch's objection is correct. Objection sustained! Doofinch has a hit."

"Thank you, Your Honor," Uncle Jasper says, giving me a little victory nod.

The judge scowls. "I'm not finished yet. Jurors, you must try to forget the last question and the answer. I know it is difficult to forget something you've already heard, but you must try your best in order to be perfectly fair. Which I always am." He lets out a chuckle at his own joke. "Get it? Judge FAIR? Judge I.M. Fair?"

"Thank you, Your Honor again," Uncle Jasper smiles.

I am beginning to think maybe Judge Fair isn't such a bad guy after all.

The judge glances at Uncle Jasper, and says, "Jurors, let me remind you that in my court, you will have an open mind and a closed mouth. You'll hear all the witnesses and then decide that Jack is a murderer."

"I object!" Uncle Jasper shouts, realizing he's been caught off-guard by the judge.

Judge Fair is leaning over, an angry look darkening his face. "You can't object to me. I'm the judge."

"You called my client a murderer."

"I did? Oh sorry." Judge Fair sneers. "It was an accident."

I get it. There is no way Judge Fair is going to be fair. He is a giant, and I suppose giants stick together. He smiles down at us, every white tooth in his head, gleaming like sharpened sword blades. "Let's get on with this, shall we?"

My uncle sits down, simmering mad. "He's prejudiced against humans," he whispers to me.

Welcome to Monstrovia

I let my eyes circle the gallery. It is wall-to-wall giants. Who isn't prejudiced against humans among this crew, I think, as I realize this is going to be an almost impossible battle! It's us puny humans against this gigantic gang of giants. It doesn't seem fair, and when things don't seem fair to me, I get mad, and when I get mad, I fight.

I look at my uncle and make up my mind that I will do anything and everything to help him win this case. No wacky goose, no backstabbing witnesses, no giant lawyers or judges, are going to stop me. At least that's what I think until I catch Mrs. Bulk eyeing me like I am a chicken nugget she can't wait to gobble down in one cruel bite.

CHAPTER 48

Goode shoots my uncle a sly grin and continues, "As I was saying, you're the wife of Mr. Eugene Bulk?"

"Yes, I was, until that miserable, rotten, killer..." She points a threatening finger at Jack.

"I object," Uncle Jasper says again.

The Judge sighs. "Mrs. Bulk, you can't call that killer over there a killer until he's found guilty."

"That's better," Uncle Jasper says, "Thank you, Your Honor."

"Grrr," the Judge growls, his eyes spearing my uncle.

I realize exactly what the judge just said, but it is too late for my uncle to object. This judge is getting away with murder. He's murdering my uncle!

Emily pinches my arm.

"Stop that," I hiss, prying her nails out of my skin.

Goode is gloating as he continues his questioning. "Tell me, Mrs. Bulk, when did you first meet the defendant, Mr. Beanstalk?"

Mrs. Bulk smiles sadly for the jury. "The first time I saw him, he looked so sweet, so innocent. He was standing outside my beautiful house looking lost and forlorn."

Beautiful house? She can't be serious! It makes my room look super-neat! And the smell!

"The poor dear moaned he was lost and hungry. I felt sorry for him. I invited him inside. Little did I know what the little beast was plotting!"

"I object! My client wasn't plotting anything. He doesn't have enough brains to plot anything. Just look at his face?"

The jury looks at Jack who lets loose an idiotic nervous smile.

The Judge sighs. "Objection sustained, but I wish you'd stop with all these objections already?"

Goode turns back to the giant. "What happened after you invited Jack in?"

"I fed him bacon and eggs."

"What happened then?"

"Jack burped."

"He what?"

"He burped!" She makes a loud burping noise that shakes the room and startles the pixie photographers into flight.

Uncle Jasper jumps up. "Objection! The fact that my client burped has nothing to do with this case."

Goode fires back, "Your Honor, this burp is very important."

The Judge lets out a huge burp. "I think burps are important too. Allowed."

Goode throws Uncle Jasper a gotcha smile. "What happened after Jack burped?"

"I went to get him some Tummy Seltzer from the bathroom. Gas, you know?"

"Oh yes, we all know about gas," Goode jokes, and everybody laughs, except Uncle Jasper, Emily, Jack and me.

The giant continues, "When I returned with the pill, Jack was gone. I was so worried. I thought he had to get home before dark. Some mothers care about where their children are."

Uncle Jasper looks like he is going to object, but decides not to call attention to Mrs. Beanstalk's absence. "I wish I knew where she is," he scribbles on his pad.

"When did you see Mr. Beanstalk again?" Goode asks.

"A few days later. I was happy to see him. I thought he wanted to be our friend. My dear Eugene and I love little boys."

"Yeah, for dinner," Emily blurts.

"I object," Goode shouts.

"Not you too." the Judge turns to us, poison in his eyes. "Keep her silent."

"Sorry, Your Honor. It just came out," Emily says, a coy smile on her face.

"Doofinch!" The judge aims his eyes at my uncle.

"Sorry, sir. I won't let it happen again."

The D.A. is chuckling, but quickly gets back on task. "How many times did Jack visit you at your home?"

"Oh at least three times. We always treated him well. That's why he kept returning."

She is pretending to be so sweet it is making me sick. My uncle isn't reacting. He's too busy taking lots of notes.

"I can't understand why he repaid our kindness by stealing from us…and then killing my dear husband!" Mrs. Bulk breaks into courtroom-shaking cries again.

"You poor, poor, dear," the prosecutor says.

Emily pinches my arm. "Isn't there anything you guys can do to stop this?"

"Write it down," I hiss, rubbing my arm. "And stop pinching me!"

"Are you all right now?" Goode offers another tissue to the tearful giant. "Can you tell us exactly what Jack stole?"

My uncle pops out of his seat like a jack-in-a-box. "I object! It has not been proven Jack stole anything."

The Judge glares at him again. "Mr. Goode, please use the word 'allegedly' to show that the defendant has not been convicted of stealing YET. Allegedly means supposedly…like we can't be sure yet." He gives Jack a 'death-look', like it's all over but the hanging.

Goode throws my uncle an insolent grin and gets back to work. "Can you tell us what Jack 'allegedly' stole?"

"Allegedly nothing! That thief stole a bag of gold coins. Then he stole our singing harp, and finally he stole my sweet Eugene's favorite, his goose that lays golden eggs, Annabelle."

There was a lot of murmuring.

"What happened after you discovered these items were missing?"

"I couldn't believe it. I told my darling Eugene I suspected Jack stole from us, but he didn't believe me. He had such a good heart. I made him set a little trap for Jack. We both hoped it wasn't him." She turns an icy stare at Jack. "How could you do this to us? We trusted you. We loved you. Shame! Shame on you!"

Jack sticks out his tongue.

"Don't do that!" I grab his arm. "Things are bad enough already! You have to behave in court."

My uncle smiles at me approvingly. "You're learning, Brodie."

I really am learning, and find myself listening hard for every clue, watching every movement, every facial expression. It is fascinating and challenging. I never realized how much I love solving mysteries, and this is a toughie.

"What was your little trap for Jack?" Goode asks. "I'm certain it was painless."

"Oh, for certain. My husband pretended to be asleep when Jack came in. When Jack grabbed our cow that gave chocolate milk, my husband said to him ever so gently, so he would not frighten the dear lad, "Jack, why are you stealing from us? We're your friends." The giant sobs into the tissue. "That boy grabbed the cow and smashed it on my poor husband's head!" She unexpectedly grabs one of the guards and swings him in the air to demonstrate. Around and around he goes. The guard screams and she releases him, sending him flying across the room.

"I'm sorry. So sorry. I've been through so much because of THAT KILLER," she moans, as the badly shaken guard staggers to his feet.

The courtroom bursts into excited murmurs.

Emily pinches me again. Am I going to have any arm left by the end of the day?

Judge Fair rises to his feet. "That's it! No more! Court is adjourned until tomorrow morning! And Mrs. Bulk, you have a right to be upset at the murder of your husband, but this kind of behavior is not allowed in my court. Do you understand?"

Mrs. Bulk sniffles."Yes, Judge Fair. I'm just so upset."

"I understand, dear lady, but let the courts punish this criminal act, not you."

"I object! I object!" Uncle Jasper is shouting again, but the judge leaves the room without replying."

I pry Emily's nails out of my arm and she leaves without a word too.

My uncle is packing his briefcase. "Not one word, Brodie. Please, not one word."

All the way home, through dinner, and later in his office, Uncle Jasper is unusually silent.

I can't think of anything to say that would make him feel better.

Suddenly, he pushes away from his desk stacked with papers about this crazy case. "We've got to find that mother and goose. They are our only hope. Good night, dear nephew. Tomorrow is another day."

I have never seen him look so discouraged. He shuffles slowly toward the door and then turns back toward me. "You should get some sleep. I will need you to be alert in court when Mrs. Bulk testifies again."

"Okay if I stay up a little? I'm not tired."

He nods. "Good night, Brodie. I'm glad you're here to help."

"Goodnight."

It is a mistake to leave me alone. I have the chance to escape, from him, this case, these monstrous creatures, and Monstrovia. I could be home soon and playing with my friends. All I have to do is be brave and take the chance.

I wait until I am certain he is gone before I make my move.

CHAPTER 49

It isn't difficult sneaking out of the house. All the doors warn to, "STAY OUT!", but none say, "STAY IN!" And the alarms that keep people out of the house, are not meant to keep anyone in. So all I have to do is find my way from the office, back through that awful tunnel, with all those scampering scampers, and find the exit door.

I pull open the office door and force myself to enter the dark tunnel. Instantly there are the squeaky noises and orange eyes that tell me the scampers are not sleeping. "They can't hurt me," I tell myself, searching for the door to the outside. I have to be perfectly quiet or the echo will give me away. The dirt floor reminds me that this is not your average hallway, but nothing is average in Monstrovia... except maybe me.

I find the door that leads to the back entrance and carefully turn the knob. Any second I expect to see Uncle Jasper waving that gargantuan sword in my face. I can imagine his look of disappointment at seeing me about to escape from this madhouse. Even that does not stop me, and soon I am closing the exit door behind me.

Wow! It's cold out here! I weigh going back for a sweatshirt, but no time. I have to move quickly. Horace would be a huge help, but I have never been able to open the garage door, and I still don't trust this gargantuan meat-eater.

I am shivering, not from the cold, but from the sight of those black serpents in the sky. "You're hardly a snack," I hear my uncle's voice warn, as I hurry from our silent street, toward the main drag, where I hope to hitch a ride.

Even at night the traffic is racing by. I can't help gawking at some of the strange vehicles racing along the multi-level highway that is minutes from Uncle Jasper's house. Even the moon seems to have strange creatures flying swiftly past. I am beginning to wonder if this is a good idea, when I hear brakes screeching inches from me. "Oh no! Not you?"

"Master Brodie, be it you?"

I am afraid to look. It can't be? It is. There, face full of a huge smile, stands the worst cab driver in the world.

"Silas Bumbernickle at yer service, Master Brodie," he says, and then looks puzzled, as he whispers. "What are ye doing out here in the danger of night? T'is not safe fer yer kind…not for mine neither." He casts a furtive glance at the sky.

I am tempted to let him scoot away, but need a ride, and he is a cabbie…sort of. "I need yer…your help, Mr. Bumbernickle. Can you drive me--"

"Anywhere. Anywhere at all, me lad. But does yer uncle know? He'll be worried about ye."

I can understand that, with these ferocious looking creatures rushing all around, I am worried too. "I'm doing it to help my uncle," I say, wishing we can get going before some other vehicle stops and 'snaps' me up to goodness-knows-where.

"Well alrighty then. Hop in me cab, Master, and we'll be off. I know Monstrovia like the back of me hand."

Wait! What am I doing? Am I really voluntarily getting into this lunatic driver's cab again?

Bumbernickle must notice my hesitation because suddenly he says, "I'll go a wee bit slower this time. Okay?"

Before I have a chance to reply I feel his powerful hands shove me back into that mushroom-top-shaped cab of his. "Buckle up me boy and we'll be off. Yer safe with Bumbernickle at the wheel."

Safe? Will I ever feel safe in this crazy place not on any map of Florida, the United States or the World? "Can you drive me to this address?" I hand him a slip of paper and buckle up quickly. I know this driver 'like the back of me hand' and I'm not taking any chances.

"Are ye sure ye want to go here," Bumbernickle asks, "Tis a good distance off." Before I can answer, I'm thrown back in the hard seat and we're zooming.

"I thought you said you were going to go slower," I gasp, as the crazy cabbie throws me all over the seat with his zigging and zagging around all the insanely racing 'cars' and vehicles.

"This is slow," he replies, a wild gleam in his eye. "We'll be there in a dragon's swallow," he adds, and thankfully turns back to his window and veers away from a certain crash with a vehicle heading at us, its animal-head passengers raising fists as we barely miss colliding at break-neck speed.

"We're 'ere," The cabbie announces minutes later, as I am thrown back by the screeching brakes.

I pull myself up from the crumpled mess I have become and stare at the massive gate. At night, with its spear head spikes, it really does look like heads should be peering at us with lifeless eyes. I step eagerly out of the cab and reach for the button on one of the columns.

"Are ye sure ye should be doin' that?"

Bumbernickle is looking at the spiked gate with doubt on his face.

I push the bell before he can try and stop me.

At first, nobody answers. Within seconds I hear a loud yawn and a familiar voice say, "Go away. There's nobody home."

CHAPTER 50

"She says there's nobody 'ome, Master Brodie." Bumbernickle shrugs his shoulders. "Too bad. Too bad. A long trip for nothin'."

"How can there be nobody home when she answered," I ask the crazy cabbie. "I know you are there, Emily Beanstalk. Now open up!" I turn to the cabbie. "There's nobody home, huh?"

He shrugs his shoulders again and looks sheepish.

I wait for what feels like hours, but finally the gates move apart.

"Do ye want me to drive ye in?" Bumbernickle sounds like the last thing he wants to do is enter the gate. "Who lives here? Dracula?"

"Yes, please. But SLOW. REALLY, REALLY SLOW." I brace myself and buckle up the shoulder harness again, and hold on. Between him and Horace, I'm beginning to feel like a Monstrovian milk shake.

To my surprise the cabbie rolls his vehicle slowly down the long road. "This be some place," he mutters, looking all around, which is why he is driving so slowly for once.

"They used to have a lot of 'spaghetti'." I automatically use my Uncle's expression.

Emily is standing in the front doorway as we pull up. "Looks safer than that other thing you were in," she says with a smirk. "Where's your yellow helmet? Very high fashion."

"I haven't time to waste," I say, cutting her off. "You know what I want."

"No. I have no idea what you are doing here in the middle of the night. Where's your uncle? Are you out here without his permission?"

"Mr. Bumbernickle, would you mind?" He has been listening in while taking in the house's size with wide eyes. "I'd like to speak to Miss Bordenschlocker in private."

The crazy cabbie looks hurt, but stumbles toward the side of the house. "Nice place ye have here. Can ye use a great driver, Miss? I knows Monstrovia like the back of me hand."

I shoot at Emily, "No. You don't want him as your driver."

Emily smiles that infuriating impish grin at me and calls to Bumbernickle, "We'll discuss it later."

I can tell from her cat-like smile she is not in a mood to cooperate with me. I don't care. I am on a mission. I only have a little time before my uncle realizes I am gone and sends the cops after me. "Where is she?"

"Who?" Emily's eyes are defiant.

I realize she is in her robe. She really did not expect me. "Your mother."

"How should I know?"

"I think you do. I think she is hiding here, somewhere in this house."

"I told you I don't know where Mom is." She looks more stubborn than usual.

"All I want to do is talk to her."

"Why would I lie to you? I want to help Jack."

"So does my uncle. We need your mother and that dopey goose or our goose is cooked." I would laugh at that accidental pun, but I am tired, shaken, cold, and suspect Emily is not telling the truth.

Emily crosses her arms over her chest, not a good sign. "Okay. Search the house if you don't believe me?"

I look at that gargantuan mansion and know it is hopeless. I also want to believe that she doesn't know. So where could the missing mother be? And suddenly it hits me. "I know where she is," I say, about to head out the door.

"Where, oh great detective?"

I hate sarcasm. "Where nobody would ever think of looking. That's what you said, and I think you're right." I run toward the back of the mansion.

"Wait," Emily shouts. "Please Brodie. Let me get shoes? I'll go with you. It's too dark. There are all kinds of creatures at night."

I'd forgotten about that. I look up at the sky and see she is right. A thin black serpent is hovering right above us. It seems to be looking down at us with more than a little interest. Meat-eater? "Emily, get your shoes, but hurry."

I don't think anyone ever talked to her like that before because she looks mad. "You can't tell me what to do! This is my property! Now get out! Get out before I call the police!"

"Okay. If that's what you want?" I push my way past her through the door. "I'll go there by myself!"

Her eyes are blazing when she jumps in front of me. "You have no right--"

"You don't get it. A lawyer has every right to do whatever he can to help his client. So get out of the way or help me find your mother now!" (Who do I sound like?)

"Wait. Please wait?" Emily looks desperate. "You really think Mom is hiding in that run-down shack? Okay, I'll get dressed. Give me five minutes?"

She looks sincere. "Okay, but if you are not back here in five minutes, I'm going to search that place by myself."

She turns toward me with an evil smile on her face. "Did you forget about... the spiders?"

I actually had, but leave it to her to remind me.

Her smile is demonic and her voice chilling. "Just imagine how much worse it is at night out there... all those gigantic, hairy, eight-legged spiders, just waiting for something fleshy to bite into...just waiting for a sip of your blood."

I refuse to let my fear get me this time. "I'll wait five minutes. Now get!" I kind of like ordering her around like that and seeing her obey for a change.

I should have known it was too good to be true.

CHAPTER 51

I'm asleep on the cold tile floor when I feel something bony grab my shoulder. I almost jump out of my skin. "You scared the heck out of me," I bark at Bumbernickle whose fingers are digging into my flesh.

"Ain't ye ready to leave yet, Master Brodie? It's not safe out 'ere, what with them serpents and beasties racing around all overand all."

I'd forgotten about the little cabdriver. "Hey, Silas," I call him by his first name, as if we are the best of buds. "How would you like to help me?"

"Anything fer ye, Master. Yer uncle is an 'ero around 'ere--"

"Yes, yes. I know. But this could be a bit dangerous."

"How dangerous, Master Brodie? Ye shouldn't be doing dangerous things without yer uncle"

"Not that dangerous." I call into the house. "Emily? Emily? I'm leaving!"

And there she is, Miss Emily Bordenschlocker-Beanstalk, the queen of the prom, all dressed in gold jeans, matching tee shirt, sneakers, and jacket. Without a watch that works in this Special Sector, I have no idea how long she's kept me waiting, but it has to be more than five minutes.

"Do you really want to go to that horrible shack now? In the middle of the night?" She has the nerve to ask after making me wait this long? "I could make you a nice cup of tea, Brodie, and we could have cookies--"

"Let's go." I am now absolutely positive Mrs. Beanstalk is hiding in that awful shack just like Jack had hidden in the giant's castle because it was the last place on Earth anyone would guess they would be.

Emily hands me a candle. "Is he going with us too?"

The candle makes Bumbernickle's face look evil, the face of a demon.

"That I am." He takes a candle, and then another. "T'isn't too dangerous? Is it?"

Emily is about to answer when I jump in, "You'll be fine. No more stalling, Emily. Let's go!"

Emily leads the way and Bumbernickle brings up the rear. I can hear him mumbling all the way to the orchard. "Ooh, tis dark and witchy back 'ere. I don't likes this place at all."

Emily stops by the trees. "Brodie," she says softly, as if someone might overhear, "Do you really want to do this now? Look up in the sky."

I do and see slinky shadowy creatures slithering in the moonlight.

"Them's the serpents I been telling ye' about, Master Brodie," Bumbernickle says, fear in his voice. "If they sees us vulnerable they comes screaming down and gobbles ye' up in one bite. Me? Maybe two."

"Nonsense! Stay together!" I catch Emily smiling at the cabbie's frightened face. "Emily, I am not leaving until I see that cabin for myself, so stop trying to scare my friend over here."

"Friend, did ye say?"

It had slipped out. I really didn't think of anyone here as a friend. They're all too weird.

"Well then, me dear friend," Bumbernickle says with a broad smile, "Though I still be plenty afeared, I be yer man fer certain. Lead on, Mistress Borden... Mistress B. I won't disappoint me good friend, Master Brodie, the brave nephew of a great 'ero, not fer anything in this world."

Just then I feel a warm swirl of air and hear Emily scream, "Brodie, duck!"

"Duck?" *Why is she so afraid of a duck?*

Bumbernickle grabs my arm and hurls me to the ground as a huge, black serpent swoops down and barely misses me with its gnashing teeth.

"He's diving again," Emily shouts. "Run for the shack!"

Bumbernickle helps get me to my feet with his powerful hands and we run after Emily. Our candles have been extinguished by the swirl of air, so we are in the dark... except when a long plume of flame shoots just overhead from the mouth of the serpent.

"He's tryin' to roast ye'," the cabbie shouts. "Ye run and I'll fight 'im off ." He shoves me ahead and plants both his stubby legs on the ground, his fists pointed toward the sky. "Come on ye rotten monster! Ye've met yer match in Bumbernickle!"

"Run with me," I shout to the little maniac, as I'm stumbling in the dark, barely keeping Emily in sight.

I hear a loud swooshing noise and then Bumbernickle shouting, "C'mon ye' ugly big snake! I'll mash up that gruesome face so yer mother won't recognize ye'!" And then I hear a loud scream and see another plume of flame shoot high into the air.

I stop running, listening for his voice, that accent. Silence...

Suddenly I scream as something is touching my back.

"It's me, you idiot," Emily hisses. "He's gone. I warned you and now he's gone."

I want to yell at her for scaring me again, but her words finally penetrate. "Bumbernickle is gone?"

Emily nods. "I'm sorry. I tried to warn you. We have to go back--"

"It's my fault. He was here because of me." I look back, but all I see is darkness. Do I hear teeth chomping? "It's my fault..."

"Let's go," Emily says. "I told you it's too dangerous at night. We can come back tomorrow to look for him."

"Not on your life. I'm not going to let my friend's sacrifice be for nothing. We're here now and I am going to see for myself." I begin to walk, on guard for any sound coming from above.

"Oh, you are so stubborn," Emily says, still rooted in place, as if deciding what to do.

"It takes one to know one. Now let's go!" I don't wait. I grab a thick branch that is still burning from the serpent's flame and head for the dark shed I can see now in the near distance.

Emily catches up to me. She is silent for a few seconds and suddenly says, "Brodie, you're braver than I thought."

Brave? No. Stupid?

The next few minutes will tell.

CHAPTER 52

The serpents don't like the flaming branch. They screech and flutter to avoid the flame. That seems strange since they breathe fire, but a lot of things here don't make much sense. At any rate, with the torches held high, they don't attack again. Soon, we're at the steps.

I wave my torch and the spiders crawl creepily away. Good. "Are you ready?"

"You can see nobody is here," Emily says, her nose almost touching my cheek. "Nothing here, but the same messy, spider webs."

She's right, it is a great nest for spiders and that's about it. "They can keep it," I say and get ready to sneak back to the house without getting unwanted attention from the serpents.

"Are you satisfied now? Can I go home to bed so I won't look like a mess tomorrow in court?" Emily lets out a really loud yawn.

Suddenly I hear a noise. "Shhh." Was she warning her mother with that yawn? "Listen, I hear something."

Emily yawns again and says, "Brodie, it's just--"

Before she can finish her sentence, a few dozen black bats come racing out of the windows, their wings flapping around me as I try to fight them off with my arms. I struggle to hide my face and hair, but the wings are brushing my skin, sending ice-cold shivers to my brain. The screaming of the bats is terrifying, but I can't run. They are everywhere.

Welcome to Monstrovia

The wings are hitting against my face like leathery fly swatters. I try to whip them away, but there are too many and I fall to the ground, still fighting them off. They are all over me. I'm throwing them off, but they keep flying back.

Suddenly I see a flame lashing out at me and I see Emily's face. She is trying to set me on fire! Why? "Emily," I shout up at her, but the bats' wings are hitting my mouth, nose and eyes like stinging leather belts. I can't fight them much longer. The flaming torch is streaking back and forth over my head. A bat is stuck in my hair. Another bat is biting my ear. I swat him away, but another lands on my cheek.

"Get off my friend!" Emily is yelling, chasing the bats away with the flaming torch.

I still feel them, their wings pummeling me, their teeth snapping. I close my eyes, but still see the flame through my lids as Emily is still screaming and chasing off the last of the bats.

"It's okay, Brodie. I chased them off." Emily sags on the ground next to me.

I close my eyes again, not knowing which is worse, being attacked by a bunch of disgusting, smelly, bats or being saved by Emily Beanstalk? I taste blood and smell bat all over me. Disgusting.

"Have you had enough yet," Emily asks, holding her torch so close I can feel its heat.

I can smell the odor of bats burning. I can't believe they're gone. I force myself to my feet and brush off the bat guano and acidy bat-spit that made holes in my shirt and jeans.

I can hardly talk, stand, or think, and everything smells nasty, but I am not giving up. "Inside," I gasp, catching my breath, still overwhelmed by the smell of the rodents. "I want to see… inside…now."

"Fine." Emily stands, looking angry. "But to be sure you're safe, follow me." She holds the torch high so the spiders scatter. "Look, the webs are all still intact over the door. If someone is here, they'd be broken. Wouldn't they?"

"Inside," I repeat, knowing I am being stubborn, knowing she is probably right.

Emily pushes the door open and I peer inside. "Torch," I gasp, still smelling bats.

She moves the torch past the door. It all looks the same as it did when I first saw it. It is a horrible mess of broken glass, rotting leaves and rickety furniture, a motel for all kinds of creepy insects. There is nothing that shows Mrs. Beanstalk, or the goose, were ever here. It is time to admit I'm wrong, but I'm learning to be stubborn, like Emily. "In," I say, my throat still clogged by the scent of bat and all the dust I've swallowed. "In."

"Oh, come on, Brodie! You can see she isn't here!"

I am inside the cabin when I can't stop coughing. I double over and spit dust and muck on the floor. "What's that?" I grab the torch out of Emily's hand and kneel close to the floor, pulling at something thin poking out between two planks.

"I didn't know," Emily says, staring at the golden feather in my fingers. "You have to believe me. I didn't know she was here."

I croak, "Where is she...your mother? Where did she take the goose?"

"Brodie, I can't tell you. Please believe me? I would if I could."

I have learned not to trust anyone, but Emily sounds so sincere. I can finally talk. "You really didn't know your mother was here?"

"Why wouldn't I tell you?"

She looks so miserable, so pathetic, so truthful. "Okay." I cough, a real cough this time. "If you hear from her, you've got to tell my uncle." I take another breath, still choking. "Without her and that goose, Jack is a dead duck."

Emily nods. "Can we go now?"

"Yes. I'm tired, covered by bat gunk... and I'll have to get a cab." I feel awful. I had forgotten all about poor Silas Bumbernickle. Does he have family...maybe kids? "Emily, I'll never forgive myself for what happened to that crazy cabbie—"

"Do somebody 'ere need a cab?"

I turn and there is that crazy cab driver, his clothes shredded, his face blackened, and his hat missing...but he is alive! "How did you get away?"

He holds up his fists. "Being little doesn't mean ye can't fight. Always remember tis' the brains that counts. These 'ere serpent brains, no matter the monster's size, is no match fer Bumbernickle, once I figures out 'is nose is a marshmallow to me fists."

"I'm glad you're okay," I said, feeling relief flowing through my exhausted body. "You're a bit of an 'ero' yourself."

He blushes and looks down at his shoes. "Did ye find what ye were seeking, Master Brodie?"

"Yes." I said, not quite telling the truth. "Can you drive me home now?" I hated asking, seeing how beat up he looked. "Do you feel well enough to drive me back?" I can't believe I am asking him to let me ride in that crazy contraption of his.

Silas Bumbernickle smiles. "Of course, Master Brodie. But would ye mind very much if we drive a little slow?"

"I don't mind at all."

We walk Emily back to the mansion. She doesn't say anything and I don't either. I'm still searching the sky for more of those serpents.

We arrive at Emily's door. Suddenly she gives me a glance and says, "Brodie, I'm sorry." And then she does the strangest thing. She leans forward and gives me a tiny kiss on the cheek. I would have pulled back, but it is a total surprise.

"Whatever happens," she says, pearly tears in her eyes, "I want you to remember I...I...." She rushes inside and closes the door without finishing.

I've no idea what she wanted to say, but that tiny kiss ends any doubt that Emily told me the truth. She was as surprised as I was that her mother had been hiding in that crummy shack with that crazy goose. I wonder what the heck she wants.

"Master Brodie's got a girlfriend, I thinks," Bumbernickle teases.

Girlfriend? Emily? She drives me nuts... but I don't have any friends here. I don't plan on staying, but it would be kind of nice to have someone to talk to while I am here. But Emily?

I had planned to surprise my uncle by producing the elusive Mrs. Beanstalk and the goose, but failed to find them, so what is the point of telling him about my hair-brained adventure? "Silas, I wonder, can you keep this night a secret, just between you and me?"

"Yer secrets be safe with me," Silas says, as he holds the door open for me. "We be friends now fer real." He extends his gnarly hand.

"We be friends." I shake the hand of my first friend in the special place they call Monstrovia.

I had left the garden door to Uncle Jasper's mansion slightly open with a piece of gum holding it ajar, so I have no trouble getting back inside. I climb the three flights of stairs as silently as a spy and stumble into my bed fully dressed and covered with dirt. I am about to fall asleep when I feel something staring at me. It's the Perry Mason poster's eyes.

"Okay, I'll tell him the truth," I say, unnerved by the probing eyes, "someday." I also swear to myself that I'll pick up some posters of some cute little female singers or actors...if they have any human posters here? If not, maybe Emily will give me a photo?

I shoot up in my bed. "Emily? Friend? You've gotta be kidding! What's wrong with you Brodie?"

CHAPTER 53

Nightmare after nightmare barely let me sleep, and each time I wake up, there are those deep-set eyes staring down at me and making me feel guilty.

"Day two," Uncle Jasper says, buried under papers at his desk.

I am worried he'll notice how tired I look, or the bruises on my arms and face. He is too busy getting ready for the next skirmish with Mr. Hugh B. Goode and his star witness, Mrs. Bulk.

"Maybe I'll call a cab today," Uncle Jasper says. "I should give old Horace a day of rest."

He's going to call Bumbernickle? I panic. "I like riding on Horace," I lie quickly, surprised at how good I'm getting at this.

"You do? I thought you were rather frightened of the poor thing?" He scratches his head.

"Oh no, Uncle, Horace and I are becoming great friends." One lie leads to another.

"Very well. Horace it will be. Anything for my wonderful assistant."

I really did it this time. No sooner does Horace come gallumphing out of the garage than Uncle Jasper insists we become better acquainted. "Rub his nose," he coaxes as Horace gives me a suspicious look and a snort of purple green smoke.

"We have to go," I say, not eager to trust my hand to those 'meat-eater' teeth. "How about later?"

Uncle Jasper shakes his head. "You must overcome your fears, my nephew. Fear paralyzes us, and is mostly born of prejudice against the unknown."

Oh please, not a lecture? Not today. I take a deep breath, and reach my hand up toward Horace's massive bobbing head. "See, Uncle, I'm doing it."

Horace pulls his head away, gifting me with a blast of hot air.

"He's almost lost his ability to make fire," Uncle Jasper says, as if we should be sorry about that. Believe me, I'm not.

"He doesn't like me," I say, holding my hand out of reach of his teeth.

"Give him time. Old fears take time to overcome." He gives me a warm smile. "Come Brodie, let's get to court."

I climb up Horace's back and settle into the sidecar. "Ready." I brace myself against the sides of the tub.

"Put on your helmet," Uncle Jasper reminds me.

"Do I have to?" As much as I hate that thing, with those tiny horns sticking out of its rounded surface, I strap it on.

"Nice and easy, Horace, old boy," my uncle says, rubbing the thick neck. And we're off!

At a slower pace, we take the lower roadway. I notice there are fewer vehicles and less horn blowing and squealing of brakes. I actually relax a little, take in some of the scenery. Being in the city, there are only a few trees, and these are thin and sickly looking compared to the ones I'd seen on Emily's land. Why am I thinking of 'her' again?

There are stores and houses not visible from the speedways above. At first glance, the stores look like storefronts in any American town, but I spot signs with strange names like, The Magic Potion Shop, Peter Pan's Youth Pill 'Pothecary, and The Pixie Photography Photo Emporium.

The houses are a bit curious too. Some look ordinary, box-like, with sloped roofs, but in between these 'suburban-style' American-type homes are some styles I've never seen before. One lot has three small homes on it, one built of straw, another of sticks and a third of brick. On another street, there is a remarkable house shaped like a pirate ship, with a 'skull and bones' mailbox for a Captain J. Hook. To my surprise, his neighbor's house is shaped like a large alligator head and on its mailbox is a label for one P. Pan and Lost Boys.

The Court House parking lot is almost full. Uncle Jasper secures Horace, warning him once again to not topple the statue of the Dragonslayer.

Horace snorts his frustration.

By the time we enter the Giant Court room many others have arrived. The place is packed with more spectators and reporters than on the first day. Apparently the pixie photographers' photos from Mrs. Bulk's outburst have gotten a lot of attention and everyone wants to be in on the 'fireworks' today.

"Are we ready to proceed," Judge Fair asks, once he is seated behind the bench. "You may continue with your witness, Mr. Goode."

"I call again, Mrs. Bulk," Goode announces, giving the judge a broad smile.

"I want to continue from yesterday afternoon, when you were describing how Mr. Beanstalk, the defendant, smashed a cow over your husband's head."

My uncle groans. "I can't stand much more of this." He pushes back his chair angrily. "A cow? Come on Your Honor, just look at my client! He's too weak and puny to lift a glass of milk, let alone a cow."

"Many people have amazing strength when they need it," Goode explains. "Think of Super Mouse."

"Who?"

"Super Mouse. He is just a mouse, but when he bites into super cheese—"

"Your honor, now we're talking about super mice?" My uncle shakes his head.

Judge Faire frowns. "Mr. Goode, Mr. Doofinch is correct. Please stick to the subject. Objection sustained. Leave Super Moose out of this."

"Super Mouse, your Honor, not Moose," Goode corrects.

"Leave him out of it too."

Goode nods. "Very well. Mrs. Bulk, what happened next?"

"That killer over there grabbed the golden goose, and kidnapped her while my poor Eugene was helpless."

"Alleged killer," Mr. Goode says before my uncle can object.

"You're the lawyer so you gotta say that. I just has to say the truth," Mrs. Bulk says, aiming her eyes at me. "I ain't no trickster of a lawyer like some."

"Objection."

"Sustained."

"So the defendant ran off with the goose while your poor husband was coming to from his beating?"

"Yes. That killer made a beeline for the beanstalk and scooted down that huge thing so fast my poor Eugene couldn't catch him. Suddenly I heard an awful scream and saw my sweet husband falling, landing dead as a doornail, while that boy was holding that axe." Tears started dripping down her face again. "You didn't have to kill him. He wasn't going to hurt you. He just wanted his Annabelle back."

Jack's face has a murderous look. Could he have meant to kill that giant? I wish I knew.

"Is there anything else you want to add, Mrs. Bulk?" Goode hands her another giant tissue.

A juror who looks like he was asleep jumps up at the soggy blast.

Mrs. Bulk dabs at her eyes. "I just want to say, I saw my Eugene fall down to the ground. I saw it all. And I saw you, holding that axe, and grinning from ear to ear. Confess you wanted him dead and…maybe I can forgive you."

I gaze at Jack and see he isn't reacting, but I think he looks guilty, and if I think that, the jury will think even worse. After all they are human. Wait a minute! No they aren't. They are giants and monsters! There's not one human here! Boy, is Jack in trouble!

CHAPTER 54

We are waiting for Mr. Goode to continue when I hear a loud rumbling noise. It is coming from the judge. It's his stomach!

"Lunch," Judge Fair announces without warning and rises from his seat.

I can't believe the stampede.

Goode leaves the courtroom surrounded as always by flashing cameras and reporters.

"Do you want lunch Brodie?" my uncle asks.

"I'm not hungry. I think I'll stay here." I'm feeling a little sorry for him. He looks so alone without the reporters that are flying around Goode like planets circling a golden sun.

"I'm starved. Trials always make me hungry. I'll be back in a few minutes. Don't go anywhere." He gives me a smile. "I know you won't."

"Don't worry, I'll be fine." I don't tell him I was thinking of having lunch with Emily, but she disappeared, without a word, as soon as lunch was announced. In fact, she hardly spoke to me all morning. Heck, she didn't even pinch my arm. After last night, I kinda thought we could be friends. I don't know what I was expecting, but Emily never seems to do what I think she will. She sure doesn't seem to want to be my friend today. So why did she kiss me?

Uncle Jasper waddles from the courtroom. I actually think of joining him, just to make him feel better, but I need time for myself. I am exhausted and achy from last night's adventures. I'm also confused, about Emily, and about my uncle.

I decide to relax in the lounge a few doors from the courtroom. I've just plopped down on a massive red leather couch when I hear a horrible racket outside the doors. It sounds as if someone is clucking.

Clucking?

"It can't be?" I peek into the hallway.

Two giants, in dark red uniforms, are pushing a large object on wheels a few yards away. The noise is coming from this object, which is covered in tan canvas.

"What is that thing?" I enter the corridor. "It sure is noisy."

One of the giants snarls, "That's the star witness in some case on this floor!"

"The what?" I can't believe the barrage of noise coming from under the canvas cover.

The second giant leans on the wall. "We gotta keep IT under there. IT was leaving the Sector. Can you believe the noise?"

"It sounds like clucking? Don't tell me that's the goose?" I reach for the canvas.

"Goose?" The burly guard steps in front of me. "It's gotta be a chicken with all that awful clucking. I ain't never heard of no goose making clucking noises like that."

"Cluck! Cluck! Cluck," the so-called goose cries out.

"See what I mean? It does that all the time." The giant covers his ears.

"I think she's upset," the other giant says, "stuck in a crate like that."

"I think she's nuts," the first one replies.

"Cluck! Cluck! Cluck!" the witness continues to cry from under the canvas.

"Maybe it's a hen," I say. "Maybe Jack's confused? I'd better check. Can I talk to her?"

"Sorry, kid," the giant says, still blocking the object. "We has strict orders that nobody removes this cover or talks to this character."

"Who on Earth gave you those orders?" I am about to reveal that I am the assistant to the famous, Jasper Doofinch the Defender.

"I did," a voice replies from behind my back.

"Who are you?" I whirl around to see who took this authority on themselves.

"I'm Amelia Beanstalk. I'm Jack's mother."

I almost fall over. "Where have you been? We've been looking everywhere for you. Didn't you know your son is on trial for murder?"

She looks like a slightly older Emily, her hair shorter, with no freckles and much darker eyes.

"I'm pleased to meet you too." She extends a delicate hand. "You might say I've been on a wild goose chase."

"My uncle and I have looked everywhere for you! I even looked in the shed--"

"I know. Emily told me."

Lightning could not have hit harder. *Emily knew? She lied?* I try to keep calm, but I have to know the truth. "Did Emily know where you were?"

"You have to understand. I told her she couldn't tell anyone. I knew you'd have to tell the cops."

"She knew." *Emily lied to me. I trusted her. The rotten traitor!*

Amelia Beanstalk smiles sadly. "It's not Emily's fault. I made her promise. I had to find this crazy goose before she got away from Monstrovia. It wasn't easy. I chased down every feathered fowl I could find until I finally caught Annabelle here about to hop a plane for Australia. Believe me, it's not easy going after a galloping golden goose going gallivanting."

"She should have told us. Emily should have trusted me...us." *How could I have been so stupid? I should know better than to trust anyone.*

"I'm sorry, but I knew if Annabelle got away, Jack's goose would be cooked. I brought her to the shed where nobody would look for us, especially the giants. It wasn't safe for her. The Bulks' friends might have got her. She would have been fricasseed for sure."

"Uncle Jasper could have helped!"

Mrs. Beanstalk looks into my eyes and I see Emily's eyes. "You're Brodie. Emily told me how much you've done for us, and what a good friend you are. Thank you."

"Where is Emily now?" I'm wondering if it is Emily's turn to pull a disappearing act.

"She didn't want to be here when you found out."

"Did she know the whole time?" I am biting my lip, holding in my temper.

"She couldn't disobey me. I'm her mother." She gives me that same stubborn Emily look. She is just as pig-headed as her lying daughter! I am fuming mad, but I'll do what I can to help them win this case because of my uncle. I hope I never see another Beanstalk woman again once this case is over. Even their name is a lie.

I hate Emily Bordenschlocker. It's time to return as I see others rushing to the courtroom.

CHAPTER 55

The court is filling up for the afternoon session. How will my uncle feel when he learns that Emily knew about her mother all this time?

Uncle Jasper returns from lunch. "What's up, Brodie, dear boy? Did you eat something that disagreed with you? You look positively green?"

"Uncle, I have something to tell you."

"Nephew, by now you should know you can tell me anything." He sits down in his chair and waits, a sappy smile on his face.

"Uncle, don't kill the messenger. Emily knew where her mother and the goose were--"

"Anything but that." He looks like he's been shot and then struck by lightning and then smashed in the face by a pie. "Are you serious? Where is that girl? I told her and told her--"

"Her mother said Emily couldn't disobey her. I can't believe it either. Mrs. Beanstalk sounds and looks just like Emily. And you should hear that crazy goose!"

"Wait! She's here? The goose is here too?" Uncle Jasper looks like he is going to explode. "And Emily knew the whole time?"

"And you're not going to believe it," I added, "The goose really sounds like she's clucking!"

"I don't care if that goose is clucking, honking or passing gas! I haven't even had a chance to ask one question of either of my two witnesses! Brodie, I have no idea what that crazy goose is going to say."

Uncle Jasper looks worried. "They're coming back. Pretend everything is normal."

'Normal'? In Monstrovia? I don't even know what is normal at home.

The courtroom is almost full. I can't look at Emily who is entering just as the doors are closing. I thought we could be friends....

She doesn't look at me either. She gives up her seat next to Jack to her mother.

I'm cool with that. I won't have to feel her nails digging into my arm. She can't bother me.

Once she is seated, Emily casts me a questioning look. I guess she wants to see if I am really mad.

I ignore her. I've other things to worry about now besides a pesky, lying, rich girl, who I will never see again once this trial is over. Good riddance! She has guts, but she is nuts! I can't believe she was pretending to help us while all the time she was lying.

Judge Fair enters the room. He opens his eyes wide when he spots the elegantly dressed Mrs. Beanstalk. "I see Mrs. Beanstalk has finally joined us."

My uncle whispers, "Do not say anything!"

"And what on earth is that?" Judge Fair asks, pointing his gavel toward the large covered object at the rear of the courtroom. "It looks like a circus tent."

"That's the goose," a guard replies, looking doubtful.

"That's the goose? Let me see her," Judge Fair demands, putting on his black-rimmed glasses.

The guard pulls off the canvas cover.

I get out of my chair to see better and am surprised to see what does indeed look like a large gold colored goose cowering in the rear of the cage.

"Why is the witness caged?" the judge asks.

Goode replies, "She was leaving the Sector when--"

"You can't escape the law!" Judge Fair interrupts.

I am shocked when I hear the goose crying, "Cluck! Cluck! Cluck!"

Jack was right? This crazy goose definitely did say, "Cluck!" I burst into laughter. This is insane! This whole case is insane! Jack was right! But why should such a silly thing like this matter?

"Ahem," Judge Fair aims his eyes at me. "If you don't mind, I'd like to continue."

I stifle my laughter, but I can't stop staring at that clucking goose. She is sitting in a corner of the cage, eyes aimed anxiously at the Judge while she fidgets with her feathers. She is a nervous wreck. Suddenly her eyes grow wider.

I look to see what has caught her attention.

She's staring at Mrs. Bulk.

I keep looking at that crazy goose and wonder why she seems so terrified of the giant. I am so lost in my thoughts that I almost miss Goode starting his final questions for Mrs. Bulk.

"So to refresh our memory after that delightful lunch, you said Jack kept attacking your husband?"

As if on cue, Mrs. Bulk sobs pitifully. "Yes. It was terrible! Over and over that evil creature smashed my husband with that cow! My poor husband couldn't see. He was mumbling…his brain damaged by the vicious attack."

My uncle didn't object when she called Jack an 'evil creature'. Maybe he is. Emily sure is.

Mrs. Bulk sighs. "My poor husband tried to stand, but fell. But then he got up. Then he fell again…and got up again. It was so sad." She dabs at her eyes. "When he got up again, I tried to hold him back. I hugged him, but he bravely pulled away, saying, "I must save that sweet goose…Annabelle." She bursts into tears.

Goode waits patiently then asks, "Where was Jack while your poor, brave husband was suffering from this attack?"

No objection? Has Doofinch the Defender given up?

"Jack was calling my sweet Eugene toward that beanstalk." She lets out another pitiful sob. "I tried to warn him. 'Eugene! Eugene!' But it was too late. I couldn't get to him. He was stumbling blindly, and suddenly…he was gone… gone…gone. You murdered my poor Eugene." She bursts into tears and loud cries again.

"There, there," the judge is comforting her.

"There, there," Goode hands her another tissue.

"There, there, "I hear the spectators and jury chime in.

Jack's mother, looks numb. Emily appears to be in a trance too, staring straight ahead.

My uncle is studying Mrs. Bulk's face. He draws a large question mark next to a drawing that looks something like the goose.

Goode is holding Hortensia Bulk's hand. "Thank you, Mrs. Bulk. You have 'egg-spressed' yourself 'egg-cellently'."

The goose jumps up. "Was that an egg joke? Cluck, cluck."

I am surprised the goose is talking. All I'd heard before was her clucking.

"You!" Judge Fair fires at the goose. "I do not want to hear one more cluck out of you in my courtroom. Is that clear?"

The goose shivers and returns to sulking in a corner of its crate.

"I have no further questions at this time." Goode sits down, but not before giving his loyal gallery a brilliant smile.

The Judge casts my uncle a disdainful look. "It's your turn Mr. Duckfinch, although I think this case has been 'cracked' already." He lets out a loud guffaw at his own joke as he looks at the goose to see if she caught his pun. But the goose is frozen, staring at the giant who is giving her a look that could boil feathers.

CHAPTER 56

Uncle Jasper walks toward Mrs. Hortensia Bulk, careful to keep out of her reach. Her eyes look like they want to boil me in oil as she stares past my uncle.

"Mrs. Bulk," Uncle Jasper begins, "I am truly sorry for your loss."

"Humpf! I'll bet! That's why you're helping that miserable murderer?"

I hear the whole jury snort.

The judge leans over. "Mrs. Bulk, please say "that alleged miserable murderer.""

Mrs. Bulk nods. She points at me. "That little rat next to you. He said he was my lawyer." She makes a fist and shakes it at me. "I'll get you later."

My uncle gives me a wink. "Mrs. Bulk, let's stick to the subject. You allege that Jack stole three things from you?"

She points her finger at Jack as if it is a knife. "I ain't ALLEGING nothing! That little ungrateful beast stole all of our goodies from us!"

"Was one this singing harp?" Uncle Jasper points to the harp.

"Yes. That little crook!"

"And the others were this bag of gold coins and this goose?"

The goose ruffles its feathers and mumbles a volley of "cluck, clucks!"

The judge aims a terrible, silencing look at the goose. "I'll warn you one more time."

The goose claps a wing over its beak, but several more clucks escape.

"Whoever heard of a clucking goose," the judge grumbles. "Crazy, mixed up bird."

"Yes," Mrs. Bulk answers, "That little crook stole our Annabelle too. I love you Annabelle."

The goose clucks nervously into her wing. "Cluck, cluck, cluck."

My uncle turns to Jack. "Jack, will you please stand up?"

Jack looks around anxiously and stands behind our table.

"Now look carefully at this boy," Uncle Jasper continues. "You called him 'little'. That's true. Just look how weak he is." He instructs Jack to roll up his sleeves and flex his arms. "Look how puny his muscles are. Now how on earth do you expect us to believe that this 'little boy', your exact words, could carry off that great big chicken?"

The goose bursts out of her corner, feathers bristling. "I'm a goose! I'm a goose! I'm not a chicken, a hen, a turkey! I'm a goose! Cluck! Cluck! Cluck!"

Instantly the Judge is flying too. "I warned you. Shut your beak!"

"Cluck! Cluck! Cluck!" The goose lets loose.

"I'm sorry," Uncle Jasper says to the cowering goose. "It's that clucking. You sound like a chicken?"

"I'm no chicken!" the goose screeches. "I'm a goose! I deserve respect."

She sure looks like a goose, but why the clucking? Crazy bird.

Uncle Jasper shakes his head. "And that huge harp? Are you saying Jack lifted that huge thing too?"

"I should have gone on a diet," the harp mutters, turning red.

The giant shifts in her seat. "Well...I...that is..."

"No answer huh?" Uncle Jasper smiles. "You also said Jack hit your husband with a cow." He lets that sink in. "Where is that cow now?"

Goode rockets to his feet. "Objection! Where the cow is now is no concern of ours, no way, no how."

Uncle Jasper shouts right back, "Oh, yes it is! That cow should be a witness. Where is the cow now?"

The Judge shouts, "Overruled! I want to know where that cow is now too."

Hortensia Bulk looks nervous, her eyes searching Goode's face.

"Where is the cow now?" Uncle Jasper repeats, looking at the jury.

"Hamburger," Mrs. Bulk mumbles.

"What did you say?" The Judge leans in to her.

Mrs. Bulk gulps. "HAMBURGER! We had no food! That brat, 'alleged brat', stole everything that wasn't nailed down."

"She would've eaten me next. Cluck, cluck." I catch the goose whispering. I make a note on my pad for my uncle.

"YOU ATE THE WITNESS?" Uncle Jasper asks. "Your Honor, I ask you, what kind of person gobbles up the witness to a case?"

"She was just a cow," the giant sputters. "Just a cow."

Emily bursts into sobbing, "Poor Elvira! Poor, sweet, smelly, Elvira!"

"Wrong cow," I whisper. "Shhh." It feels great to shush her for once.

Mrs. Bulk is shifting anxiously in her seat. "I was hungry. I had to."

"So when you're hungry, you eat your favorite cow? What else do you and your dear, kind, husband eat when you're hungry?"

"Objection," Goode shouts, jumping up again.

"Overruled. Say, I'm getting hungry from all this talk of food. Hey chicken, could you spare an egg?" The judge gives the goose a winning smile.

"Never!" The goose clucks angrily. "And I'm not a chicken! I'm a goose! A GOOSE! Cluck! Cluck! Cluck!"

"Spoilsport," the Judge growls, looking at his watch.

Uncle Jasper waits patiently and then continues, "Okay, so tell us what else you eat?"

"Well, if you must know, we love weedy pudding, snot-grass tacos, brown booger hotcakes and spinach quiche."

"And that's all?" Uncle Jasper pauses and then attacks. "What about hamburgers, hot dogs, juicy little kids?"

Goode is up screaming, "Objection! Objection!"

"Never!" Mrs. Bulk smiles. "We're vegetarians."

Uncle Jasper fires back. "But you just said you ate a cow!"

The giant squirms. "Alright! I admit it! I ate one lousy, little cow. But it was just a cow!"

I am beginning to understand that a good lawyer has to listen very carefully to every word a witness says, pay attention to every detail. Suddenly, I remember something and quickly jot it down and hand it to my uncle:

She said Mr. B <u>mumbled something</u>? What?

My uncle gives me a questioning look, but smiles when he sees the word "mumbled" on his pad.

I had remembered something strange from when I had been up in the giant's bean-can castle. She had also mumbled some words I had never heard before. Jack had mentioned them too. I know it is a long shot, but I've got a feeling there is more to it...there was something frightening about those words.

"By the way, Mrs. Bulk, you said that after Jack 'allegedly' hit your husband with this currently non-existent cow that your husband mumbled something. What was it?"

"What was what?" Mrs. Bulk is twisting her hands in her lap.

I am getting better at seeing how witnesses behave, and I see the word mumbled made her nervous.

"What did your husband mumble?"

"It was nothing, nothing important." She is really squirming now. Her butt is moving around like she is crushing ants with it.

"I'd love to know anyway," Uncle Jasper coaxes gently. "We'd all love to know since they may have been his last words."

I remember Jack said something about a rhyme the giant had said. I also remembered Mrs. Bulk saying what may have been the start of a rhyme, when I'd paid her a visit, but didn't think much about it at the time. I jot down another message and hand it to my uncle:

Ask about the rhyme.

My uncle gives me another puzzled look.

I nod and mouth, "Ask her."

Uncle Jasper shrugs his shoulders and asks, "Mrs. Bulk, by any chance were those words a rhyme?" He gives me that puzzled look again.

"What rhyme," Mrs. Bulk asks. "Your honor, this is crazy--"

"The rhyme your husband sometimes said before he ate," I whisper to my uncle.

"The rhyme Mr. Bulk said before he ate," Uncle Jasper repeats my words, moving closer to where I am sitting.

I detect a nervous twitch in Mrs. Bulk's right eye. I also see beads of sweat on her forehead. Are we getting close?

"Oh, you mean, "Mary had a little lamb. I like that one."

I shake my head.

"No. Try another," Uncle Jasper says.

"Humpty Dumpty sat on a wall?"

"No."

"I know! Three blind mice!"

"I'm sure he loved mice almost as much as children...but no."

"Your Honor," Goode protests, not even bothering to get up. "Haven't we wasted enough time on this ridiculous rhyme?" He looks surprised, realizing he made an unintended rhyme.

Judge Fair sighs. "Mr. Doofinch. I will let you continue, but don't make it last. Time is going very fast." He giggles. "Oh my, now I've made a rhyme too. This is fun. Go on. I want to hear this rhyme."

Mrs. Bulk is sweating. I can smell the farty bean stench all the way over at our table. He's doing it! He's nailing her! Go, Jasper, go! My uncle isn't a hero sandwich! He is the real thing! And I am helping! I can almost taste the discomfort we are causing Mrs. Bulk, and it feels really good. For the first time I smell victory, and it is just a few words away.

CHAPTER 57

What do you know? My uncle was right all along. A tiny detail, easily overlooked, can win a tough case. In this trial, a poem, a silly rhyme, may be the clue that is nailing the case for our client. I keep searching my brain to remember the strange poem I heard Mrs. Bulk mutter during my perilous encounter with her. I was so frightened at the time I really didn't pay much attention to it…like in school, I guess. How many important things had I missed out on by not paying attention?

"Your honor, she's stalling," my uncle says and looks meaningfully at the jury.

The judge points his gavel at the giant. "Mrs. Bulk, you will answer about the rhyme at this time! Do not delay. We haven't all day." He laughs. "I love this! Every trial should have a rhyming poem. I'm going to practice when I get home?" He writes on his pad his latest rhymes.

The giant shifts in her seat. "It was just some dumb rhyme. A kids' poem, I guess. Not important." She looks directly at the Judge. "It was nothing, Your Honor. I give you my word."

The Judge frowns. "Now, I'm curious too. Aren't all of you? Hey, another rhyme!" He hurriedly writes it down too.

The jurors nod their heads.

Uncle Jasper moves closer to the witness box. "What was the rhyme, Mrs. Bulk? Why are you afraid to repeat it?"

"I told you it was just nonsense! Some silly syllables…" Her eyes are looking at Goode, pleading for help. She is sweating rivers now. Nearby spectators are coughing from the baked bean sweaty smell she is giving off.

"Would my assistant, Brodie Adkins, please stand?"

I am startled. What does he want? The giant terrifies me!

"Brodie, dear nephew, don't worry." Uncle Jasper gives me a smile of encouragement.

I stand up, staring uncertainly at the giant, who looks like she is ready to throw herself on me and crush me to death. She is like ten Principal Feeneys!

"Do you remember the rhyme you told me you heard Mrs. Bulk say when you visited her castle?"

"Yes, I think I do," I reply, my voice shaky. "Fee Fi Fo Fum?" I say it almost in a whisper. I really don't want to be up here. I don't like the way Mrs. Bulk is glaring at me.

"Louder please?"

Why did he have to call on me? I am getting those dragons in my belly again. I look at the glaring giant and know I have to do what I can to help my uncle. "FEE FI FO FUM!" I drive each syllable into Mrs. Bulk's brain. "I don't know the rest. Sorry, Uncle."

Mrs. Bulk grips the railing. "You knew already, so why waste the court's time and ask me?" She appeals to the judge. "He's just wasting time. It's just a dopey rhyme."

"Thank you, Brodie." My uncle smiles as I return to my seat, my legs still shaky. "Mrs. Bulk, what does this poem mean?"

"Nothing. It's just meaningless syllables. Can't you hear them? Are you deaf?"

My uncle looks at me, but I have nothing else to add. I wish I'd heard the rest of the rhyme, but she mumbled it as she went into the kitchen.

"Mr. Doofinch," Judge Fair says with a frown. "Are you telling me you have wasted all this time, just for a meaningless rhyme? Oh my, I did it again." He giggles, but then grows stern again. "I think you'd better bring this to an END right now, my friend. Is that another rhyme?"

A light seems to go off in my uncle's face. He glances at me and asks, "By the way, Mrs. Bulk, what was the END of that rhyme?"

"Your Honor," Goode says, "I think we've had quite enough of this waste of our time with a silly rhyme!" He giggles at his rhyme.

Uncle Jasper addresses the judge, "I would agree with my learned colleague, Your Honor, but every rhyme has another rhyme. That is why it is called a rhyme."

"I demand that we understand," Goode said, now locked into rhyming too.

"Mr. Doofinch--" The judge is shaking his head.

"Just please make her answer the question? Please, Judge Fair?"

"Oh, Your Honor, can't we move on?" Goode points to his watch. "Soon we'll have to be gone."

"Sit down, Mr. Goode," the Judge orders. "I think I want to hear this. I find I like these rhyming poems." He turns to the giant. "You will answer the question please or you will not be…released." He sighs. "Not a very good one."

"I forgot his question," Mrs. Bulk says, shrugging her massive shoulders. "I'm still in shock from all this pain this brat caused me. Shouldn't we be talking about that and not some stupid rhyme?"

"Answer his question," Judge Fair repeats.

"I don't remember his question!"

My uncle isn't giving up. "What was the end of the rhyme? That is my question."

I just can't remember the last part of the rhyme. It sounded like nonsense to me at the time. Oh no, I'm rhyming now too! It really is catching!

"I told you I don't remember! It was silly… just a child's game."

"What was the last part?" My uncle won't stop. "Come on! Fee fi fo fum…."

The harp jumps up. "I remember it now!"

All eyes turn to the harp as he recites loudly:

"Fee fi fo fum!
I smell the blood of an Englishman!"

"SHUT UP YOU STUPID HARP!" The giant is out of her seat, two guards hanging onto her legs trying to slow her down, as she reaches for the harp who is reciting the rest of the rhyme. He is so pleased he remembers it that he doesn't see the danger he is in and continues:

*"Be he alive or be he dead,
I'll grind his bones to make my bread."*

The harp beams with triumph. "I told you I knew it!"

"Now look what you've done, you big mouth!" The giant struggles against the guards to reach the harp who now looks terrified. I hear loud plunking noises as his strings snap from the stress.

The Judge shouts, "MRS. BULK, BE SEATED NOW!" He hammers his table with his huge gavel. "Guards, return Mrs. Bulk to her chair now!"

"But your honor," the guards sputter as they struggle to hold Mrs. Bulk back.

"Mrs. Bulk, be seated now or I'll throw you in jail myself!" The judge towers over her.

Mrs. Bulk's hands are inches from the harp, but the guards are pulling her back.

I watch as the giant, escorted by the weary guards, lumbers back to the witness stand, rasping at the harp, "You big mouth! I'll fix you good."

The spectators that had run from their seats in panic watch her cautiously as they return.

Two guards shake their heads sadly. "He's gone, sir," one says, and they carry the broken-down harp from the room.

I feel sorry for the poor harp but hopeful that the tide has turned. The giant is about to fall, and my uncle, the great Jasper Doofinch, Defender of Monstrovia, is little 'David' about to topple the seemingly overpowering 'Goliath', the smarmy Hugh B. Goode! Who'd have thunk it?

"I ask again," my uncle, now smiling broadly at me, addresses the panting witness.

"It was just a stupid nursery rhyme," she screams. "Everyone knows that harp is 'unstrung', totally crazy."

Uncle Jasper doesn't wait. "A nursery rhyme about 'grinding bones for bread'?"

The jury's eyes are riveted on the giant. Uncle Jasper has raised a doubt, but it is still possible that the rhyme was only a stupid nursery rhyme that the giant muttered after he had been allegedly beaten silly by Jack with the cow. A poem is not the proof we need to end this case, but at least Amelia has finally stopped pinching me.

"I'm curious," Uncle Jasper continues, after looking at his notes. "It occurs to me this harp and goose are very unusual…very rare. Do you know where Mr. Bulk got the goose and harp in the first place?"

The giant grunts, "At garage sales."

"Garage sales?"

"Yeah, garage sales! My husband and I love a good garage sale. You got a problem with that?"

"Do you have the receipts," my uncle asks.

"From a garage sale?" Mrs. Bulk laughs rudely.

"No more questions," Uncle Jasper abruptly says and returns to his seat.

"What," Emily and Amelia hiss.

"Shhh," Uncle Jasper hisses back.

I lean toward my uncle. "You had her. Why did you let her go?"

His eyes meet mine. "To be honest, Brodie, I thought about continuing my questions, but decided if I kept her on the stand, I risked her saying something that could make things worse. Sometimes you're better off quitting while you're ahead. I can always call her back for more questions later."

I nod, but I'm not convinced. I'm itching to see if we could have nailed her. We? It's funny how this lawyer thing is catching… like chicken pox. You have to scratch the itch, but it's kind of a good thing.

The judge looks at Goode to see if he has any more questions for Mrs. Bulk. Goode waves his hand and the judge dismisses the giant.

Mrs. Bulk lifts herself off the chair and stomps heavily toward the gallery. As she passes my uncle, she waves her dress and his papers fly off the table. Her eyes are blazing at me. "I'll get you, you little rat! And your uncle too!"

"We'll adjourn until tomorrow morning," the judge announces.

As I am packing, Emily approaches. "Brodie, can we talk?" She looks nervous.

"No."

She bites her lip. "Maybe later."

I watch her leave out of the corner of my eye. Man, she ticks me off! I still can't believe she lied to me like that.

At home, I am so exhausted I barely am in the door when I say goodnight to my uncle.

"Goodnight, Brodie. Today was a good day."

"It was," I reply, and climb the staircase to my bedroom. I pull open the small, red, door that says, "STAY OUT!", and throw myself on the bed. I try not to look at the posters. They remind me of that smarmy Mr. Goode. I need sleep, but as exhausted as I am, I can't doze off. Every time I close my eyes Hortensia Bulk's awful, vicious, face reappears.

I lock my window, double-lock my door, brace a chair against the doorknob, and leave on the table lamp. Once I am certain I have taken every possible precaution, I flick on the television.

The only channel I can get is showing <u>Abbott and Costello meet Jack and the Beanstalk!</u>

I have nightmares all night.

In those nightmares, I keep hearing the giants' roaring, "Fee, fi, fo, fum."

CHAPTER 58

I am 'egg-shausted', but 'egg-cited', when Uncle Jasper drags me to court next morning. Yesterday convinced me we can win. I feel great because I gave my uncle a clue that might win it.

The second witness is the peddler, Sylvester McClean. It was McClean who traded the magic beans for Jack's cow.

"What do you do for a living?" Goode, looking fresh as a clean shirt, asks McClean.

"I'm a traveling salesman." McClean smiles, all teeth. He is wearing a blinding, checkered jacket and red bowtie on his six foot, dare-I-think, possibly human, frame.

"Have you ever seen the defendant, Jack Beanstealer...er...Stalk?" The D.A. corrects himself with a sheepish glance in Jack's direction.

"That kid tried to sell me a beat-up cow with an odor problem," the peddler says.

"You didn't buy it from him?"

"No way! But he kept pushing me to buy this run-down thing. I finally got so fed up I offered to trade with him."

"How did he react?"

"He wanted cash. I wasn't paying cash for an old cow, especially one with an odor problem, but he kept on and on. I finally gave in and gave him a few magic beans for the bony thing. It was the only way I could shut that brat up. I lost my shirt on that cow." He addresses the jury. "Who wants a cow that's skinny, gives no milk, and has an odor problem?"

"Thank you! You've been moo-velous! Your turn, Mr. Doofinch."

"Do you have a lot of magic beans?" My uncle asks after studying his notes about the peddler.

"No. These were the only ones I had. The kid got a really good deal and I got a lemon of a cow, stinky thing that it was. These magic beans are really rare. I did hear of someone about twelve years ago who may have had some." He shrugs his shoulders. "Just rumors."

"Where did you get your beans from?"

"I don't recall. I'll have to check my records."

Another dead end. I wonder where my uncle is headed.

"Did you ever see these beans work yourself?"

"If I'd seen them work, how could I sell them? Who's going to buy USED MAGIC BEANS?"

The jury and gallery laugh. I do too, but not for long.

"So there was no real reason for you or Jack to believe they really were magic?"

McClean frowns. "I guess not. But I gave my word."

"But how could you give your word if you never saw these beans work? For all you knew, they could have been worthless. That would have been cheating the poor boy--"

"Hey, that's not fair! I'm a salesman! It's not my fault if Jack was greedy! He thought the magic beans would make him rich. That's why he kept bugging me for them."

Uncle Jasper didn't expect that answer and looks a little nervous. "What did you tell him these so-called 'magic' beans would do to make him rich?"

"I never told him nothing!"

"Nothing? He traded a perfectly good cow…all right, a slightly skinny cow with an odor problem, for beans that don't do NOTHING?" Uncle Jasper is moving in for the kill. "Why would anyone do that?"

"I'm not a crook, if that's what you think," McClean abruptly shouts, rising out of his chair.

"No shouting in my court!" Judge Fair bangs his gavel.

"You told him the beans did **nothing** and he still traded a good cow for a handful of so-called magic beans?" My uncle is really closing in. I can't wait. I never liked bow ties. Mr. Feeney wears one all the time.

"A cow with an odor problem! He even admits that!" McClean looks at Jack. "Wait! I remember! I told him a legend I'd heard about the beans. Yes, that's it."

My uncle is inches from McClean's nose, poised like a lion about to spring on his defenseless prey. "What legend?"

"I told him the beans would grow into a huge beanstalk that could help some lucky soul climb up to the sky and steal the pot of gold at the end of the rainbow." McClean smiles victoriously. "That's why he wanted them beans. He was greedy for gold!"

My uncle looks like he's been shot. I see now why he worries about surprises. He just got a big one!

I try to imagine what the jury thinks of McClean's testimony. They just heard that Jack wanted the magic beans to steal from someone who had gold high in the sky. Now everyone knows there isn't a pot of gold at the end of the rainbow, but who did live high in the sky? The giants!

The peddler made it appear as if Jack planned to get gold from the Bulks. He made it look as if Jack knew exactly what he was doing when he bugged McClean for those magic beans. I turn to the jury and I can see they are mulling over this new evidence.

Uncle Jasper's face shows he is aware that he made a huge mistake. But my uncle is not someone to give up, even if he should. He begins again, "Mr. McClean, surely Jack didn't believe your legend? I mean a pot of gold at the end of the rainbow?"

"Nah. Everybody knows there ain't no gold at the end of the rainbow." He laughs.

The spectators laugh too.

But then McClean continues, "But that brat believed me about the beanstalk. That's why he wouldn't let me go to sleep until I gave him my magic beans. That kid knew exactly what he wanted. He wanted that beanstalk so he could go up to the giant's castle and get their GOLD! GOLD! GOLD!"

"No more questions," Uncle Jasper says in a hushed voice and falls into his chair. Even I know McClean's story gives the impression that Jack planned the burglary, and since Bulk died during that crime, Jack is guilty of murder. Case closed! Put on the shackles! Go to jail and do not pass "Go"!

The worst part is my uncle was the one to squeeze the information from the peddler. He accidentally sank his own case!

"It's okay," I whisper to Uncle Jasper, but the butterflies in my stomach, more like dragons, are eating me alive. "Please stop pinching me," I beg Amelia yet again.

Emily looks like she has gone into shock. Jack just stares blankly straight ahead.

Goode stretches his arms in triumph, that smarmy 'gotcha' look on his face. Then he rises to speak. "I have just two more questions, your honor. "As a salesman, you have to be a pretty good judge of character. Don't you?"

McClean smiles. "Absolutely. I gotta be an expert at telling about people."

Uncle Jasper's fingers grip the side of the table.

"As an expert on character, do you think—and I know it is just an opinion—but do you believe Jack Bordenschlocker, aka Beanstalk, is capable of murder?"

"Objection, your honor! He's calling for an opinion--"

Judge Fair gives Uncle Jasper a glare. "He said it was an opinion. I will allow it."

McClean straightens up in the witness chair, as if he is the greatest star witness ever, and says, "As an expert on character, I believe Jack was very capable, and did kill Mr. Bulk."

Uncle Jasper sags in his chair.

"Get up and tear his story apart," I urge him, pushing him forward.

"No, Brodie. Sometimes it is better to let a witness go before he causes more damage." He said it so softly, sounding as if he was accepting defeat.

It can't be. My uncle never gives up.

The peddler swaggers past us, stopping when he comes to the goose. "You and I should go into business, my fine feathered friend. We could make a fortune selling them gold eggs of yours."

"Cluck. Cluck. Cluck," the goose says, sticking her beak indignantly into the air.

"Court adjourned until tomorrow morning," Judge Fair proclaims, and sneers in my uncle's direction. "Unless you're ready to quit and plead guilty? I would be inclined to be lenient if we end this circus now?"

My uncle glares at Judge Fair, badly shaken.

"Very well, it's your funeral," Judge Fair says.

I didn't sleep the night before because of the nightmares I had of the giant, her teeth gnashing at me, her claws reaching for me, seeking revenge. Now I can't sleep because I have the awful feeling we've lost the case. My arm hurts where Amelia's nails dug in. Will I ever be able to talk to Emily again? How could she lie like that... to me? All these thoughts are circling around in my 'eggs-hausted' brain, so who can sleep? And through it all, like a haunting, irritating echo, repeating in the background, I hear a ghastly, ghostly, goose taunt, "Lots of cluck! Lots of bad cluck! Cluck, cluck, cluck."

CHAPTER 59

Jack looks comatose the next morning, with black raccoon markings around his eyes and bloodshot pupils.

"Not sleeping well?" I ask, after an awful night.

"How can you and your uncle sleep after what he did to me yesterday?" Jack fires at me.

"Hey," I reply with fake cheer. "We've got plenty of chances left. The most important thing is you're innocent. Don't forget." I hope if I keep repeating it, eventually he'll believe me. And I will too.

Amelia and Emily arrive, both wearing pale blue suits. Amelia whispers, "Today will go better." Emily gives me a fast look and goes to her seat.

It better, I think, moving my arm away from Amelia. Can a lawyer sue a client for abusing his nephew, I wonder, rubbing my sore arm.

Emily looks at me again.

I turn away.

"Good morning, Jasper," Goode is beaming. "You ready today to be whipped again?"

"Sure. Let's see what other shockers you have to support your weak case," Uncle Jasper replies.

Goode laughs, "You sound like every other defense attorney I've whipped. Well, good luck Doofinch. You're going to need it." Pixie cameras click blindingly as Goode offers his hand. He presses a folded paper into my uncle's palm. It reads, "You should've taken the deal."

My uncle shows it to me. "I guess I should have," he mutters, crushing it and tossing it in the small trash-can below our table.

"We're not beaten yet," I say firmly, but I don't really believe it.

"I call the chicken," Goode announces.

"I keep telling you I'm not a goose! I'm a..." The goose smacks her head. "Now I'm doing it!" She shakes her wings furiously. "I keep telling you, I'm a goose! I'm a goose!" She repeats this amid a stream of clucking, as she is led to the witness box by two watchful guards.

The over-stuffed goose pulls herself up on the chair, but slips off, falling on her back, her wings flailing wildly.

Everyone rocks with laughter, even Judge Fair.

The goose clucks angrily, unable to turn herself over and get back on her large orange feet.

"Officers, will you help that goo...ha, ha, ha... goo... goose...before I die here," the judge manages to say between his laughing. "Oh, this hurts! Ha! Ha! Oh!"

A guard reaches his hand toward the goose's bottom.

"Cluck! Cluck!" The goose whirls on the guard. "What are you doing with your hand on my bottom?" The goose tries repeatedly to poke the guard with her beak. "It's RUDE! RUDE!"

"I was only trying to help," the beak-dodging guard shouts.

"I don't want hands clawing my rump! Cluck! Cluck! Cluck!"

"I've an idea," the second guard shouts, dropping to the floor. "Step on my back!"

The goose clucks loudly and places her sprawling foot on his back. She lifts her other leg to reach the chair. The guard's back sags under her weight and he falls flat, the goose falling with him.

"Oh," the judge roars with laughter, "Please no more? I'm dying! No more!"

The goose is now in a furious rage, shaking her wings at everyone in the room. The angrier she gets, the more she clucks, the more everyone laughs, including me. It is quite a sight.

The judge, choking on his laughter, signals the court officers to try again.

They both get down on hands and knees, forming a step for the goose to climb.

She finally makes it onto the seat, glaring at the spectators and clucking under her breath.

"Worth a fortune on one of those home video shows," a pixie camerawoman says, clutching her camera and rushing out of the room.

My stomach hurts. The only ones not laughing are Jack, Amelia, Emily, and my uncle, who appears to be studying the goose intently.

I don't see much to study. This goose is beyond a doubt the craziest and clumsiest creature I have ever seen.

"I feel like such a fool," the goose mumbles pitifully from the witness chair, hiding her face under a wing.

"Let's get on with this," Judge Fair bellows, finally under control. "Mr. Goode, ask your questions!"

Goode begins. "Are you the goose that lays gold eggs?"

The audience gets quiet at the word 'gold'.

"Yes, I am. Cluck! Cluck!"

"And you really lay eggs made of solid gold?"

"Do you think I lay fake gold eggs? Cluck! Cluck!"

I realize Goode is trying to show that Jack knew the eggs were gold and that was why he went back to steal the goose. That would certainly be a good motive.

"Is this one of your eggs?" Goode produces an egg that glows like the sun.

"That's my baby," the goose cries out. "Cluck! Cluck!"

Goode tosses the egg in the air and every eye in the courtroom bounces up with it. "Everyone can see your eggs are gold. Can't we?"

The jurors' heads nod like bobble-head dolls, all following the bouncing egg.

"So Jack saw your eggs and knew they were gold?"

"Are you kidding? Of course he did! That's why he goose-napped me! Would you please stop throwing my babies around? Cluck! Cluck!"

"Objection," my uncle shouts. "Only Jack can tell us what Jack knew or didn't know, unless this goose can also read minds?"

"Sustained," the judge mutters, mesmerized, like everyone else, by the flying egg.

"How did the Bulks treat you?" Goode continues.

The goose hesitates, looking toward the gallery. "Oh, good. Cluck. Cluck."

Goode nods. "And when did you first see the defendant, Jack Beansteal...stalk?"

The goose scratches her head. "It was after dinner one night, several weeks before he goose-napped me. Cluck. Cluck. Cluck."

My uncle isn't objecting. He had written the words, "dumb cluck" on his pad, followed by a huge question mark.

"What happened when you were 'allegedly' goose-napped by Jack," Goode proceeds.

The goose shivers. "I was asleep when I was shocked to feel cold hands on my...my...bottom! How humiliating!" She goes off into a fit of clucking.

"What happened next when Jack allegedly stole you?"

"He carried me down the beanstalk and gave me to his mother. She insulted me!"

"How did Mrs. Beanstalk insult you?"

"Objection! Mrs. Beanstalk is not on trial here," my uncle says from his seat.

"Overruled," Judge Fair says.

Goode smiles. "How did she insult you?"

"She said I was a fake, a phony…that I wasn't really the goose that lays golden eggs! Cluck. Cluck. Can you imagine? Cluck! Cluck! First, hands all over my backside, and now she calls me a FAKE! Cluck! Cluck! Cluck! Cluck!"

"Why did she do that?"

Even I know my uncle should object, but he seems distracted, staring at his pad and drawing circles around his picture of the goose.

"She was greedy for my gold," the goose hisses. "Nobody understands that I can't lay gold eggs when I'm nervous. Could any of you? Cluck! Cluck! Cluck!"

I am getting a bad headache from all that clucking.

"Where were you when the giant was mur…'allegedly' murdered?"

The goose hesitates again. "Cluck! Cluck! I was at the bottom of the beanstalk."

"Did you hear Jack say anything about the giant after he died?"

"Objection! We are taking the goose's word for what Jack said. How do we know this goose is telling the truth?"

"I'm not a liar! Cluck! Cluck! Cluck!"

It is Jack's word against the word of this insane goose. I don't know who to believe, so how can the jury know? Uncle Jasper was right, it really is impossible to know who is telling the truth.

"Over-ruled," Judge Fair says. "Answer the question! I'm getting 'egg-stremely' hungry."

"Is that an egg joke?" The goose glares at the judge.

Judge Fair out-glares the goose.

No contest. The goose backs down, hiding her face again.

Goode repeats his question. "What did you hear Jack say?"

"Cluck! He was bragging, 'I killed the giant and stole all his treasure!' He was happy and proud! Happy and proud I tell you! Cluck! Cluck! Cluck!"

I notice something. The goose was looking straight at Hortensia Bulk the whole time she spoke.

"Thank you," Goode says, but the goose continues, "That boy kept shouting, "Revenge! Revenge at last!"

"Thank you! Thank you!" Goode says again. "That will be all! You were egg-cellent!"

"Cluck. Cluck. Cluck," the goose says in a low voice, her eyes on Mrs. Bulk.

"That will be all for today," Judge Fair says. "Anyone for a chicken dinner?"

"Cluck, cluck, cluck, cluck, cluck!"

Something is bothering me, and it isn't just Amelia's nails poking my arm again. I am focused on the goose as she is returned to her crate, still clucking under her breath...a crazy goose in a crazy case...cluck, cluck. What am I missing? What is everyone missing?

CHAPTER 60

"We're in big trouble," Uncle Jasper says, waking me up from a deep sleep.

"What's wrong now?"

"The goose. Somehow she got away. They just called me from the hotel where she was being guarded."

I yawn as this news sinks in. "I'll bet its Emily and her sneaky mother. I wouldn't put anything past those two."

"I don't think so. They say she snuck out of the bathroom window."

"A goose going to the bathroom?" Why should I find that strange in this crazy place?

"She was terrified," Uncle Jasper says. "I am not surprised she ran off."

"I just hope the giants don't find her," I reply sleepily.

"That would scramble our case but good," he says, getting up from my bed. "Anyway, I'm off to help find her and didn't want you to worry when you got up and I'm not home."

"I'm going with you." I start to get out of bed, but fall backwards.

"No, dear nephew, you need your sleep."

"No, I need to be with you." I put my feet on the floor.

"Are you sure," Uncle Jasper asks. "I can use your help, but I understand if you prefer to stay here. It isn't safe at night--"

I have a flashback picture of my battle with those serpents and bat-things in my head, but I slide my feet into my sneakers anyway. "I'm going with you. Nothing will stop me."

"Thank you, Brodie. I never expected this from you."

I almost change my mind when I see we are rushing to the garage. Horace in daylight is scary enough, but at night?

"Can I please try?" I ask when we reach the massive door.

"Make your voice deeper. You need to sound like a man."

"Open sesame," I command in as deep a voice as I can manage.

The door doesn't budge.

"Don't worry, Brodie, you will do it someday. I have confidence in you. Don't be in a rush to grow up. It isn't always that great. He takes a deep breath and bellows, "Open Sesame!"

Sure enough, the door moves and Uncle Jasper is inside his garage in less time than a 'dragon-swallow'.

I am surprised I don't hear Horace's frightening roar, but suddenly there he is, the giant meat-eater. He looks exhausted, his eyes drooping and his tail down.

"I'm afraid I woke the old boy," Uncle Jasper says, already seated behind his bicycle handles.

Just then Horace lets out a huge yawn and bathes me in a stench like a garlic explosion.

I stink! I am tired and I stink!

"We've got to find that darn goose," Uncle Jasper says, once I am seated in the sidecar. "But where do we begin looking?"

"Where is the last place anyone would look for a crazy goose," I ask, trying to use Bordenschlocker logic.

"I have absolutely no idea. I am incapable of thinking like a goose."

"Well, Jack hid in the giant's castle...Amelia hid in that horrible shack...."

Uncle Jasper scratches his head and puts on his helmet. "I'm still clueless."

"I don't think the goose would go back to the Bulks. She looked terrified of Mrs. Bulk. So where would a goose on the lam hide?"

"Maybe back at Beanstalk mansion," Uncle Jasper suggests.

"How would she get there? She can't fly. She can hardly walk. She has no money...she can't lay a golden egg. How far can an overstuffed golden goose go?"

"Not very far," Uncle Jasper says. "Hmmm? Not very far..."

Horace has reached the highway and I brace myself for yet another bouncing ride on that multi-leveled nightmare of a racetrack, but suddenly Uncle Jasper veers to a side street.

"Where are you going?" I am surprised at his sudden change of direction.

"Brodie, my brilliant assistant, you are a genius. Thanks to you, I think I know where our feathered fugitive fled to, the last possible place anyone would think of looking."

"This is the hotel where she was being protected," I say, as we pull up to the Giant Trampler Towers, across the street from the Giant Courthouse. "There are Giant Cops everywhere."

"They don't have my brilliant nephew with them." Uncle Jasper leaps off Horace.

I shudder as a bear dressed in a blue uniform takes Horace's reins. He looks like the guards I'd first seen when we entered the buoy in Key West. That seems like ages ago.

"I'll be a few moments," Uncle Jasper says to the bear, handing him a dollar bill.

The bear looks unhappy, so Uncle Jasper slips him another dollar.

"I didn't know you use American money here," I say, as we enter the lobby.

"We're part of the United States, so why wouldn't we use your currency?" he replies, as if this is the most normal thing on Earth in a place that seems to do whatever it wants, except when it wants to do what the rest of the United States does. Totally confusing.

Quite a few heads turn when they see us enter the massive lobby. On some bodies, more than one head!

"This place is full of giants," I mutter, trying not to stare at the nightmarish creatures all around the room. "Where do you think our goose is?"

Uncle Jasper signals me to follow him as he crosses the carpet in the lobby and heads to an elevator. "I can't reach the button. Someday I'm going to sue for equal rights for short people."

"Why don't you say, Open Sesame," I tease. "Just sound like a grownup."

He is about to answer when a huge shadow is reflected on the wall.

A chill races down my spine. I whirl around and almost bang into a giant's knee. "Uncle Jasper," I gasp, backing away.

"May I help you?" the giant asks in a surprisingly polite tone.

I am hiding behind my uncle. I do not like giants, not after Mrs. Bulk, Mr. Hugh B. Goode and Judge I.M. Fair.

"Would you mind pushing the elevator button for us," Uncle Jasper asks, looking as if he isn't afraid, not even for an instant. (I guess you get used to things after a while?)

"My great pleasure, Mr. Doofinch," the giant replies.

He recognizes my uncle?

"Do I know you, sir," Uncle Jasper asks, stepping back from the elevator.

"You were kind enough to help my brother several years ago. He spoke very highly of you." The giant pushes the button and the elevator doors open.

"Thank you, sir. Please call on me if you should ever need my help." Uncle Jasper hands the giant a business card.

Please don't, I think, still shaky from the unexpected meeting.

"Uncle Jasper," I ask, as the elevator moves down to the basement. "Do you help giants too?"

He looks at me with a warm smile. "Brodie, I try and help anyone who needs me."

We reach the bottom floor and the doors open. I smell baked beans. "Not again?"

"Shhh, Brodie."

I am speechless anyway. We are in the largest kitchen I have ever seen in my life. There are huge pots simmering on stoves, and more pots on wire shelves, but it is the knives hanging from the ceiling that catch my eye. They are the biggest and nastiest knives I've ever seen! We are definitely in giant country, and those knives are a giant reminder that I am hardly a snack to these carnivores. "Uncle, can we go? I don't think the goose would be silly enough to come here. Even she, as mixed-up as she is, couldn't be crazy enough to hide in a giant's kitchen where she might end up in one of those pots."

"Look Brodie." He points to the floor which has a thin coating of flour on it. (Giants aren't very neat.) See them? Footprints... goose footprints I bet... leading right to the back of the kitchen. You were right, my boy. The last place a goose would hide: a Giant's kitchen."

Bordenschlocker logic strikes again.

"I think we've found our runaway," Uncle Jasper whispers, as he moves toward the rear of the massive room, checking cabinets along the way.

I kind of feel bad for the goose, but we need her for the trial.

Suddenly, I hear a loud squeal, and there, staring at us with panic in her eyes, is the one and only Annabelle Goose.

CHAPTER 61

"Miss Goose, please remain calm and come with us," Uncle Jasper says in a very soft voice. "We won't hurt you."

The goose stares at us with narrow eyes. "Are you alone?"

Uncle Jasper nods. "We're here to help you."

"Cluck. Cluck. If you want to help, please, just let me go? Cluck, cluck."

"You know we can't do that."

Before he can say another word, the goose lets out a stream of panicky clucks, flaps her wings, and charges full-speed, straight at my uncle.

"Brodie, block the door," he shouts as he tries to grab the goose.

I run for the door, but the flour makes the floor slippery. I am sliding everywhere and suddenly the goose is waddling behind me, her beak shooting out to peck me. "Cut it out," I shout as she keeps going for me. "Uncle Jasper!" I leap to one side and the goose slides past me. She is sliding on her bottom toward a door.

I see my Uncle racing after her, trying to grab her. "I can't stop," he screams as he slides past her.

"I'll grab her this time," I shout, and run for the goose, who is waddling and sliding and slipping all over.

Suddenly she slides under a counter.

"There she is," I scream, about to grab her.

"Stop where you are!" A loud voice orders.

The goose scrambles to her feet and heads for the door.

"Stop her," Uncle Jasper shouts, picking himself up. "She's a fugitive!"

I burst into laughter. He is covered in white flour. He looks like a snowman, or that marshmallow guy.

"I said 'stop or I'll shoot'," the voice orders.

Too late. The goose is gone out the door.

"You let her go," I say, struggling to get up.

"Calm down, Brodie. That's not the exit. And these are Giant police."

I brush flour out of my eyes and find myself facing a giant in a dark blue uniform.

"Who are you guys?" the cop with the rifle asks. "You're causing a disturbance and the hotel called us."

"You look like snowmen," the second cop says. "I didn't know we had snowmen in Monstrovia."

"Gentlemen," Uncle Jasper replies, brushing flour off his clothes. "I am Jasper Doofinch--"

"The lawyer?" The first cop asks. "Hey, Bucky, this here is that famous lawyer, Jasper Doofinch."

Holy cow! Does everyone know my uncle? I lower my hands. Everything is going to be okay now.

"You mean the guy what gets all them criminals we catch free," the second cop asks, not looking as friendly as I would like.

"Yeah, that guy," the second cop answers, rapping a thick club in his palm.

"My dear sirs, I am, like yourselves, only doing my job," Uncle Jasper says, still brushing flour off his clothing.

"Looks to me like you're breaking and entering here," the first cop says, pulling handcuffs off his belt.

"And destroying property," the second one adds, rapping the club harder. "I'd say you're about to get a taste of your own medicine, lawyer. You're going to jail."

"But gentlemen--" Uncle Jasper looks flustered.

"And who is the kid," the first cop asks, looking down at me, still covered in white flour. "I suppose you're this rotten lawyer's son?"

"Oh no, sir," I get out real fast. "I'm his nephew from New York."

"So kid, what're you doin' out here in the middle of the night?" The second cop asks, as the first opens his cuffs, trying to adjust them for thin human wrists.

"Allow me to explain--" Uncle Jasper says.

"Be quiet you! I want to hear from the boy. You lawyers can't be trusted to tell the truth."

I can tell my uncle is sputtering mad, but eyeing the huge cop and the handcuffs he wisely decides to keep quiet.

"Go ahead, kid, we're waiting."

I think fast. "Do you know about the Beanstalk trial?"

"Sure. Who doesn't? That rich kid killed that kindly Mr. Bulk."

"Yeah, he should fry," the first cop snorts. "Killing a giant is a terrible crime."

"Well, my Uncle and I are here because the star witness, the goose that lays golden eggs, escaped, and is hiding in that closet, right over there."

"You're kidding? The goose that lays gold eggs is here?" The cop with the rifle edges toward the closet. "I always wanted to see that rich goose thing for myself."

"She's right in there. And if we don't catch her, the judge will not be able to finish the trial and the killer of Mr. Bulk will go free." I don't tell him that we are working for Jack. I'm not lying exactly. I'm just sort of leaving things out.

"Is that true, Doofinch?," the second cop asks.

"My nephew is telling the truth. We need that goose to finish this trial."

"That's different. We want that kid to get his just desserts." They both move toward the tall steel door. "Goose, this here is the Giant Police. Come out now with your wings up and you won't get hurt."

I wait with my uncle, but the door stays closed.

"Has the goose got a name," the first cop asks, his ear against the door. "I hear clucking? You sure it's a goose?"

"Annabelle," I reply. "And crazy as it sounds, she's definitely a goose."

"Annabelle Goose, if you don't open up, I'll huff and I'll puff and blow this door down."

I take another look at the second cop and gasp. The Giant Cop has the face of a huge wolf! "Uncle, it's a wolf! The goose isn't safe."

Uncle Jasper shakes his head. "Brodie, when will you learn that you can't judge everyone by one bad apple? Just because one wolf gave the three little pigs a hard time doesn't mean all wolves are evil."

"What about the wolf that went after that Russian boy, Peter? Or the wolf that almost ate up Red Riding Hood? Nope, I don't trust wolves or half the creatures here. I am not going to leave that poor goose until I am sure she is safe."

"Last chance Goose," the wolf-cop threatens and takes a deep, deep breath.

"I'm coming out. Cluck, cluck, cluck," the goose cries, and with head down and wings up, tears flowing from her eyes, Annabelle Goose, frantic feathered fugitive, surrenders herself to the Giant Police.

Uncle Jasper walks over to her and I can see he is trying to tell her she will be okay now. "You have nothing to fear. These guards will take you back to your hotel room and protect you." He looks at the cops and says, "Thank you gentlemen."

"You just better make sure that Mr. Bulk's killer gets what he deserves."

"Yeah, we'll protect Goosey here," the first cop says, brandishing his odd-looking rifle.

"Cluck, cluck, cluck," the goose moans. "Nobody can protect me. Nobody."

CHAPTER 62

After a terrible day in court and a wild goose chase hunting down our frantic feathered fugitive at night, I am pooped, and expect Uncle Jasper to have run out of steam too, but there he is, at his desk, eyes bent low, studying all those endless piles of paper. "Good morning, dear nephew. I hope you are well rested?"

I can barely speak I am so tired, but he appears to be full of energy, and full of hope? It amazes me how my uncle is like a boxer, taking punch after punch, being knocked down, but refusing to quit. I find myself wishing I could be like that. I also wish I could help him solve this perplexing puzzle.

By the time Horace has bounced us back to the courthouse, I make up my mind I am going to do everything I can to stay focused and help my uncle win this case.

The first witness is Anabelle Goose again. This time the guards walk her all the way to the witness chair where specially constructed steps are waiting for her. She looks around, as if she is searching desperately to escape again. Seeing there is no way out, she shakes her feathers, sighs, and climbs up the steps. She looks like someone headed to the gallows.

As we wait, I keep looking at the goose, and sure enough she seems unable to take her eyes off Mrs. Bulk. Why?

Uncle Jasper approaches the goose and says gently, "Miss Goose, yesterday, you were saying Jack kidnapped you from the Bulks' house? Is that right?"

The goose nods slowly. "He stole me. Cluck. Cluck."

"So you liked staying with the Bulks? If you could have, you would have wanted to stay with them? Is that right?"

What is he asking? Won't this help the other side?

The goose ruffles her feathers nervously. "I don't understand? Cluck. Cluck."

"Let me put it simply. You liked living with the Bulks?"

I catch the goose sneaking another look at Hortensia Bulk before answering. "Yes. They were okay. Cluck! Cluck!"

"Just 'okay'? My uncle uses Anabelle's words.

I am doing it too. I understand now that a lawyer must pay attention to every word and every signal a witness gives with their body or facial expressions. I think I see something now... I'm just not sure what it is.

"Yeah. They were okay." The goose looks at Mrs. Bulk again.

I look too. The giant's eyes are drilling holes in the goose's face.

The goose bursts into rapid chatter, "I mean they were good. Good people. Very nice. Yes, very, very, nice. Cluck! Cluck! Cluck!"

"But you said they were only 'okay' before?" My uncle sees me signaling him. He approaches the table and reads what I've written on my pad:
Watch A's eyes!

He walks away. "Just 'okay'? You said, they were just 'okay'?"

The goose looks again at the giant.

This time my uncle follows her eyes. "Why only 'okay'? Why not 'great'? Or 'excellent'? Or even just 'good'?"

"Objection," Goode says, sounding bored. "Answered already."

"Overruled," the Judge says. "Answer the question."

I catch Mrs. Bulk drawing a long-nailed finger across her throat.

"Cluck. Cluck. They were really good and kind and wonderful…wonderful…wonderful! Love the Bulks! Cluck, cluck, cluck."

"You said a moment ago they were only 'okay'?" My uncle is again using the goose's own words to poke a hole in her story. I get it now. I know what he is up to.

Annabelle sneaks another look at the giant. "Well, I said they were good…" She looks again.

Uncle Jasper waits. He waits. He waits.

I know this strategy. Mom uses it on me all the time…waiting quietly until I say something that will 'hang' myself. I have my fingers crossed and am silently coaxing my uncle, "Stay quiet. She'll say something…wait for it…wait for it…"

The goose is sweating, fidgeting anxiously, eyes on the giant, and then down at her feet, and then she finally says, very quietly, "Well, cluck, they were a little greedy."

"WHAT?" Mrs. Bulk's voice rips through the chamber. "WHAT DID YOU SAY?"

"Oh, cluck, cluck. Like everybody else! They were like everybody else! GREEDY! SELFISH!" Her eyes meet Hortensia's again and she is trembling violently, clucks coming out in a gushing stream. "I'm sorry. I'm sorry. I'm just so nervous."

"Calm down," Uncle Jasper says. "Nobody can hurt you here." He glares at Mrs. Bulk who now looks as innocent as an angel.

The goose heaves a big sigh. "Oh me! Oh my! Cluck, cluck, cluck!"

Uncle Jasper waits until she is calm before he begins again. "You said, the Bulks were like everyone else? How would you know that they were like everyone else? Does that mean you had other owners?"

"What do you mean? Cluck! Cluck! Cluck! Cluck!"

She sounds like a geiger counter, the more frightened she is, the faster the clucking. I am getting an awful headache. Maybe we should have let this mixed-up bird escape after all? But then we would never have learned her secret.

CHAPTER 63

I know Uncle Jasper feels sorry for the goose, but also know that can't stop him from grilling her with tough questions to help his client. I understood now, that even if he hates what he has to do, he will do everything possible, as long as it is legal, to help Jack. And that means he will wring the truth out of this crazy clucking creature no matter how it hurts her, or him!

"Did you have other owners before the Bulks?" My uncle steps in front of the goose, blocking her view of Mrs. Bulk.

He listened to me! I helped him! I'm paying even more attention now, excited that I am part of this battle. I'm a member of the team.

"Please look only at me," Uncle Jasper says, smiling warmly at the goose.

That seems to calm the poor goose a little. She scratches her head with a wing. "Nobody ever asked me that before. Did I have another owner? I remember that my mother used to say, when I was barely out of the egg, we lived with someone else. I don't remember. Cluck. Cluck. Cluck!"

"Objection. We don't have to know every nest this bird was in, do we," Goode says, again sounding bored.

Uncle Jasper replies calmly, "We do if one of those nests was **her real home** and she was **stolen** from it!"

Hortensia Bulk explodes, "That's a lie! My Eugene would crush you if he were here!"

"I'm sure he would," Uncle Jasper says, as she is pushed back into her chair by the guards, her lawyers and three giant soldiers called in for just such an emergency.

Judge Fair leans toward Mrs. Bulk. "Mrs. Bulk, I've told you before I will not accept any more outbursts. Sit down now and be quiet or I will have you removed from this courtroom."

Mrs. Bulk is sputtering, but settles back into her chair.

"Did your mother say how she came to live with the Bulks," Uncle Jasper asks, once he sees Mrs. Bulk is seated again, guards all around her.

"It was a long time ago. I don't know. Cluck. Cluck. I don't remember! Please stop asking me?"

"So she could have had an earlier owner? It is possible?"

"I don't know! Stop asking me! I don't remember…"

"It's possible then that she could have been stolen from that earlier owner?" Uncle Jasper presses on even though the goose is quaking with fear.

The Judge interrupts. "Mr. Doofinch, a court of law is no place for guessing games. Do you know what happened or not?"

"I think I do."

"You 'think' is not good enough. You're wasting time. Do you have other questions?"

My uncle looks at me, but I'm out of ideas!

He walks to our table and looks at his notepad. "When you were allegedly stolen by Jack, whose hands lifted you off the nest?"

The goose is thinking, the pain of thinking hard on her face. "Jack's. Cluck! Cluck!"

"Are you sure?"

The goose's face is scrunched tight. "No. I remember now. She was showing me off to him. It was her hands." The goose glances toward the giant, who is no longer blocked by my uncle, and shivers. "No! It was him! He carried me down! Cluck! Cluck! Cluck! I was wrong! Sorry. I was wrong!"

"Him and what truck," I shout out.

"I beg your pardon! Cluck! Cluck!"

My uncle looks angry, but I continue. "Well, look at you! Jack couldn't carry a big over-stuffed goose like you all the way down that huge beanstalk." *Holy Goosearolli! I sound like Uncle Jasper!*

"I...I...Aye, aye, aye! Cluck! Cluck! Cluck!" Her eyes race around the courtroom.

"Isn't it true you escaped by yourself?" I keep my fingers crossed.

"I don't know what you mean," the goose whimpers. "He's not allowed to ask me questions, is he?"

"Objection!" Goode is out of his seat. "He's not allowed to ask questions, is he?"

"Boy, sit down!" Judge Fair roars. "Doofinch, get him down now!"

"Ask her about "Fee Fi Fo Fum," Jack hisses, as Uncle Jasper gently pushes me back into my chair.

Uncle Jasper looks confused.

I look at Jack and wonder if he is finally helping us. "Uncle, ask her about that. I have a hunch," I whisper urgently.

Uncle Jasper sighs. "Miss Goose, I have another question." He slides closer, blocking her view of Mrs. Bulk again. "Fee Fi Fo Fum. Does that ring a bell?" He looks doubtfully at Jack.

"CLUCK! CLUCK! CLUCK!" The goose screams, backing into the far reaches of the witness box, clearly in terror. "Why didn't you let me run away? Why? Why? Cluck, cluck, cluck!"

Uncle Jasper looks surprised by her frantic reaction. "FEE FI FO FUM!" he repeats louder, his eyes never flinching from the goose's panicked face. He steps away.

"Oh stop! Please stop?" The goose turns anguished eyes toward the giant who is staring at her with daggers in her eyes.

My uncle steps back in front of the goose's line of vision, pushing himself as close to the goose as he can get. "You know what it means! Fee Fi Fo Fum! Don't be afraid."

"NO I DON'T," the goose is clucking crazily. "Cluck. Cluck. Cluck. Cluck. Cluck. Cluck."

"Objection! Objection!" Goode is shouting and flailing his arms.

"Yes you do!" I join in. "FEE FI FO FUM!"

"Brodie!" My uncle is fire-eyed. He looks so angry that I sit back down.

The goose jumps up and takes a terrified look at the giant's lethal eyes and cries, "All right! All right! I'll tell you the truth! I ran away! Cluck! Cluck! Cluck! I had to! You have no idea! All that pressure! Oh my! Oh my!" The goose is trembling hysterically, sobbing into her wings.

My uncle is still trying to block the goose's view of the giant. "What pressure, my fine feathered friend? You can tell us. I'm here to protect you."

The goose is still cackling wildly and shaking her feathered wings. "Cluck! Cluck! They were so greedy! Cluck! Cluck! I knew if I stopped laying those stupid golden eggs, my goose would be cooked! I had to escape! Cluck! Cluck! Cluck! I had to! Jack was my chance!"

The giant leaps out of her seat. "SHE'S LYING! We were always kind to her! You crazy, mixed up, bird! Tell them you're lying or you're goose liver!"

"SIT DOWN MRS. BULK!" Judge Fair outroars her. "If you get up again, I'll have you carried out! I mean removed…well you know what I mean. No more outbursts from anybody!" He scans the courtroom with angry eyes. "Continue, Mr. Doofinch."

My uncle casts me a grateful smile. "So Jack didn't steal you at all? You left of your own free will? Don't be afraid."

The goose looked up from under her wing. "Yes…Yes. Cluck. I had to escape…I didn't want to be…goose liver. Oh, cluck. Oh, cluck. When I saw Mr. Bulk leave, I knew I had to make my break…I had to try…cluck, cluck."

"Victory at last," Amelia whispers.

"I feel sorry for her, the poor abused thing," Emily mutters, staring at the quivering goose.

I do too. But Jack has to be our first concern.

The goose sags in the chair, a pitiful crying mess. "My life is terrible. Woe is me. Woe is me. Cluck. Cluck. I hate my life. I hate my life. Cluck, cluck, cluck, cluck."

"That's all," My uncle says kindly. "I feel truly sorry for you. Maybe things will be better now." He looks at the Judge. "I have no more questions."

"YOU'RE DISMISSED!" Judge Fair roars. "NOT ONE MORE CLUCK!"

The goose is shivering uncontrollably as she slowly drops down from the witness stand. She makes a wide path away from Mrs. Bulk who eyes her like she is Southern-fried.

My uncle is back in his seat. "Thank you, Brodie," he whispers. "You were a big help. I'm proud of you."

I feel kind of funny about that. I have never heard anyone say that to me. I want to thank him, but there is still much to do. We can't afford to be distracted. Even though the goose has admitted she escaped from the Bulks on her own, meaning there had been no goose-napping, we still hadn't gotten Jack off the hook completely for Mr. Bulk's murder.

Emily leaves without a word to my uncle or me after giving Jack a kiss on the cheek. I try not to look at her, but I remember her kissing me that way too.

"That is one poor, strange, creature," my uncle mumbles, as we walk out of the courtroom. "The goose, I mean, not the Beanstalk women." He chuckles.

"One very frightened creature. She's had a very sad life." I really feel sorry for her.

Uncle Jasper nods. "Some talents doom their owners to such a life."

I hadn't thought about that. The goose had gotten her ability to lay gold eggs from her mother. Do I have any inherited talents? I don't look anything like my uncle, but is it possible I inherited something from him too? I kind of like solving mysteries and thinking my way out of tight spots, like in this trial, but do I really have a talent for it like him? Only time will tell.

I stare at the exotic monsters and fairy tale folk of Monstrovia as we walk together toward the underground garage. They are strolling around like normal people do in other parts of the United States. They don't seem to realize how strange and unique they are. Or are they?

Even Emily, Amelia and Jack aren't really human. Am I the one truly out of place here? How did my uncle, a human like myself, cope with living among such monstrous beings? Can I do that someday too? Can I overcome my fear and disgust at their horrifying appearance? The truth is, do I really want to?

"I think you were right," I say, as we reach Horace. "You said this case was a 'stinker'."

"I just didn't know how much of a stinker it would be." He winks at me and suddenly lets out, "Cluck! Cluck!"

"Not you too," I moan, as he rockets Horace into traffic with me hanging on for dear life.

"Do you think we won today?" I ask, when we stop for a parade of knights crossing an intersection, Horace snorting indignantly at them.

My uncle smiles. "Brodie, with your help, we definitely scored some points, but you never know what the other guy has up his sleeves, and Goode has never been beaten."

There's always a first time, I think, almost happy that my Uncle is allowing Horace to zig and zag through the traffic as he sits in his saddle, steering with the handlebars. We are winning at last. There is no doubt about that in my mind.

The strange thing is Uncle Jasper isn't smiling. In fact, he doesn't seem happy at all.

CHAPTER 64

I am looking forward to court today. I want to help my uncle win, and am eager to solve the mystery of who really did kill Mr. Bulk. I think we are getting close.

The Judge doesn't scowl at me for once. Maybe he is getting used to me too?

Emily and Amelia enter late. And do they make a grand entrance! All the pixie photographers are fighting to take their pictures, and the Bordenschlocker women look like they are enjoying the 'red carpet' attention, posing with glamorous smiles and being chummy with the reporters.

"I don't believe it," Uncle Jasper grumbles, "I told them not to wear gold. I told them to act like normal people."

As she finally makes it down to her seat, I see what he means. Mrs. Beanstalk is dressed in an obviously expensive gold dress, a large diamond necklace and matching diamond earrings. She looks like a movie star, or a princess, with a diamond tiara on her perfectly piled-up hair.

"I thought they didn't have anything left," I whispered to my uncle.

"They're fake," he hissed back, "but I told them to look simple. I don't understand them at all." He is furious, and doesn't even say good morning to them.

Goode calls his next witness. "I call Mrs. Amelia Bordenschlocker, aka Beanstalk!"

She is on our side! The D.A. finally has made a mistake.

The Judge appears entranced by Amelia as she walks in high heels to the witness stand. "In case your lawyer didn't advise you," he says, "you don't have to testify if you feel it may hurt your son."

"I have nothing to hide," Amelia responds, giving the judge a flirty smile.

Goode winks at me a 'gotcha kid' look if ever I saw one.

Uncle Jasper sighs. "What is that woman up to now?"

"I'm glad you could make it today," Goode begins, sarcasm dripping. "You sent Jack to the market with a cow. What did he bring home?"

"He traded my cow for three 'alleged' magic beans!"

"How did you feel about this?"

"Are you kidding? I was furious! My boy is so kind-hearted he never suspected a scam!"

"Kind-hearted, you say?" Goode smiles. "But did he not steal from the Bulk family that had been so kind to him?"

"No. He's always been a good boy."

"Then how do you explain the police found the coins in your house?"

"Just unlucky I guess." She gives a tinny laugh.

None of the jurors laugh.

My uncle hisses at me, "She sounds like a rich phony. She should just tell the simple truth. They hate her."

The alarm in my head is ringing off the hook as I see the jury members have frowns on their faces. They do hate her. I don't blame them.

"Just unlucky? Hmmm? Has your 'wonderful' son ever been accused of any crimes before?" Goode holds up a manila folder.

"What's in it?" I ask my uncle.

He looks up and says calmly, "Objection! This is not about other accusations. Stick to this case!"

"I'll allow it," the judge says, eyeing Amelia with a dreamy expression on his face.

Amelia smiles at Judge Fair and says, "Nothing was ever proved."

Even I catch that. In other words, yes, he was accused. What is wrong with her? Her whole attitude seems 'off', put-on. I feel my uncle growing tense, eyes glued to Amelia's face, but she's not looking at him, or Jack.

"I see." Goode is a shark about to bite down hard. "Wasn't he accused of stealing Tom Thumb's pig, Bo Peep's sheep and Peter Pan's shadow?" He waves the folder at Amelia.

Goode is way off base. This is too funny. Like one kid coulda' done all that?

Uncle Jasper writes, "absurd", on his pad and doesn't even bother to object.

Amelia sighs and tosses back her hair.

"Nothing was ever proved."

Why did she say that? She just admitted the accusations.

Goode smiles at Uncle Jasper and I see he is moving in for the kill. "Or moved the candle on Jack Be Nimble? Or placed the banana peel on the hill for Jack and Jill? Were all those false accusations too?"

"Objection," Uncle Jasper says, still amazingly calm. "These accusations have no importance to this case. This was never brought up before."

"Overruled," Judge Fair says. "Mrs. Beanstalk has already answered to some of these charges so I will allow her to answer to the others."

"You are not denying that Jack was accused of all those things? Are you?" He aims his best 'shark' smile at the jury. "Doesn't this prove he has a history of trouble with the law?"

Amelia faces the judge. "Well, yes, but, as I said, nothing was--"

"Enough already!" My uncle finally explodes out of his seat. "We get the picture. Why don't you just blame every hurricane, earthquake, train wreck, volcano and other disaster on Jack too?"

"I didn't know he did those things!" Goode smirks with his toothy smile dripping Beanstalk blood.

"Objection! Objection!" Uncle Jasper screams.

The gallery of giants bursts into laughter.

Goode waves his hand and says with a satisfied grin, "I have no more questions for this 'wonderful' mother about her 'perfect' son. I believe the jury can make up its mind after her 'performance'."

I stare at Amelia and then turn to Emily. She is looking down.

I want to shake her and scream at her and her mother. "My poor uncle, what the heck are you trying to do to him?" I try not to show any emotion to the courtroom, but this is bad! Really, really bad.

Uncle Jasper rises slowly from his seat. He looks like he is deep in thought. He's certainly deep in something. Why would Jack's mother want to help the other side? It makes no sense…and then it hits me like a punch in the belly. She really thinks Jack is guilty! She doesn't believe her own son is telling the truth.

CHAPTER 65

I'm a lawyer now. Just like my uncle, I am listening to every word and catching clues. And just like him, I know he just made a big mistake. What would I do if I were him? Would I let Amelia go without questioning her, or risk her doing even more damage? This lawyer business is tough.

Uncle Jasper is still standing there, the wind knocked out of him, studying his notes, trying to figure out what he can do next. Keeping Jack's mother on the stand is dangerous. She has already hurt our chances with her outlandish outfit and her snobbish, attitude. The jury hates her. I'm glad it isn't me standing up there, responsible for Jack's life. I would have strangled Amelia...and her daughter.

My uncle glances back at me.

I'm no help at all, but I have to make it look like I believe we can still win. I have to for his sake. "Go for it," I whisper to my uncle. "Tear her apart."

He nods his head and turns to face the enemy. "Mrs. Beanstalk, was Jack ever convicted of even one of these acts he has been accused of?" He closes his eyes.

I'm guessing he's praying she will give a helpful answer for a change.

"No." She smiles weakly, but adds, "Most people still believed he did them."

My uncle glares at her. "Will you please answer "yes" or "no" only?"

I can't understand it. Why is she giving the wrong answers? What's wrong with her? I have to warn my uncle. I write it on my pad:

She thinks he did it. Stop! Let her go.

He peers at the paper, but continues anyway. "Why did people still believe he did these things?"

I brace for an objection, but it doesn't come. Maybe Goode is feeling too confident to bother. He is smiling, stretched out, totally at ease, while my uncle is sweating like a pig.

Amelia replies, "I don't know."

"You don't know?"

Goode interjects, "She said she doesn't know."

"So you have no idea why people still thought your son was guilty even if he was never convicted of even one crime?" Uncle Jasper looks at the jury. "He was never even put on trial. Is that right?"

"Yes." It is like she just realizes this fact herself because she adds after some thought, "Maybe they were prejudiced against him…against us."

"Prejudiced against you… because you were rich?"

Amelia shakes her head. "No. Because we were poor. We lost everything. Remember?"

"Objection! How can she know why people think the way they do," Goode says, his arm along the back of his assistant's chair. He oozes confidence. It's over and he has won.

"Sustained," the judge says. "Mrs. Beanstalk, you can't know why people think the way they do. It would mean you could read their minds."

Amelia's eyes play with the judge. "Your Honor, everyone blamed my son for everything that happened."

"Why do you think people did that?" Judge Fair asks, his voice surprisingly gentle.

"Objection," Goode interrupts. "It's the same objection as before."

The judge sighs. "They have a right to defend themselves against charges which you brought up in the first place, Mr. Goode. Overruled."

The judge turns back to Amelia. "Mrs. Beanstalk, I ask again, why do you think people believed these charges against your son?"

"I think, Your Honor, most people believe the poor are more likely to commit crimes." She turns to the jury. "You all know that. It's probably happened to some of you too. A crime gets committed and who gets blamed?"

Several jurors nod agreement, while others look unconvinced.

Amazing! Amelia suddenly sounds humble, like a real person.

Goode sits up, apparently taking notice. Did she throw him a curve ball?

The judge is nodding his head. Has Mrs. Amelia Beanstalk somehow reached him?

I see Amelia tremble. "We were so poor when my husband, C.C. left..." She chokes on the words. "It was hard being so poor. People laughed at us...they made fun of Jack...they accused him of all kinds of things. It was pretty awful for us...especially for him."

Goode shrugs. "Like she looks poor," he mumbles, loud enough for the jurors to hear.

Uncle Jasper moves in carefully, eyeing the judge, who is silent. "So when crimes were committed, everyone suspected Jack, you believe, because you were so poor and desperate after your husband, C.C. abandoned you?"

Amelia looks at Jack and gives him a sad smile. "Mr. Doofinch, I had a hard time with Jack. He hated school and got in lots of trouble..."

I hear Mom talking about me. The divorce changed me.

"Emily was smart and liked school. Jack was difficult... he didn't do his homework...argued with me about all kinds of things...had no friends."

Amelia tried smiling at Jack again, but he was looking down. "Jack caused me a lot of trouble. He was not an easy child, not at all like his little sister." She gave Emily a loving look.

Like Emily Bordenschlocker isn't trouble? I'd lost count of all the annoying things she did to me...and that dopey kiss on the cheek that made me think we could be friends...before I found out about all of her lying.

Amelia shrugs her shoulders again. "Mr. Goode is right..." I see Uncle Jasper wince. I brace myself for what is about to come out of her mouth.

Amelia is now speaking in a low, calm, genuine, voice, "Jack was an angry, hurt child...and he did get in trouble... but I know now he didn't do any of those things."

"Objection!" Goode is standing now.

"Why are you objecting to your own witness, Mr. Goode," Judge Fair asks. "You know you can't do that."

Goode sits down. He puts on a smile of confidence, but Amelia is not saying what he was expecting of her, nor what I was expecting either. I am glued to her face, holding onto every word.

"My poor Jack was just an easy target. He always was." She slumps back in her chair. For the first time her make-up isn't perfect, with dark smudges under her eyes. She is fighting off tears. She pauses.

"Are you able to continue?" the Judge asks.

"Yes, sir." She replies and wipes her eyes with her fingers. "I know you all think of us as those rich Beanstalks." She gives them an earnest look, "but I was a struggling, single mother, and my children, especially Jack, had to suffer because of that. I hated C.C. for leaving us. I hated my life. I hated…Jack." She begins to sob. "I hated Jack…Jack."

I had never really thought about how difficult things must have been for my Mom after my dad left us. Amelia's testimony is making me think about Mom and how angry I have been…how wrong I have been. Maybe Mom had no choice but to take that stupid job selling dentists those tiny rubber bands for braces in China! As Amelia spoke, I realized I hadn't made it any easier on Mom.

I had been so angry about the divorce, so worried about myself, about being poor, I'd never thought about the effects on her.

Who worries about grownups? Being a single mother isn't easy. I made it worse.

Uncle Jasper is still questioning Amelia. "So Jack never did those things that the District Attorney brought up?" He looks like he is praying again.

Amelia gazes at Jack, tears in her eyes. "No. I know now my son is not capable of hurting anyone. Not ever."

"But you believed he did? Why? Why would any mother not believe in her child?"

Amelia sighs. "I hated Jack. I'm sorry, but its' true. He reminded me of... my husband." She turns to Jack. "I'm so sorry, Jack. I know that was wrong, but I couldn't help it. He abandoned us and I hated him for that. I hated you because you were so much like him."

Uncle Jasper peers at Goode as he asks, "Mrs. Beanstalk, what happened to your husband?"

CHAPTER 66

There is silence in the court. Everyone is waiting for her answer, but Amelia isn't saying anything. You can almost see the icy mask being reinstalled on her face as she glares at my uncle. "I don't want to talk about this."

"Mrs. Bordenschlocker, I understand, but please tell the court what happened to your husband?" My uncle is refusing to bend under her continuing glare.

Amelia shakes her head and mumbles, "He ran off one night. You know that. Can we drop it?"

"How did it happen?"

"Objection! Answered already." Goode looks relaxed again.

"Overruled. Please answer."

Amelia gives my uncle a warning look, her hands tight on the railing. "He went out late one night. Poof! He never came back. Can we now drop it? Please?" She casts hopeful eyes at the judge who is silently studying her.

"That's it," I whisper to Emily, forgetting my vow of silence.

"I don't know. Are you talking to me now?"

"I don't know," I reply.

She pierces me with her eyes and says, "I had no choice, she's my mom."

I turn back to the trial. Her words do stick with me though.

"So he just vanished," Uncle Jasper asks. "No explanation? No contact afterwards? Just poof?"

"He left! He just left! I figured he ran off with another woman. We couldn't keep the mansion. He left. It happens all the time. Drop it!"

"So all these years you **assumed** he left of his own free will?"

Amelia looks stunned. "What? What do you mean?"

Goode leans forward as does Judge Fair. I do too. What does he mean?

"Did you notice anything strange that night?"

"Objection! He's fishing again!" Goode is about to say something else when the judge says, "I want to hear this. Please continue, Mrs. Beanstalk."

Amelia frowns. "It was a long time ago. I was shocked. I thought C.C. had taken everything of value and left with someone else…someone younger… prettier. He dumped me…he dumped us." She gazes apologetically at Emily and Jack. "He abandoned me and my two little kids."

My hopes drop. I try to think of another question my uncle can ask when suddenly Amelia's facial expression changes. "Funny thing though, I do remember something strange. I never thought about it much. Our animals were very upset the next morning."

"Animals?" Uncle Jasper asks, looking confused.

Amelia looks at the Judge. "We had a few chickens and a couple of geese left…and Elvira, our sweet cow."

"Elvira," Emily moans.

"Although she did have an odor problem," Amelia adds with a shrug.

"Objection! What do we care about some upset animals?" Goode looks impatient.

"Doofinch, I tend to agree with the District Attorney." Judge Fair says, gazing at Amelia Beanstalk, "Even though I must admit I would like to hear the rest of your story sometime. But we must move on."

"With your permission, your honor, I just have a few more questions?" Uncle Jasper looks hopefully at the judge.

"Only a few. But let's get to it!" Judge Fair shakes his robes, a sign of impatience.

"You said the animals were upset? Try to remember what else happened?"

Amelia sighs, and appears to be looking back into the past, her eyes closed. "I do remember one more thing. The geese kept honking that one of them was missing. I didn't care about a missing goose...my husband, C.C., was gone."

"Did you call the police about your husband?"

"Yes. But they said he just ran away. They said it happens all the time..." Amelia doesn't look very glamorous for a change. She looks like a woman who had been abandoned by her husband...she looks like... my Mom...

"Were there any other clues that night?"

"Objection! This all happened years ago," Goode says. "This is a waste of time. It has nothing to do with this case."

"Overruled. I'm curious to see where this 'wild goose chase' takes us," Fair says, looking at Amelia.

"There you go again," the goose rages, feathers flying. "Chicken jokes! Cluck! Cluck! Cluck!"

"I said, "goose" not "chicken"! Stop being such a cluck," Judge Fair shouts. "Crazy, mixed-up fowl."

"Were there any other clues?" Uncle Jasper repeats, staring hard at the goose.

I had almost forgotten about the goose.

"Nothing I can recall," Amelia says.

"There were footprints," Emily says. "You told me, Mom. Remember?"

Uncle Jasper nods. "What about these footprints?"

"I remember now. There were large footprints by the goose pen."

"Really large footprints?" Uncle Jasper asks.

Please say yes, I pray, finally understanding where my uncle is headed with this.

"I know what you're doing," Hortensia Bulk screams. "My hubby would never do anything like that! He was a good, kind man!"

Uncle Jasper whirls on her. "A good, kind man who just happened to say, "Fee Fi Fo Fum!""

"That's unfair! My Eugene wouldn't hurt a fly!"

"Only humans!" Uncle Jasper shouts back.

The giants in the gallery are screaming at my uncle. They look murderous. I'm frightened for him. The Giant Court system was created to keep things peaceful between the giants and other Monstrovian residents, but could it protect my uncle?

The Judge hammers his gavel. "Hold her back," he orders. "And you," he aims his angry eyes at Uncle Jasper, "Finish now!"

Uncle Jasper nods. "So you never found out what really happened to your husband, C.C. Beanstalk?"

"Everyone assumed he just left us. I did too...until now."

Emily slides her hand over her brother's arm.

My uncle hitches up his trousers and says, "Mrs. Beanstalk, do you now believe your son committed the crimes he is accused of in this court?"

"No. Absolutely not! I know now Jack could never hurt anyone."

"Do you believe he killed Mr. Eugene Bulk?"

"No. Absolutely not! Jack could never kill anyone." She smiles again at Jack. "It's my fault. I should have believed in him." She trembles. "I should have believed in C.C. too. I was so wrong. I was bitter. I was angry. Please forgive me, Jack?"

Jack's eyes close and I see tears on his face.

"Thank you. I have no more questions." Uncle Jasper moves to help her off the chair. "You did fine," I hear him whisper as he returns her to her seat.

"Prosecution rests, Your Honor," Goode announces.

"How about you?" Judge Fair asks. "Do you have any witnesses?"

"Only one," Your Honor, Uncle Jasper says. "I call Jackson Bordenschlocker, aka Beanstalk."

Oh no! Anyone but him!

CHAPTER 67

Amelia Beanstalk hisses, "Jack can't take the stand."

"It's okay, Ma, Mr. Doofinch knows what he's doing." Emily gives Jack a thumbs-up. "Come on Bro, cut that giant down to size!"

Emily's words really mean a lot, almost enough for me to forgive her, but not quite.

Jack walks toward the witness stand like a man to his execution.

"Did you kill Mr. Bulk?" My uncle asks once Jack is sworn in and seated.

"I never killed no-one. He was going to kill me!"

"Liar!" Hortensia Bulk shouts, but shuts up as soon as she sees the judge's gavel raised.

"Why would Mr. Bulk want to kill you?" Uncle Jasper asks.

"How could he know why someone might 'allegedly' want to kill him," Goode objects.

"Sustained," the Judge rules. "He isn't a mind reader, Doofinch."

"What did the giant do before he allegedly tried to kill you?"

"Ooooh, he screamed at me! Then he pounded his fist on the table. Then he picked up a knife and fork." Jack's voice is shrill and annoying, and the jurors look like they don't believe him. I am getting good at reading their facial expressions.

Goode laughs, "So Mr. Bulk was going to eat his dinner? So what?"

Jack shakes his head. "No, Mr. Goode, he was going to eat ME! That giant was going to grind my bones for bread! You heard the poem. He was going to "grind my bones" and then cook me!"

Goode shouts, "Objection! Objection!"

Jack persists, "He was going to eat me!"

"I object! I object!" Goode is frantic. "Can't you hear me, Judge?"

"I hear you fine, but this boy deserves a fair trial. We need to hear his story," Judge Fair says. "Go on, Mr. Beanstalk. We're all listening."

Goode falls back into his chair.

"So you had no intention of killing Mr. Eugene Bulk at all?" Uncle Jasper looks confident now.

"Golly no! It was an accident. He chased me, slipped, and fell from the beanstalk. I didn't know he was dead until I heard a big crash. I thought it was an earthquake. I tried to wake him up."

"Why didn't you tell everyone what happened right from the start?" Uncle Jasper asks.

Jack hesitates. "I banged my head really hard so I forgot a lot. And then I didn't think anyone would believe me if I told them a giant was trying to gobble me up for dinner. I thought it was my fault. I was scared, really scared, so I ran away."

"Slow down, Jack." Uncle Jasper sees the jury is getting lost.

"I'm not smart," Jack says slower. "Bad things happen to me all the time. I don't mean nothin', but they just happen."

"But you don't think what happened to Mr. Bulk was your fault now," Uncle Jasper said forcefully, trying to steer Jack away from taking blame.

"Sometimes I do."

No, Jack, No! I feel like wringing his neck.

"Why would you possibly think this was your fault," Uncle Jasper asks, struggling to keep his cool.

Jack screws up his face. "My father ran away and my own Ma hated me…I got used to believing everything was always my fault."

"It was your fault, you ungrateful little brat!" Hortensia screams. "You came to our house to steal! You're a greedy pig! You're a murderer!"

"Shut that woman up," the Judge roars. "I've had enough of her outbursts!"

Goode reaches over and instructs Mrs. Bulk to be quiet.

"Oh shut up yourself," she replies, pushing him away.

My uncle is making progress, but something still isn't right. The clue that can nail this case is in front of us. I know it is. What are we missing? I rush through my notes while listening to my uncle, knowing we are almost at the end.

"What about the goose? Did you plan to steal her?"

"That goose begged to come with me. She was afraid of being eaten too. That guy would eat anything alive!"

"How dare you!" Hortensia roars again.

Goode shouts, "What about the gold coins? Surely they didn't beg you to save them from the giants too?" He laughs loudly, but it sounds fake to me.

Jack is silent.

"No answer, huh?" Goode casts a triumphant look at the jury. "Guilty as charged."

"What about the coins, Jack?" My uncle asks patiently. "Try to remember."

I pray Jack has an answer...one that will help.

"I didn't know I had them."

Oh no! You idiot! How could anyone not know they were carrying a big bag of coins?

Uncle Jasper shows no reaction. "You didn't know you had a bag of gold coins with you?"

Goode laughs again, a huge, boisterous laugh that signals the jury that this is totally unbelievable.

I find it unbelievable too. We are sunk. I feel miserable. What a fool Jack is!

Jack sighs. "I really didn't know. I found them in my coat pocket when I almost fell off the beanstalk." Jack looks at Mrs. Bulk and his face lights up. "Oh my gosh! She put them in my coat when I wasn't looking! Didn't you?"

Hortensia Bulk's voice cleaves the air. "Why would I do that? You liar! You ungrateful thief!"

Jack is thinking hard, his face scrunched up like a prune. "So I would fall off the beanstalk and break my neck. I know now--"

"Know what?" Hortensia screams. "You little jerk! You know nothing! You're a fool!"

"You tried to kill me. You didn't want me to tell the truth about you." Jack is standing in the witness box glaring at Mrs. Bulk. "I remember. I remember now."

I am amazed. He doesn't look afraid for once. He isn't backing down.

"What are you talking about? You're the criminal here! Everyone knows that." Mrs. Bulk gives the jury a confident smile. "You, my fellow Giants, you all know he did it. He's just a lying weasel even his own mother hates!"

"You can't fool me. I know the truth," Jack repeats.

"What truth, Jack?" Uncle Jasper asks.

Jack's voice is low, as if he has just discovered the truth himself. "It was you. You and your husband killed my father."

CHAPTER 68

There are loud murmurs in the court. I hear a few laughs from some of the giants in the gallery.

"Oh come on," Goode exclaims, "How long must we listen to this fiction?"

Jack jumps up, his hand shaking as he points at Mrs. Bulk. "Your husband killed my father when Dad caught him stealing the golden goose's mother."

"That's a lie!" Hortensia Bulk tries to laugh. She is sweating again. "This brat has some imagination!"

"Objection! Objection! Objection!" Goode is shouting into the judge's face.

"Sustained! The jury will disregard all references to the--"

"Your Honor," Uncle Jasper interrupts. "How can we ignore such serious charges?"

"The Bulks aren't on trial," Goode counters.

"Maybe they should be," Uncle Jasper argues back.

"There's no proof of any of this," Goode shouts. "This is all make-believe! It's all a big fairy tale being made up by this desperate defense attorney."

The courtroom is filled with the noise of excited spectators. Emily is pinching Amelia's arm. Judge Fair is hammering his gavel. The goose is clucking wildly, her eyes glued to the giant. "Cluck! Cluck! Cluck!"

My head is banging like a drum from all that clucking. Why doesn't she ever stop? Why doesn't she honk like a normal goose? All this annoying clucking!

Clucking?
Clucking!!!
CLUCKING!!!!!
It had been in front of me all the time! "Yes there is," I shout. "I have proof!"

"There's no proof," Hortensia roars. "It never happened! No one's going to listen to you, you little human rat!"

"You can't prove anything!" Goode bellows. "Your Honor, there is no proof, so we should end this comedy already. Beanstalk is guilty and that's that."

I look hard at Jack. He looks confused. What else is new?

Uncle Jasper corners me. I think he is going to yell at me for shouting out in court, but instead he says, "Brodie, I have confidence in you."

"Uncle Jasper, it's the goose. It was in front of us all the time! The goose is the proof!"

Amelia drops her face into her hands. Emily's eyes are huge.

Goode bursts into raucous laughter. "Come on, your Honor? This crazy goose is proof?"

Hortensia Bulk joins in. "The goose? Cluck! Cluck! Cluck!" She rolls up with laughter. She sounds like a runaway train, huffing and puffing with laughter, at our expense.

"I have no idea what he's talking about," the goose clucks, anxiously watching the giant. "Cluck!"

My uncle's eyes are studying me. "Brodie, do you really have proof? This is very serious."

I hesitate, staring at that crazy, mixed-up, goose, knowing this is either the home run we've been praying for, or the fatal last out. Game over. Goode wins.

My uncle repeats patiently, "Brodie, do you have proof or not?"

"Yes, Uncle, I think I do."

Uncle Jasper leans closer and I whisper to him my suspicions. He listens in silence and then asks, "Are you sure?"

I gaze at the goose and show my uncle my notes. It had been there all the time, but we missed it.

"Mr. Doofinch, do you have proof or not?" Judge Fair looks like a thunderous Zeus staring down from his high perch on Mount Olympus, ready to obliterate us with lightning bolts. "Do you have proof or not?"

Uncle Jasper gives me an anxious smile. "Yes, Your Honor, thanks to my assistant, I believe we have the proof."

"There is no proof because it never happened," Mrs. Bulk roars again.

"SILENCE YOU," Judge Fair shouts. "This is your last chance. What is your proof, Mr. Doofinch?"

My uncle gives the judge a weak smile. "Your Honor, the goose is my proof. Jack, the goose can prove what happened to your father."

"I don't understand," Jack mumbles. "How is the goose proof?"

Goode explodes. "This goose doesn't even know she's a goose! Just listen to her! She clucks like a chicken, the annoying thing."

"I do too know I'm a goose! Cluck! Cluck! Cluck!"

Goode laughs. "I rest my case! Whoever heard of a goose that clucks? This is the most ridiculous, absurd--"

Uncle Jasper approaches the goose. "Your Honor, with your permission, I'd like to ask this goose just one question." He looks at me.

I hope I am right. I pray I am right. I can't believe how much I want this to be the answer for my uncle. Yes, I want this for him, and for Jack.

"Cluck, cluck." The goose backs away. "I don't know anything. Do I?"

Uncle Jasper smiles at the goose who is obviously terrified. "Yes, my poor dear Annabelle, you do. You keep saying it over and over again. That's how my brilliant assistant, Brodie, finally discovered the truth. It was here all the time, but it took him to see it."

The goose is shaking all over, her eyes intently aimed at the giant's face. "I don't know anything. Cluck! Cluck! Cluck! I'm just a big chicken. Yes, I admit it, I'm a chicken."

The giant's face is bright red, her teeth bared and her eyes deadly.

"Cluck! Cluck! Cluck!"

"What nonsense," Goode sneers. "Just look at that poor, mixed-up, thing."

"I agree," Judge Fair says. "It's time we end this. If you have nothing else?"

I know I have found the missing piece of the puzzle. It really was here all along. "Please, just one more question? One teeny little question? PLEASE?" I cross my fingers, my toes, my eyes…I pray.

Judge Fair shakes his head. "Alright! Just one more question. Just one."

Goode is arched over his table, his face reminding me of a vicious hunting dog, aimed right at my uncle's jugular. It is now or never.

"Jack," my uncle asks, "What was your father's first name?"

"That's your question?" Goode springs toward the bench. "Your Honor--"

"C.C.," Jack answers, a puzzled look on his face. "You know that already."

"No, Jack. His real first name, the name he hated so much that he only used the initials."

I hold my breath. Please, let me be right? Please? Please?

There is a long, tense pause.

Tears well in Jack's eyes, but he finally manages to say, "Cluck. My father's real name was Cluck!" He turns to the goose and says, "Oh my gosh! Dad's real name was CLUCK!"

"Cluck?" the goose asks. "Cluck?"

"What?" My uncle asks, holding a hand next to his ear. "Would you repeat that louder?"

"CLUCK! That was my dad's real name," Jack repeats, a look of realization crossing his face. "He hated his name. He never used it. I almost forgot it."

"That's right. Nobody else knew his name. He hated it!" Emily exclaims. "That's why we all called him C.C."

Amelia gasps, "My dearest Cluck Cornwell Bordenschlocker, all this time I thought you deserted us. Oh. I am so sorry."

The goose flops onto her rump in a state of shock. "I always wondered why I kept saying, 'cluck'. Every other goose said, 'honk'. I was a freak, a fool, an outcast. They only liked me for my gold! They all thought I was crazy! You thought I was crazy!"

"No, you aren't crazy." Jack smiles warmly at the goose. "It was because your mother kept saying it when you were a little goosie, shortly after you were born in the Bulk's castle. Your mother loved my father almost as much as I did. He was always so kind to her. He was kind to everyone."

The goose sobs. "I'd forgotten how my momma loved her sweet, kind, Cluck Bordenschlocker. She always told me that if I ever needed help, just call Cluck." The goose whirls angrily on Hortensia Bulk, "You two monsters stole my Momma! Oh Cluck! Cluck! I remember what Momma said, "Someday we'll go home again to my wonderful, kind, warm-handed, Cluck Bordenschlocker! How could I forget?"

Goode falls into his chair, sputtering to himself, "Cluck. Cluck. Cluck?"

Hortensia Bulk looks like she's been struck by lightning. "I told that idiot, Eugene, if we stole that gold egglayer our goose would be cooked!"

"But he never listened to you, did he?" Uncle Jasper asks, approaching the giant.

"No, he never listened! Never!"

"He was always the boss…and you…you were his servant."

"I was his maid! I did everything, everything for him! I had to clean that castle! I had to iron his horrible clothes! I had to cook all those beans! BEANS! BEANS! BEANS! Always beans! I was sick of them horrible, brown, beans! He was always looking for those miserable magic beans so he could sneak down to earth again and grab more loot. But did that big jerk ever find any? No!"

"And then that dopey Cluck Bordenschlocker comes along, climbing that beanstalk of his, and my imbecile husband says all we have to do is climb down and grab it all. How did we know that dopey Cluck would hear us and try to protect that goose's gold-laying mother? So after he slams that dumb Cluck over the head, he says 'nobody will miss him, the poor fool.' That's what my husband says. 'Nobody will miss him.' Bleh!"

"You poor dear. You were his slave!"

Why is my uncle being nice to Mrs. Bulk?

"I ain't nobody's slave! I showed him." Mrs. Bulk pounds her fist so hard the seats around her jump into the air.

"You did," Uncle Jasper says. "You showed him nobody could make you a slave."

"I sure did. He'll never make me cook those darn farty beans again!"

"You did it. You showed him once and for all, didn't you?"

"I showed him! He was always yelling and cursing at me! All those beans to try and find stupid magic beans that didn't even exist! No more! No more!"

"It was you. You did it, didn't you?" Uncle Jasper asks, getting dangerously within reach of her gigantic fists. "You did what anyone would have done after so much abuse."

Hortensia Bulk thrusts her fist in the air. "Yes," she says with terrifying calm, "Yes. I did what anyone bullied for so many years would have done." She laughs insanely. "I pushed the big, selfish, ogre. I pushed him. I saw my chance at freedom and I pushed him off the beanstalk!"

The spectators gasp, and the giant realizes she has just confessed. "I didn't mean to kill him. He was just so clumsy that one push and..." She falls backwards into the chair, giant tears falling to the floor. "I never meant to kill him."

"Cluck! Cluck!" The goose doesn't seem frightened for once.

It is over! We won!

"Your Honor, I ask you to dismiss all charges against Jackson Bordenschlocker, aka Jack Beanstalk," my uncle says in a booming voice.

The Judge glares at District Attorney Hugh B. Goode who is just sitting in his seat clucking.

Emily throws her arms around me. "You did it! You did it! Brodie, you solved it!"

I am blushing with embarrassment.

"Guards, arrest Hortensia Bulk for perjury, theft, suspicion in the murder of Mr. Cluck Beanstalk, the death of Mr. Eugene Bulk, and a million other things we can throw into the omelet," Judge Fair roars. "I've never seen a case so full of beans in my whole life!"

"Oh no! No!" Hortensia Bulk moans, as the guards approach her very, very cautiously.

"I don't have any beans in my case," Goode mumbles, turning his brief case upside down and placing it on top of his head.

The goose waddles over to Amelia. She looks very nervous again. "I'm sorry. I never suspected what really happened. I was just sick and tired of laying those miserable golden eggs."

"Being a goose that lays gold eggs isn't all it's cracked up to be," Uncle Jasper says.

"Is that another 'egg' joke?" the goose scowls, and then bursts into laughter.

EPIL-EGG (Oops! EPILOGUE)

My uncle is sitting on his chair in the courtroom. Everyone has left. Goode had been picked up by four giants in white coats. He is going away for a long rest, the newspapers report.

The reporters and Pixie photographers are waiting in the hall for Uncle Jasper, but he appears to be in no hurry.

I feel a little disappointed. He hasn't said anything to me about how I helped solve the case. How can he be so ungrateful? And then I remember I am nothing more to him than a pesky adolescent, a nuisance nephew, he had to take care of because my mother sent me to him for the summer while she is selling tiny rubber bands for braces to dentists in China.

"You know," Uncle Jasper says, his eyes kind of glossy, "I couldn't have won this case without your help."

"Thank you," I reply, thinking it's about time, but knowing that really isn't what is bothering me.

"When you first showed up on my doorstep, I didn't know what I was going to do with you," he continues.

"I didn't know either."

He studies my face with those deep, dark, all-seeing eyes. "I think you could become a fine lawyer someday. Brodie, I think you can be anything you set your mind to."

"Thank you." I feel tears in my eyes. What's wrong with me?

I had hated this roly-poly man, this poor excuse for a superhero, and I had hated this strange world. I still am not sure about this weird Special Sector, Monstrovia, but now I want to ask Uncle Jasper to let me stay while Mom is away. I want to, but I can't. I know he doesn't want me. He is a busy hero, and I will be in his way. I am just his burden for one summer and he will be glad to be free of me.

I wonder if he would change his mind if I told him Mom had arranged a foster home for me after the summer, until she gets back. I had thought that would be better than this insane place and my crazy uncle. But that was before I got to know him. "Never judge a book by its cover."

"I am proud of you Brodie," my uncle says, sounding odd, as if he is choking on something. "You know, Brodie, my brilliant nephew, even though they are divorced, your parents still love you, very, very, much. They would be very proud of you too."

"I'm proud of you, Uncle Jasper. You were amazing. You never stopped fighting." I smile at him. "Mom was right. Uncle Jasper, you are a hero."

"I'm no hero, Brodie. If I were a real hero, I wouldn't be so frightened of asking you to…to stay with me." He looks into my eyes. "There, I've said it… Brodie, my dear, brilliant, nephew, I would love if you would stay with me until your mother returns."

"Are you serious?" I jump up, almost knocking him over, but giving him the biggest hug I've ever given anyone in my entire life, except Mom and Dad. "I thought you'd never ask!"

So what happened after that? Well, Jack was cleared of all charges. He became a social worker helping the poor. He later ran for President of the United States…and lost. But at least he tried.

Hortensia Bulk received a life sentence in prison, and was ordered to eat baked beans for every meal, for the rest of her life. Serves her right!

Amelia Beanstalk went to Hollywood and starred in such films as *Franken-egg* and *Psycho Chicken*. She married Judge Fair, and with Anabelle, they opened up an egg-cellent chain of restaurants called, 'Cluck's Golden Eggs'. They are very happy.

And what about Emily? We're still friends. She threatens to become a lawyer and my partner. She plans to specialize in women's causes. I think she'll do it too. Just don't tell her I said that.

As for me? I'm still living with my uncle. He hired a housekeeper and a driver for us. You got it. Silas Bumbernickle now lives in the house, with his wife, Mavis. He still calls me 'Master Brodie', but he's a true friend. Even if he is the worst driver ever!

Uncle Jasper is like a father to me, and a genuine hero. He takes on the crazy cases nobody else wants, defending every mythical monster and unfortunate fictional character who needs help. And I am his Dr. Watson, his assistant, proudly recording his strange adventures. Together, we do our best to ensure everyone in Monstrovia gets a fair trial.

And oh yes, one more thing. All the doors in my uncle's mansion now say:

STAY OUT! EXCEPT FOR BRODIE!

THIS CONCLUDES BOOK 1.

Look for new adventures of Brodie, Uncle Jasper, and Emily in the Land of Monstrovia in the next book coming soon:

Who are the most dangerous creatures on Earth?
You're in for a big surprise.

Like what you've read? Check out more from Brodie's Co-author Mark Newhouse

Visit www.bullystoppersclub.com for free anti-bullying materials, and get news, contests and fun freebies at www.markhnewhouse.com. Look for all of Mark's books, including The Rockhound Case Files and The Midnight Diet Club on Amazon and wherever books are sold!

Look out for more great books from AimHi Press coming soon!

Coming Just In Time for the Winter Holidays :

<u>SANTA'S SPEEDING TICKET</u>, a picture book hysterically illustrated by Monstrovia cover-artist Dan Traynor. Someone's in big trouble! But who?

About Co-Author Mark Newhouse

(since you know all about Brodie from his book)

When Mark heard the story you have just read, he knew he had to work with Brodie to ensure that the Monstrovia Chronicles would be shared with all the children looking for the truth.

In his previous career, Mark loved teaching in Central Islip, New York, and was voted Teacher of the Year (New York State Reading Association). As an author, Mark has won numerous awards for his children's and adult books, stories and articles.

The Rockhound Case Files, featuring Rockhound, the dog detective, and his crew of canines catching crazy crooks using science experiments, won Learning's Teacher's Choice Award and are now available including as bilingual individual cases.

In the Midnight Diet Club, there's something strange about Esme's bullies, and the dark secret will be revealed in this darkly humorous nail-biter. That book won 1st Prize in the Royal Palm Literary Awards of the Florida Writer's Association and is now a great audiobook as well.

Mark hopes to continue sharing Brodie's adventures in the Monstrovian Chronicles for years to come.

Made in the USA
Columbia, SC
08 November 2019